A SECRET PARCEL

by

SERENITY WOODS

ISBN-13: 978-1522908319
ISBN-10: 1522908315

DEDICATION

To Tony & Chris, my Kiwi boys.

CONTENTS

Chapter One

Even with her eyes closed, and without him saying a word, Georgia knew that the person who'd just walked into her office was Matt King.

She was sitting on the sofa under the window, cross-legged, her hands resting palms up on her knees. Everyone at the office knew not to disturb her when she was meditating, so when she'd first heard the approaching footsteps she'd kept her eyes closed and hoped they'd go away.

Then the footsteps paused, and her nostrils filled with the distinctive smell of his aftershave.

She inhaled, her trained nose separating the notes of myrrh, cardamom, warm amber, and bergamot. In her relaxed state, she observed the way her heart rate increased and heat spread through her at the thought of seeing him again. Hmm, that was interesting. She'd thought she was over her schoolgirl-style crush. Apparently, that wasn't the case.

She kept her cool though, and just said, "Matt King," before opening her eyes.

He was leaning against the doorjamb, hands in the pockets of his jeans. He was a fine figure of a man, she thought, tall without being lanky, slender and yet muscular, with short sexy hair and an irreverent, 'I don't give a shit' air about him that drew the attention of most women he met. Today, he wore a pair of tight jeans and an open-necked blue shirt, with his usual surfer's necklace around his throat. He looked gorgeous, and he smelled even better.

She'd never tell him that, though. Instead, she scowled at him, irritated that he'd interrupted her quiet time. "Go away. I'm busy."

He remained where he was, oblivious to her glare. "How did you know it was me?"

"I would have known it was you from a mile away. You smell like a tart's boudoir."

He grinned. "Boudoir? Been reading the Marquis de Sade, have we?"

That made her laugh. She couldn't stay cross at him for long. "Come in." She shifted into the corner of the sofa to make room for him.

He pushed off the doorjamb and walked in, passing through the golden bars of sunlight that lay across the tiles of the second-floor office. It was a beautiful, early summer day in the Bay of Islands. Through the open window, the sounds of people having lunch at the café down the road filtered through—light conversation, the clatter of cutlery against plates, and the higher ting of spoons stirring lattes in glasses, accompanied by faint jazz music from the shop further down that sold musical instruments, CDs, and second-hand vinyl.

Matt sat next to her, a piece of summer himself with his tanned skin that brought with it images of surfers riding the waves and beach cricket on Christmas Day. "What were you doing?" he asked.

"Meditating. Until you ruined my concentration."

"Meditating?" He gave her an amused, quizzical look.

She turned to face him, still cross-legged. "What's so funny about that?"

"You can be so flaky sometimes."

"Meditation isn't flaky. It's an effective treatment for stress, worry, addiction, and lack of focus. It gives peace of mind and wellbeing. It can even help creativity. You should try it."

"Maybe I will." He sighed. "I could do with some inspiration."

"Oh? Lost your muse?"

"A bit." He glanced out of the window.

She studied him for a moment, admiring his strong profile, his straight nose, the slight stubble on his cheeks and chin. He'd acted the playboy for so long that sometimes she forgot he was a genius.

Matt was the author of *The Toys from Ward Seven*, a series of children's picture books. The books themselves were adored by children across both New Zealand and Australia, but it was the fact that characters from the books had been used to decorate medical equipment for children that had led to an increase in the popularity of the tales. Matt and his two brothers owned the company that produced the equipment, and Georgia ran the Northland office of the charity part of their business, We Three Kings. She helped to make the wishes of sick kids come true, as well as liaising between the charity and the local hospitals.

Matt was a talented artist and a great writer. She didn't like his admission that he'd lost his muse.

"What are you working on at the moment?" she asked. "The Squish the Possum book?" He'd told her about his new character the previous week.

"That's almost done. The Ward Seven books aren't the problem."

"So what is the problem?"

He hesitated, still looking off into the distance, and she felt certain he was about to confide in her. But the moment passed, and he blinked and turned his gaze back to her, his ready smile reappearing. "Nothing. Doesn't matter."

She felt a little hurt that he hadn't told her. "Matt..."

"Those jeans are exceptionally tight." He glanced at her thighs. "Are they spray-painted on?"

She gave him an exasperated look. "What are you doing here, exactly?"

"I missed you."

The previous weekend, it had been his turn to visit Whangarei Hospital dressed as Ward Seven's Dixon the Dog to hand out presents to the sick kids with her. His brother, Brock, had swapped with him at the last minute because he'd wanted to meet a parent he'd been in contact with online for a while.

"Brock and Erin seemed to hit it off," Georgia said. "I'm pretty sure he pulled."

"He did." He blew out a breath. "He's offered to take her to a hotel at the weekend for her birthday. Fucking idiot. She's going to think he's expecting sex."

"I'm sure he'll be hoping for it," she remarked wryly.

"Well, he says he's not, but that's not the point, is it? Even if he was, he doesn't have to be so obvious about it. He should have just bought her chocolates and taken her out to dinner."

She shrugged. "Some women prefer the direct approach. She's been single for a while, according to Brock. Perhaps she's desperate for sex."

Matt raised his eyebrows. "Speaking from experience, are we?"

Oh yes. Georgia hadn't had sex for so long, she was worried it would close up down there the same way a person's pierced ears did if they didn't wear earrings.

"Let's just say I sympathize with her predicament," she said.

His eyes took on a hot, interested look. "The direct approach, huh?"

Since she'd joined the company a year ago, Matt had asked her out approximately once a week, every week, without fail. The last time had been the previous Friday, when he'd suggested she go with him to the party Brock was having on Christmas Eve. She'd said no, but it hadn't been easy. He was so tempting, like a slightly warm chocolate truffle she knew would melt in her mouth.

She had no doubt he knew his way around the bedroom. Over the past year, he'd dated—and dumped—four women. And those were the ones she knew of.

She'd spoken to one of them, Tina, or Taylor, or Trinny, something like that, after bumping into her while shopping in Kerikeri. She'd asked her how Matt was, only to be met with a snort.

"We broke up," Tina, or Taylor, had said.

"Oh. Sorry to hear that." Georgia had managed to hold back the question for about five seconds before it had burst out. "Why?"

Taylor, or Trinny, had shrugged. "This and that. It was never going to be a long term thing. He's too secretive and private. He doesn't let anyone in. To be honest, I'm relieved. The guy's insatiable. I mean, I like sex, but not *every* day." She'd rolled her eyes and walked off.

And you're complaining about that? Georgia had wanted to yell after her. She got all hot under the collar every time she thought about those words.

The guy's insatiable.

Georgia liked sex. And she hadn't had any for a really long time. The notion of dating this guy, this knowing, confident, slightly arrogant, gorgeous man, and letting him do unimaginable things to her as often as he wanted, made her feel slightly faint.

But even though it had been hard sometimes to turn him down, she'd managed to fight the urge to say yes to his requests. He still flirted with her all the time, still asked her out repeatedly, and she flirted back, a little, but she'd managed to keep him at arm's length, and because of it, they'd grown to be good friends.

Now, though, his lips had curved up in such a sexy smile that it took every ounce of willpower she possessed not to let her tongue roll out onto the carpet like a cartoon character's.

He rested his arm along the back of the sofa, not quite touching her, and yet she could feel the heat from his body, smell his glorious aftershave. They flirted a lot, but this was the closest she'd been to him.

She could see small details she'd missed from a distance. The way the sleeves of his shirt stretched across impressive biceps. A small, well-faded scar on his chin, probably caused by falling off a skateboard or playing rugby as a child. The interesting mix of green and brown in his warm, hazel eyes.

In the past, he'd always teased her as if he fully expected her to say no. This time, however, his gaze caressed her lips before returning to her eyes, holding sexy interest. This man really wanted her.

Holy moly.

The direct approach, huh? he'd asked her.

"Don't get any ideas," she warned.

He grinned. "I'm full of ideas when you're around. It's my creative brain."

She gave a long sigh, wishing she could just lean forward and press her lips to his. "Why did you come here today, Matt?"

"I have a proposal."

"Before we've even dated?"

He gave her a wry look. "Not that sort of proposal. A business one. It's the New Zealand Children's Book Awards on Friday. I wondered if you'd like to go with me?"

She stared at him in surprise. "They're in Wellington, aren't they?"

"Yeah."

"Isn't it black tie?"

"Yep."

Suppressing her shock—and more than a little pleasure—that he'd asked her, she raised an eyebrow. "Do you even own a suit?" She'd never seen him in anything but jeans.

He grinned. "It's your chance to see me do my James Bond impression."

She could think of worse ways to spend a Friday night. "You're shortlisted for the Picture Book Award, aren't you?"

"Yeah." He ran a hand through his hair.

"Aw." Warmth spread through her. "You're nervous."

"It's a big award. Of course I'm nervous."

She tipped her head to the side, amused and surprised. "I didn't think you had nerves."

"Of course I have nerves. Charlie's the robot in the family. Although apparently he's asked Ophelia out on a date this evening, so even he seems to be growing emotions."

Georgia knew he was teasing—the King brothers were tight, and only they were allowed to mock each other. She liked Charlie, the scientist of the trio of geniuses, who always looked slightly puzzled and seemed to spend most of his time staring into space, lost in thought as he worked on his next amazing invention.

"Oh," she said with interest, "so he finally got around to asking her out?"

"Yeah. He's taking her to McDonald's."

They both laughed. "He's such a sweetie," Georgia said. "So... both Brock and Charlie are getting into the dating game, eh? Are you going to join their ranks?"

"When you say yes," he retorted.

"I don't want to go on a date with you, Matt."

He pouted. She reached out and flipped his bottom lip with the tip of a finger.

He rolled his eyes. "This isn't a date. It's a business proposal, like I said. I don't want to go alone."

"But why me? You must know a hundred other girls you could have asked."

He shrugged. "I don't want just any old girl. I want you." He met her gaze. He looked completely serious.

"Why? Is this just another ploy to get in my knickers?"

"It wasn't, but tell me I'm in with a chance and I'll make a concerted effort."

"Matt..."

He shifted on the sofa. "I want someone I feel comfortable with. A friend."

"Can't you take Charlie?"

A look of impatience crossed his face. "A female friend."

"Come on, you must have other female friends."

"Not really."

They studied each other for a moment.

"Oh," she said. "I see. Every woman you've ever met is an ex."

He tipped his head from side to side. "Not every woman…"

But she could see she'd gotten it right. When he met a girl he liked, he slept with her, and then he broke up with her. And then, presumably, they refused to talk to him again. So he didn't have any friends who were girls.

"Am I the only woman in the world who's ever said no to you?" she asked curiously.

He didn't say anything, but she could see from his expression that she was right again.

Her heart sank a little. The only reason he wanted her was because he couldn't have her. It was hardly a revelation, but she was surprised at how much it hurt.

Thank God she'd had the sense to say no to him, and she was going to continue to say no. If she slept with him, she had no doubt it would be fantastic. But then he'd dump her, and that would be it. She'd be alone again, and she'd lose his friendship. And that would break her heart.

Chapter Two

Matt tried not to fidget while he waited for Georgia to reply.

Would she say yes? He found her difficult to read, sometimes. On the one hand, he was certain she liked him, even though she didn't react to him the way women normally did when they wanted to sleep with him. There was no twirling of her hair around a finger, no moistening of her lips with the tip of her tongue or leaning toward him, no batting of her eyelashes or high, girlish giggles. But there was always something in her eyes that suggested she liked what she saw. And yet every time he asked her out, she said no.

He wasn't quite sure why he hadn't given up. He rarely spent time trying to chat up a girl who obviously wasn't interested. If he discovered a woman had a partner, or for whatever reason just blanked him, he'd move on to his next target. Plenty more fish in the Pacific.

But Georgia had captivated him the moment he'd first seen her, over a year ago, and his obsession with her was only getting worse.

He could remember the moment vividly. He and Brock had been interviewing applicants for the position of branch manager. They'd arrived at the office and had entered the reception area, and Matt had stopped so abruptly that his brother had walked straight into the back of him.

"What the f…" Brock had followed Matt's gaze and his voice had trailed off. "Ah. I see."

Matt had been unable to take his eyes off her. She'd worn a navy pantsuit, the jacket buttoned up over a white shirt, sophisticated and professional, although her high heeled sandals had given it a sexy edge, as had the dark hair pinned up into an elegant chignon with one long, thick strand left free to curl by her cheek.

She'd crossed her legs at the knee, and one sandaled foot had swung slowly while she'd flicked through the pages of a magazine.

"Wow," Matt had said. "Who is she?"

"That's Georgia." Brock had drawn him toward the front desk. "She has invaluable experience and great references. Please don't drool over the poor girl and put her off before we've even done the interview."

Matt preferred to leave the day-to-day running of the business to his two brothers, but Brock had insisted either he or Charlie take part in the interviews, saying that because all three of them worked closely with the branch managers of their charity, it made sense to make sure they clicked from the start. Matt had barely glanced at the half-a-dozen resumes Brock had given him, though. "Where's she from?" he'd asked.

"Christchurch. She's just moved up here."

"Is she single?"

Brock had given him an exasperated look. "We're interviewing for the position of manager, not girlfriend."

"I'm being polite. It's good to have some background info on the applicants."

Brock had given in. "She's single, but she has a ten-year-old son." He'd looked at Matt as if assuming that would be enough to put him off.

For some reason, though, it hadn't deterred him. He'd surveyed her with interest, noting her smooth skin free of wrinkles. "She must have been young when she had him."

Brock had checked her application pack. "She's twenty-seven, so, yeah, she was seventeen."

"But single?"

"So her CV says." Brock had gestured to the office they were going to use for the interviews. "Come on. And focus on the business, please. No questions about her cup size or anything like that."

Matt had behaved himself, letting Brock lead the way and only interjecting when he had a relevant question to ask, but he'd become more fascinated with her as the interview had progressed. Although she'd been polite, she'd asked lots of questions, and it had been clear to both of them that she was there to interview them as well. She was educated and intelligent, with a degree in business management, and after only five minutes Matt had known that—irrespective of his attraction to her—she'd be perfect for the job.

When Brock had asked a few questions about her hobbies, she'd hardly sounded as if she was a fun-loving partygoer, talking instead about gardening and bushwalking. But she had a subtle, teasing sense of humor he enjoyed, they liked the same kind of music and movies, and, well, she was hot.

He had noticed that she'd carefully stepped around Brock's questions about her move to the Northland. She'd explained that she'd lost her home in the Christchurch earthquake back in 2011, and that she'd tried to rebuild her life with her son after that, but had finally decided she needed a fresh start.

She hadn't mentioned her husband, though, not revealing whether he was still alive and they were divorced, or if he'd died, maybe in the earthquake. Matt had tentatively brought up the subject twice since then, but the first time she'd neatly sidestepped the issue, and the second time she'd told him outright, "I'd rather not talk about it," so he hadn't mentioned it again.

He'd first asked her out two weeks after she started work at the office, and after that approximately once a week, but she'd continued to turn him down. After a few months, it had become a standing joke between them, and he did it more for fun than because he truly expected her to say yes.

Today, though, was the first time she'd hesitated. *Let's just say I sympathize with her predicament*, she'd said when he'd mentioned Erin, and for a brief moment her eyes had heated, her eyelids lowering to half mast, and her lips had parted as her gaze had slipped to his mouth, as if she'd been thinking about kissing him. She'd looked so sexy and sensual that it had taken willpower of iron to stop himself from pulling her onto his lap and kissing her senseless.

He'd meant what he'd said, though. He really was nervous about the award ceremony, and he didn't want to go alone. He was tempted to beg her to go with him, but he decided to save the humiliation until she'd definitely refused.

"I don't understand why you're nervous," she said. "You're Mr. Gregarious usually."

"That would be my Mr. Men title," he agreed.

"Are you worried you will win it, or that you won't?"

"Both. If I don't win I'll have to display the gracious winner's face while silently cursing the person who does, and I don't know how

I'm going to handle that. And if I do win..." He trailed off, not certain how to put his feelings into words.

"Afraid you're going to cry?" she teased.

"Maybe."

Her eyebrows rose, and she leaned back against the sofa, interested. "I'm surprised—I didn't realize it meant that much to you. You gave me that big speech not long ago about how you didn't care about awards and it was the kids loving the books that counted."

"I lied." He gave a short laugh. "Well, not completely. Of course it's the readers who count. I get letters all the time from kids and I pin them up to remind me why I write."

"You're a puzzle," she said. "I can't quite make you out. On the surface, you look like the last sort of man who'd be into writing books for children. What made you choose that genre?"

He didn't say anything for a moment. She was sitting in a shaft of sunlight, and he noticed that her brown eyes were more the color of amber. He felt as if he'd been imprisoned in them, captivated by her curious stare.

Although they'd grown to be good friends, they weren't what he would have called intimate. When he visited the office, which was usually once a week, they talked about music and movies, about the business and some of the kids the charity was helping out, and occasionally about her son, Noah, or about Brock and Charlie. But they rarely discussed themselves, their hopes and dreams.

Matt didn't discuss his personal life with anyone, not even his brothers, so it didn't come naturally to him to open up. But there was something about her gentle, nonjudgmental manner than prompted him to talk.

"I'm guessing you're aware that my sister died when I was ten," he said, assuming she would have read it in one of the articles that had been written about the King brothers over the years.

She nodded. "Yes. Asthma, wasn't it?"

"Yeah. It's why Brock and Charlie are both involved in childhood respiratory diseases. After Pippa died, they knuckled down, got their qualifications, and became intent on being doctors."

"How did her death affect you?"

"I went off the rails," he said. He looked out of the window, but he didn't see the top of the shops below, and the palm trees waving in the summer breeze. Instead, he saw his parents' despairing faces when they were called in to yet another meeting in the principal's office. "I didn't know how to deal with it. I couldn't process the fact that she'd gone. People treated me weirdly. At school the teachers gave me extra time to do my assignments and told me I didn't have to do my homework, and sometimes the other kids resented me for it. So I rebelled. Got into fights. Smoked, drank. Got worse and worse. Was generally very difficult all through my teenage years. I came close to being expelled in Year Eleven."

"But you weren't?"

He sighed. His parents had taken him home after the meeting with the principal and, for the first time ever, apart from at Pippa's funeral, his mother had cried in front of him. He'd felt so ashamed that he'd upset her, and he'd finally broken down. The two of them had sat down with him that night and they'd spoken for hours, about Pippa, about school, about what he wanted to do with his life.

"No, I wasn't expelled," he said. "My parents told me they just wanted me to be happy, and that I could leave school if I wanted, but we talked about what I'd do, and I realized I didn't want to flip burgers or stack shelves in the supermarket. I wanted more than that. I'd always been good at art, and my dad suggested I focus on that and English, because I could also write, and that maybe I should go to Art College. I didn't quite turn it around overnight, but I managed to gain University Entrance, and I loved it at Art College. I had a lecturer who was the first person to bring my art and my writing together, and it was his idea to try picture books."

"So you came up with Ward Seven?"

"Not immediately. I wrote several fairly generic kids' books first, none of which were published. But then one night I was talking to Brock and Charlie, and Brock mentioned how so many of the kids he saw were scared of hospital. It rang a bell with me. I kept thinking of what would have happened if the ambulance had gotten to Pippa in time and taken her to hospital, and how I wouldn't have wanted her to be scared."

He stopped and swallowed. He didn't want to think about how frightened she must have been before she died.

"And so you came up with the idea for Ward Seven?" Georgia asked.

Relieved she was ignoring his emotion, he cleared his throat. "Yeah. I went home that night and drafted the stories for the first few Ward Seven books, then worked on the characters for a few weeks. Jenny—my agent—told me immediately I was on to a winner, and she sold them to a publisher the next week. Then when I showed the sketches to the guys, Charlie had the bright idea of specifically targeting equipment for children using the Ward Seven characters. And the rest is history."

"Thank you for sharing that with me," she said. "I didn't realize they were quite as close to your heart. Is that why you'd like to win this award?"

"I suppose I see it as a culmination of everything I've worked for up until now. I want to win it for Pippa. And if I don't, it'll be like I've failed her."

"Matt, seriously, after what you've achieved? All the children you've made happy with the books, and the kids you've helped with the Ward Seven toys in hospitals?"

"I know. I'm being stupid."

"No." She put a hand on his where it rested on his knee. "You're not. You're being sweet—and that's not a word I would have associated with you before today."

He looked down at their hands. Her skin, though tanned, was paler than his, and she'd painted her nails orange to match her top. Apart from the suit he'd first seen her in, she always wore bright colors, blues and reds and turquoises, and he'd grown to associate her with happy feelings, like a florist who worked with flowers all day.

He raised his gaze to hers again. "So will you come with me?"

She gave him a suspicious look. "Was all that another attempt to get in my knickers?"

"Maybe." He smiled.

Her lips curved up a little. "I'll come with you. But only if we have separate rooms."

He thought about Brock and Erin, and again remembered Georgia's words, *Let's just say I sympathize with her predicament.* It didn't sound as if she'd had a partner for a while. But she was young, and she was gorgeous, and she had that twinkle in her eye that told him she enjoyed sex and she'd be great in bed, given half the chance.

"Sure," he said. He'd book two rooms. And like Brock, he wouldn't be expecting sex.

Hoping and expecting were two different things, though.

Chapter Three

Georgia continued to eye him suspiciously. It was the first time he'd opened up to her like that. Although he could be a bit of a player, she thought she knew him well enough to hope that he wouldn't pluck at her heartstrings just to convince her to go away with him.

She wasn't a hundred percent certain, though.

"Don't look like that," he said. "It wasn't a ruse, and you can back out at any time." His hazel eyes were warm, more brown than green. "I hope you won't, though."

"We'll see." She had a couple of days to think about it. She'd meditate on it and go by her gut instinct.

"What about Noah?" he asked. "Would you like to bring him too?"

That took her by surprise. "To Wellington?"

"Yes. He's very welcome."

She said nothing for a moment. Matt was such an enigma. One moment he was acting out the billionaire playboy role to perfection, the next he was being the nicest man she'd ever met. He knew Noah fairly well, but he didn't have to make that suggestion.

"It's good of you to offer," she said, "but actually it's his last day at school tomorrow. After he's finished, I'm taking him to the airport, and he's flying to Christchurch to be with his grandparents for the holidays. I'm joining him on Christmas Eve."

Matt nodded. "Your parents or Noah's father's?"

"Mine."

She could see the curiosity in his eyes. He was desperate to know about Noah's father, had even asked her outright about him a couple of times, but Georgia never spoke about Fintan to anyone.

To his credit, Matt didn't push the point. "I bet you'll miss Noah while he's away."

Before she could stop herself, she'd huffed a sigh. When Matt raised an eyebrow, she admitted, "Probably not."

"Oh. I thought he was doing better?"

She'd occasionally mentioned to him that Noah had gotten into trouble at school, but she'd rarely gone into detail. However, after what Matt had just told her about his past, maybe confessing to him wasn't the worst idea in the world. If anyone would understand, it might be him.

"I thought he was improving," she said. "Then last Thursday he got into another fight."

"Ah."

She slumped down on the sofa. "He was stood down from school for two days. I think they only let him back today because it's so near the end of term and he's graduating from the primary school tomorrow. I had to see the principal again this morning. He was, like, 'Here we are again, Ms. Banks. This is becoming a habit.'"

"Nice," Matt said. "Encouraging."

"Yeah." Should she say anything about what was really bothering her? Matt wasn't a parent, and it wouldn't have surprised her if his answer to parenting issues was just a shrug and an "I dunno," or even a smart-arse joke about bringing back the cane or something.

Then she felt ashamed. He'd just told her about his own struggles at school—there was clearly more to him than met the eye. She ought to give him the benefit of the doubt.

He was waiting quietly as if aware of her internal struggle, and gave her an encouraging smile. She took a deep breath. "I hate the way the guy this morning made me feel as if Noah's behavior is my fault. And he's not the only one—if I do mention it to anyone else like my parents, the disapproval in their voice makes me want to scream."

He didn't say anything, and she wondered if he agreed and was sitting there thinking *You only have yourself to blame.*

"I know I'm responsible for Noah," she continued hotly, "of course I am. When a youth behaves badly, I understand that everyone's going to blame the parents. I've done the same in the past when I've walked into a supermarket and seen a toddler lying on the floor screaming—I've looked at the mother and thought 'Why isn't she doing anything?'"

"I don't have kids, but I've heard that sometimes the best way to deal with that sort of behavior is to ignore it," he said. "When the child wants attention, I can see that giving it to them can be the worst thing you can do."

A little mollified, she nodded. "Parenting's hard. There's no manual as such. I've read all the books going, and tried to make the best decisions. And I'm not looking for sympathy. There are any number of children out there who live with single parents and who aren't badly behaved. But I can't work out what's gone wrong. I don't think I'm soft on him, or overly harsh for that matter. I try to set firm boundaries, and to be understanding at the same time, to listen to his point of view. I've done my best. But lately it's not good enough. He just behaves badly, all the time. I've tried everything—punishment, rewards, being harsh, being nice. Talking it through, the silent treatment. Nothing works. I can't reach him."

She stopped as her throat tightened. Dammit. She hadn't meant to get emotional.

Matt studied her for a moment as she struggled to compose herself. Then he lifted up his arm and flicked his fingers to beckon her toward him.

She hesitated for a second, but the notion of a hug from another human being was a treat she couldn't pass up. Unfolding her legs, she turned on the sofa and curled up next to him.

He lowered his arm around her shoulders, gave them a little squeeze, and kissed the top of her head. "Boys," he said. "We're a pain in the arse from birth to the grave."

She bit her lip hard so the tears that pricked her eyes didn't fall. "I honestly don't know what I'm going to do."

He slid down a little on the sofa and rested his head on the back. Oddly, it felt very relaxed and comfortable, sitting there in his arms.

"Maybe it's time to get some help," he said. "A counsellor, perhaps."

"He had a counsellor in Christchurch and she did nothing at all." Georgia's voice held more sharpness than she'd meant, showing her real feelings about the psychologist Noah had seen. "She just made him go over and over everything, like constantly stirring up a riverbed so the silt won't settle. I thought he'd be better when we came up here. I thought once we got away from everything and started afresh, we'd be able to work it out, just me and him."

Matt rubbed her arm, a gesture that was human and comforting rather than sexual, and slowly his body heat began to warm her through, relaxing her stiff spine. "It's possible he has something locked inside him," he said, "and he needs someone else to help him find the key to let it out. Someone who doesn't have an emotional investment in him. He obviously watches you working hard and having to cope alone. Maybe he feels that if he tells you what's going on inside, he's going to burden you."

She rubbed her nose. "I want him to feel that he can tell me everything. I've told him that."

"Yes, but he's the man of the house now, and part of him will feel as if he should protect you."

Georgia frowned. "I can't imagine that's the case. I've hardly brought him up to think women are the weaker sex."

"Doesn't matter. It's inbuilt in us."

"Even if I were to agree with that, it wouldn't be relevant at his age, surely? He's still a child."

"He's eleven now, isn't he? He's only a few months older than I was when Pippa died. I can remember being that age. He's ninety percent child. But he's teetering on the edge of being a man."

Georgia sat up a little and frowned. She hadn't attributed Noah's problems to teenage issues because he was still at primary school, although he would be starting high school the following February.

"He should have another couple of years until puberty hits, though, shouldn't he?" she asked. Didn't boys mature later than girls? She hadn't noticed any body hair on her son, but then he'd become more private lately, dressing in his room rather than wandering through the house naked the way he had when younger. His voice hadn't broken, but then she'd thought that happened later. She'd have to get some books on it.

"Well, it doesn't happen overnight," Matt said. "I don't know what growing up is like for girls but I imagine many of the problems are similar, like one minute wanting to sit on your mother's lap and the next minute yelling at her that you never want to see her again because she treats you like a kid."

"I can remember that confusion. The embarrassment of saying or doing something childish when I thought I'd grown up. It's a horrible age. I wouldn't go through it again if you paid me."

"Me neither. I hated being out of control. Testosterone brings feelings of anger and aggression—emotions that once upon a time would have been treasured and cultivated because they were necessary for survival, but nowadays they're seen as negative feelings. Over time we learn to control them, but it's difficult at that age. When we get angry, we fly off the handle, and we want to punch things. That's why rugby was invented."

"I had my suspicions."

"I'm serious. Sport's the best thing for boys with anger issues. They can wear off all that aggression on the field."

"I guess. I admit I hadn't thought about it before. But it can't just be that, can it? Not every boy is going to get involved in fights."

"No, I suspect there are other issues involved. But it might explain why, if he is feeling confused or angry about something, he is less able to control his feelings."

She looked down at her hands, thinking about his words, *I suspect there are other issues involved.* She didn't want to talk about Fintan, but there was something else bothering her. "I sometimes wonder if he suffers from not having a man around." She'd not admitted it to anyone else, not even her mother. Why had she opened up to Matt like this? She wondered whether he'd laugh, or maybe say something judgmental.

He thought about it. "I don't think kids in single parent families suffer in any way. But I do think children look to their parents and other adults for clues as to how to behave. You only have to look at little girls who sit and watch their mothers put on makeup and do their hair. It's the same with boys. They watch the men in their family and learn how to react in certain situations, and to understand when it's acceptable to show anger, and when it isn't."

"That's what worries me sometimes. He doesn't see a lot of men. I'm not very sociable, and I don't have any family up here. I don't have any brothers anyway, and my sister's still single."

"I bet all his school teachers are women too," Matt said. "It's great that so many women are moving into teaching, but there's definitely a shift in schools now with fewer men entering the profession, and that means fewer role models for the guys."

"You seem to know a lot about it."

"I do a lot of work with the local schools. Extra-curricular art classes. It will be a bit better at the high school, but I do think it's an issue for young men these days, especially those who don't have a father figure at home."

"You're probably the closest to a father figure he has," she realized.

"Jeez. God help him."

She gave a short laugh. "You're not so bad. You're rich and successful. Working hard in your chosen profession. I can think of worse role models for him. Apart from in the relationship department."

"Good point." He smiled, although his eyes flickered with something—regret? Had she offended him with that remark? She didn't know him well enough to know. Surely he didn't think himself the perfect example of a boyfriend?

Sighing, she checked her watch. "Anyway, he'll be here soon. School's finished."

"I might hang around and say hi, if that's okay. I've got something I want to ask him."

She narrowed her eyes. "What?"

His lips curved up. "Nothing about you, if that's what you're worried about."

His arm was still around her, his body warming hers. He sat with one ankle resting on a knee, the epitome of casual sexiness.

What was it about this man that pressed her buttons? After the trauma she'd been through in Christchurch, dating had been the last thing on her mind for years. Looking after Noah and just, well, surviving, had been hard enough.

Friends had told her that one day she would heal and love again, but Georgia hadn't been so sure. Loving again meant opening up her heart, and it had felt so frozen that she'd been certain no man would ever be able to thaw it through.

Matt was gorgeous, and he'd surprised her with his insight and concern, but he was hardly relationship material. She knew he only wanted her because he couldn't have her. He was the traditional rich, sexy bachelor who loved his independence and abhorred the idea of settling down. No doubt one day he'd fall hard for some leggy blonde, but she wasn't the sort to capture his heart.

It had been a long time since she'd had a man in her bed, though, and the thought of welcoming Matt into her arms, of kissing him and letting him touch her in places she hadn't been touched for a lifetime, was incredibly appealing.

His eyes had taken on that sultry heat again, and she knew he was thinking about kissing her. It would take hardly any movement for her to lean forward and press her lips to his. His arms would slide around her and tighten, and she'd abandon her inhibitions and let him kiss her until all her problems melted away...

Chapter Four

"Mum?"

The voice from the doorway made both their heads snap around. Noah stood there, hands jammed in his pockets, looking sullen as usual, although he did smile when he saw Matt sitting with her.

"Hey, dude." Matt lifted his arm away from her, got up, walked over to him, and held out his hand. "How's it going?"

Noah shook his hand and said, "Cool."

Georgia also came over and hesitated. Matt guessed that normally she would have kissed him, but she was aware it might embarrass him now. "Hi, sweetie."

Matt knew that Noah looked up to him the same way the boy did the All Blacks, with a kind of wide-eyed reverence. Noah loved art and design. It was the one thing he showed any interest in, and whenever they met, he usually had half a dozen questions to ask about art supplies or techniques.

"How was school?" Georgia asked him.

Noah dropped his bag onto the floor. "Usual."

"Last day tomorrow," Matt said. "Then it's high school next year, eh? Looking forward to it?"

Noah shrugged. "Kind of."

"I was a judge at the school's Art Exhibition," Matt said. He saw Georgia's eyebrows rise. He'd surprised her. He'd surprised himself, too, with how much he'd enjoyed interacting with the teenagers. That was why he'd agreed to do some workshops with them. The idea of helping them develop their inherent talent appealed to him.

He perched on the edge of the table. "They do some pretty amazing stuff there. You'll be able to get some serious artwork done, not just coloring in like at primary school."

For the first time, Noah's eyes lit up. "They do graphics too, and computer design. Not until Year Nine though, when you get to choose your options. First I have to do cooking and woodwork." He rolled his eyes.

Matt grinned. "Yeah, I know what you mean. The cool thing about trying all those other subjects though is that you might find you're really good at something you've not tried before. I like cooking—I think if you're an artist there's something fun about creating with food."

Noah nodded, his cheeks flushing a little at Matt's intimation that they were both artists.

Matt could see Georgia watching them interact, her expression thoughtful. *You're probably the closest to a father figure he has*, she'd said. That remark had shaken him a little. He'd never thought of himself as being a role model for anyone. He was touched that she thought of him that way, although her comment about him being far from an ideal example where relationships were concerned had stung a little.

"I've got something to ask you," he said, resolving to think more about it later. "I've nearly finished the latest Ward Seven book. And I've been thinking about working on something different afterward. A young adult graphic novel."

Noah's eyes widened. "What's it about?"

"I'm not a hundred percent sure yet, but I'm thinking probably a blend of a teenage secret agent and a treasure hunter. There'd be a supernatural element to it, a bit like Indiana Jones. The thing is, I need someone I can base the hero on, and I was wondering if you'd be up for it. I wouldn't use your name, and you'd only be the inspiration for the character, so it wouldn't look exactly like you. And of course, you can say no if you'd rather not…"

"I'd love to." Noah looked as if he'd been asked to go to the moon. "That would be awesome."

Matt looked at Georgia, whose expression was unreadable. "If that's okay with you?" Maybe he should have asked her first. Perhaps she didn't want her son splashed all over the pages of a novel. "I wouldn't tell anyone if you'd rather I kept it a secret," he said.

Her lips curved up a little. "It's fine," she said. "We're both thrilled you asked. Do you have an idea for the book?"

"I've been scribbling down notes for a while, and sketching here and there to come up with a sort of storyboard. Once I've finished Squish, I'll get going on it properly. Maybe in the New Year you'd sit for me so I could do some sketches?"

Noah nodded eagerly. "That sounds great."

"Okay. Well, I'd better be going." He pushed off the desk. "I hope you have a nice Christmas in Christchurch."

The pleasure faded from Noah's features. "I don't want to go," he said, his face turning sullen again. "I want to stay here and see my friends."

Georgia's shoulders slumped an almost imperceptible amount—this was clearly an old argument.

"Well, Christmas is a time to spend with family," Matt said. "And your mum lives a long way from hers, so it'll be nice for her to see her folks, won't it?"

Noah examined his shoes. "I guess." He threw her a glare. "I wanted to wait until Christmas Eve so we can fly down together, but she's making me go tomorrow."

Matt suspected that Georgia felt the need for some time to herself, if Noah had been as difficult as she'd implied. And presumably Noah was aware of that, and felt as if he was being sent away.

"We all need a break sometimes," Matt said. "You as well. It'll give you a chance to do something different for a week or two. I bet your grandparents will spoil you rotten, as you're their only grandson."

Noah shrugged, and Georgia rolled her eyes.

Matt suspected there was more to the story than Georgia had implied. Noah wasn't being difficult just because his father wasn't around. No doubt it had something to do with the circumstances surrounding his father's absence. Matt wondered whether Georgia would ever tell him what had happened there. Maybe her husband had abused her—that would explain why they'd moved away. Perhaps she was frightened of him finding out where she was or something. That didn't ring true though—Matt couldn't imagine the strong-willed, independent Georgia letting any man abuse her.

Then he admonished himself for that stupid point of view—no woman 'let' a man abuse her. The surge of anger that ran through him at the thought of someone harming the sensitive, beautiful woman before him made his hands curl into fists, its ferocity surprising him.

He forced his fingers to unfurl. Georgia wasn't his property, and she wouldn't appreciate yet another male displaying aggression in front of her.

"Okay," he said. "I'm off. I'll catch you when you get back, Noah." He patted the boy on the shoulder.

"Wait." Georgia ran to the door. "Just wait a minute." She disappeared down the corridor.

Matt stared at Noah. "What was that about?"

"Dunno." The lad shoved his hands in his pockets. "Have you decided what you're going to call the character in your book yet?"

"No. Any ideas? What's your middle name?"

Noah took one hand out and scratched his cheek. "Rory. It's Irish. It means red-haired." His hair was dark, though, the same as Georgia's.

"Your dad?" Matt guessed.

"Yeah. He was from Ireland. His name was Fintan."

It was the first time Matt had heard either of them say anything about him.

He had to be careful here. Georgia was such a private person that he was sure she wouldn't want him questioning Noah. But from the boy's eager reply, Matt was certain Noah wanted to talk about him. He doubted he'd get another opportunity to find out about her mysterious ex.

He opened his mouth to ask a question. And then Noah's use of the past tense sunk in.

The realization halted his words, and he stared at the lad speechlessly. "I'm sorry," he whispered eventually, not knowing what else to say.

Noah aimed a kick at the table leg. "I'm glad he's gone. He was an arsehole."

Before he could stop himself, Matt gave a short laugh. Noah looked up and met his gaze, his lips curving up.

"What's so funny?"

Matt turned to see Georgia standing in the doorway. Out of the corner of his eye, he saw Noah's eyes fill with panic.

Matt grinned at Georgia. "I told Noah that my middle name's Sebastian. He found it most amusing." He glanced at Noah, who looked both relieved and surprised that Matt hadn't dropped him in it.

Georgia snorted. "I'm not surprised." She held out a small cardboard box. "For you. For your nerves."

Matt took it and opened the lid. He looked up at her. "Teabags?"

"It's passionflower tea. It's great for anxiety."

His gaze slid to Noah's, who crossed his eyes. Matt bit his lip for a moment, then gave her a smile as he closed the lid. "That's very sweet. Thank you."

"Try it," she said. "It works, believe me."

"I will. I appreciate it." He winked at her. "You'll let me know about Friday?"

"Sure."

"Right. See you later."

*

"Did she say yes?"

Matt tucked the phone under his chin and used both hands to fold over the front cover of his new pad of A3 paper. "Not yet." He laid the pad on the table and smoothed it flat.

He owned several easels, and he had an old fashioned wooden desk that housed his computer, but when he was sketching out ideas he preferred to use his modern architect's table with its sloped surface.

"Christ, bro," Brock teased. "I always thought you had the Midas Touch, but I'm beginning to wonder now."

"I know what you mean. It's like trying to break down the Berlin Wall. She's impervious." He opened the drawer to his right and let his fingers brush over the rows of pencils lying in the box inside. "It's one of life's little pleasures," he said, "choosing which pencil to use on a blank sheet of paper. It's a bit like looking into the future. White paper holds all the promise of wondrous things."

"Until you make your first mistake and fuck it up," Brock said.

"Yeah. Unfortunately life doesn't have an enormous eraser you can use to rub away the bad bits."

Brock chuckled. "You thinking about school?"

"Nah not really. More about Pippa."

Brock fell quiet for a moment. Matt chose a newly-sharpened 4B and placed it on the slim ledge at the bottom that stopped pencils rolling off, then pushed himself back. Picking up the mug of tea he'd just made, he stood to walk over to the windows.

His house was built on a high hill overlooking the picturesque town of Russell in the Bay of Islands. He'd spent a fortune on it, and it was far too large for him, but as soon as he'd walked into the place he'd fallen in love with it. Directly beneath it were several acres of bush in which he could hear kiwi crying and moreporks hooting forlornly at night. Beyond the trees lay the small, pretty town, and behind that, the sparkling blue Pacific Ocean.

The floors of the house and the deck were pine and the walls were white, so everything looked fresh and bright. He'd purposely kept furniture to a minimum, concentrating on chrome and glass, so the whole place was cool and clean, emphasizing the most important things to him—peace, light, and space. Most of the interior was open plan, but to one side he had a huge, separate studio which was almost self-sufficient, with a little kitchenette, a bathroom, space for all his easels and desks, and also a comfortable sofa for when he fancied putting his feet up and having an afternoon snooze.

Sliding open the glass door, he stepped out onto the deck and sipped his tea while studying the gorgeous view. He'd made the tea using one of the teabags Georgia had given him. It wasn't as bad as he'd thought it would be.

"I can't believe Pippa died eighteen years ago," he said.

"I know. It seems crazy. Where have the years gone?"

"I was talking to Noah earlier," Matt said. "Georgia's boy."

"Oh yeah?"

"He told me his middle name is Rory, which is Irish for red-haired, because his father was Irish."

"Oh, I didn't know that."

"He said 'was Irish', Brock. I'm pretty certain he's dead."

"Shit. I just assumed they were divorced."

"Yeah, me too. And there was no love lost between Noah and his dad either. He called him an arsehole."

Brock gave a short laugh, similar to the one Matt had given at the time. "What did Georgia say to that?"

"She was out of the room, thank God." He watched a pair of rosellas sweep down into the bush, bringing a flash of yellow, red, and blue to the green of the trees. "She's having trouble with him. I suspect it's because she won't talk about his dad and he's pretty messed up about it, but I could be wrong. The last thing I want to do is put my foot in it. She'd never talk to me again."

"True. Although maybe she would talk, if she had the right person to talk to."

"I can't imagine that will ever be me." As he said the words, Matt felt the truth sink in. Georgia might fancy him, but she'd made it quite clear that where relationships were concerned, he was far from being a role model.

And she was right, of course. He couldn't remember the last girl he'd dated for more than a few months. He'd always considered that life was too short to waste on being monogamous. There were so many pretty girls out there, why should he spend the rest of his days with just one?

For the first time in his life, though, Matt felt a strange twist in his gut, and a realization that he was lonely. He'd never considered having children himself before, assuming that was something that happened to other people, but just lately he'd been spending more and more time with them, at the hospital, at the local schools, and now with Noah. He liked Noah, liked the connection he had with him. Was it odd that he felt a strange urge to protect him and to want to try to help him sort himself out? Maybe he just saw himself in the boy, and that was why he was thinking about Pippa, remembering all that angst, the wrangling of emotions he'd experienced at that age.

"You all right?" Brock asked.

"Dunno. I'm feeling broody. It's very odd."

"She's really gotten to you, hasn't she?" Brock's smile was evident in his voice.

"Yeah. Don't know why. She's not interested. Maybe that's why. Maybe I am that shallow."

"You pretend you are, but you're not," Brock advised. "Is there definitely no hope?"

"I don't know. She may come with me to Wellington because I sounded suitably pathetic, but I don't know if it would lead to more than that."

"I know the feeling."

Matt grinned. "Yeah. You, me, and Charlie makes three."

"I can't believe he's taking Ophelia to McDonald's."

"I'm guessing Summer's going too, otherwise yeah, not romantic at all."

"He'll probably pull before we do."

"I know! What's the world coming to?"

Brock laughed. "See ya later."

"Yeah, see ya."

He hung up and looked across at the sea, taking another swallow of the tea. He adored this view, but for the first time he wished he had someone standing beside him to share it with him.

He remembered the way Georgia had snuggled up under his arm. She'd surprised him, but he hadn't said anything, enjoying the feel of her against him, the smell of coconut in her hair, her light perfume, the silkiness of the skin of her upper arm under his hand. She was a lovely girl, feisty, ambitious, determined, and independent, and yet there was something vulnerable about her too, like a piece of coal in a pile of diamonds, a touch of darkness amongst the light. She'd suffered in the past, he knew it instinctively, could recognize another's pain, having been through it himself.

He'd opened up to her today, something he'd never done with a woman before, always keeping them at arm's length and usually breaking up with them before they grew too intimate.

Would Georgia ever feel comfortable enough with him to do the same?

Chapter Five

"Thank you so much for agreeing to this." Georgia shook the hand of the guy in the Search and Rescue T-shirt. "The We Three Kings Foundation appreciates your help."

"Of course. That's what Mozart and I do—help people." Owen Hall released her hand and turned to the young girl standing with her parents to the side. "So… you must Ellie, the star of the show today."

Ellie Patton smiled shyly. Slender and pale, a chirpy pink hat hiding her hairless head, Ellie had Acute Lymphoblastic Leukemia. Although only eight years old, she'd undergone several rounds of chemotherapy over the last few years, and she'd been in and out of hospital so much that she'd jokingly told Georgia they were going to fit a revolving door for her.

Georgia's job could sometimes be difficult when she knew the children she was helping had life-threatening illnesses, but the older she got, the more she decided it was important to make every moment count. Helping to make a wish come true for sick children was something no other job would ever top, and seeing the joy on the kids' faces made it all worthwhile.

Ellie's parents had written to the We Three Kings Foundation to ask if they could make their daughter's wish to work with Search and Rescue dogs come true. Georgia had contacted the Northland branch of the Search and Rescue service and spoken to Owen, the branch manager, and he'd lost no hesitation in giving up a day to help. Later, he was going to take Ellie to his main training center to meet some of the other S&R members and their dogs so she could watch a proper session and then help with one of his puppy training classes, but at the moment they were on the domain—the park in the center of Kerikeri, in the warm sunshine, with the strains of Christmas carols drifting across the grass from one of the shops further down.

Owen shook hands with Ellie's parents as Georgia introduced them, and then he led Ellie over to where a chocolate Labrador was waiting patiently.

"This is Mozart," Owen said, clicking his fingers at the dog, who walked forward a few paces to sit before them. "Mozart, shake hands with Ellie."

The dog obediently lifted a paw, and Ellie shook it solemnly.

"Great," Owen said. "Now, we're going to practice a few commands with him. I'll help, but you're in charge, okay? You tell me what you want him to do, and I'll show you how to ask him. And if you feel tired, just tell me, and we'll sit down for a while and I'll tell you a bit about what happens when someone goes missing. All right?"

Ellie nodded happily, and Owen proceeded to show her how to make Mozart walk backward and forward, retrieve a ball, walk in a circle, and lie down and put his feet in the air.

Smiling, Georgia left them to it and walked the short distance across the domain to the picnic table and chairs by the children's playground, where a woman sat with a baby in her arms.

"He's so patient." Georgia took a seat on the bench the other side of the table. "He's amazing."

"I know." Skye was breastfeeding, and divided her gaze between the baby with the gorgeous blue one-piece with dinosaurs on it, and the man who was currently showing Ellie how to make Mozart jump over some small hurdles. "I guess it's the years he's spent training dogs, but he's just so good with kids. Much better than me." She sighed as the baby kicked his legs and pushed her away. "Harry! Stop wriggling."

Georgia laughed and sipped the coffee from the takeaway cup she'd brought with her. "He's going to be a rugby player by the looks of him."

"Or a wrestler. I swear he constantly wants to do exactly the opposite of whatever I want him to do."

"That's boys for you. I'm sorry to tell you that never changes."

Skye sighed, latched him on again, and settled back. "You have a boy, don't you?"

"Yeah. Noah's eleven."

"Gosh! You don't look old enough to have an eleven-year-old."

"Well thank you for that. I was a child bride." Georgia smiled. "I can't believe he's eleven, actually." She looked at the baby in Skye's arms who had settled down, his eyelids drooping as he suckled contentedly. Skye was about the same age as her. How strange that her own son was about to go to high school. "It seems like another lifetime that he was that age."

"You have only the one?"

"Yes." Georgia shifted in her seat. Normally, she would have changed the topic of conversation at that point, but since her conversation with Matt the day before, she'd felt her past weighing heavily on her mind. "Noah's father died four years ago, when we lived in Christchurch."

Skye's eyes widened. "Jeez. I'm sorry to hear that. How awful." She looked across at where Ellie was instructing Mozart to fetch different objects under Owen's patient tutelage. "These things often come out of the blue, don't they? And they just whip the rug from under your feet."

"That's very true," Georgia said, thinking about how quickly her life had changed.

"My brother died when I was young." Skye watched Owen and Ellie play football with Mozart, who was by far a better dribbler than either of the humans. "That's who Harry is named after." She kissed the baby's head. "He died in a motorbike accident. It's funny how much something like that can affect you when you're younger. It changed us all—my two siblings and I—in different ways."

Georgia thought of what Matt had said about losing Pippa, and how it had affected him. "I think maybe I underestimated what an effect it would have on Noah. I mean, of course I knew it would be a terrible wrench for him to lose his father. But the manner of his passing was… difficult. It's been hard for both of us, and I think it's had much more of an effect than I expected."

To her credit, Skye didn't push for details. "Maybe it's more difficult because he's a boy too," she said. "Boys are told that crying is weak, and he probably feels he shouldn't show emotion. Gosh, it must have been hard for you bringing him up alone."

Emotion tightened Georgia's throat. Because she didn't talk to many people about this, she was used to her parents concentrating on Noah and his feelings and problems. She'd never had the sort of relationship with them that she yearned for. They'd sent both her and her sister off to boarding school at a young age, and their attitude tended to be that she was the adult and should therefore be able to deal with her feelings. To a certain extent they'd intimated the same about Noah, that he should learn to deal with it rather than use it as an excuse to behave badly.

"It has been tough," she said. "And lonely at times. I thought moving up here would be a fresh start and we'd be able to put our sorrow behind us, but I guess you can never really escape your past."

Skye took a few swallows from her water bottle on the table, then peeled a banana and broke off a piece to nibble. "Have you made many friends up here?"

"A couple," Georgia said, although that was a bit of a reach. She occasionally went for coffee with the receptionist at the office, and she chatted to some of the other mums at the school, but she didn't have any confidantes. "It's my own fault. I don't get out much. I'm either working or in my garden. I've never been much of a partygoer."

"Me neither." Skye ate the other half of the banana. "Maybe you'd like to come around for a coffee one day? I spent a few years travelling and lost touch with most of my old school friends."

"That would be nice," Georgia said, genuinely touched. She liked Skye, who had obviously had some hard times of her own, but was devoted to her husband and baby. "Do you and Owen live in Kerikeri?"

"Yes, the other side of the inlet. My family's up in Mangonui. Have you heard of *Treats to Tempt You?*"

"The chocolate shop? Of course!"

"My sister and her friends run it, and I worked there for a while before I left to have Harry. Maisey makes the best truffles, and Elle's ice cream is to die for. Maybe we could make a trip up there one day?"

"I'd love that."

"Unfortunately I don't know any single men or I could hook you up," Skye teased. "I'll have to ask Owen if he knows anyone."

"Oh, I don't… that is… it's possible…" Georgia's cheeks grew hot.

Skye's eyebrows rose. "I see. Okay, what's his name? Tell me all about him."

"Oh, he isn't… well, he could be, but he wouldn't want to…" Georgia gave in. "His name's Matt. Matt King."

"Right." Skye nodded. Then her eyes widened. She bent to the huge tote bag tucked under the pushchair, ferreted in it with one hand, and pulled out a book. It was a Ward Seven picture book, *Carmel the Cat gets an Eye Patch*. "It's not the same guy, is it?"

Georgia's lips curved up. "There can be only one. He's like the Highlander." The thought of Matt in a kilt made her eyes go unfocused.

"Jeez," Skye said, looking suitably impressed. "He's, like, a billionaire, isn't he?"

"He is. He's a very strange guy. He's young and he's a fabulous artist. I used to think he was quite arrogant, although I'm beginning to realize that might be a front—possibly. He and his brothers run the charity I work for, and they give away millions of dollars each year. I found out yesterday that he also helps out at the local schools. He lost his sister when he was about Noah's age, and I think it's made him realize the importance of your upbringing, you know?"

Skye smiled. "You like him a lot?"

"No! A bit. Well, yes, a lot. He's gorgeous."

"But…"

Georgia sighed. "There are lots of buts. I haven't dated for a long time. I work for him. And he's not the relationship sort, for a start."

"Does it have to lead to a relationship?"

Georgia met Skye's gaze, and they both laughed. "I suppose not," Georgia conceded. "I've never… you know, gone with a guy just for sex, though."

"It can be liberating," Skye said. "Having a fling. Removing all that pressure about it having to mean something. It can be nice to just be with someone. To enjoy the moment." Clearly, she'd had at least one brief affair herself.

Georgia scratched her nose. "He's asked me to go with him to Wellington tomorrow, actually. He's up for a book award, and he was a bit nervous about going to the ceremony on his own."

"Are you going to go?"

She sucked her bottom lip. "Don't know yet."

"You should," Skye prompted. "You should totally go and have no-strings hot sex with a gorgeous billionaire."

"And I can see you're going to be terrible for me."

Skye shrugged. "I've made some doubtful decisions in my life, but I try not to regret any of them. Life is short, and the more I think of what happened to my brother, the more I try to live in the moment. *Carpe diem*, Georgia."

"Yeah." Working with sick kids was starting to convince Georgia that was the way to be. But could she extend that to sleeping with Matt King just for the hell of it?

She needed to think about it when she was on her own. For now, she decided to change the subject. "Is Mozart the dog who was injured last year?"

Skye's gentle gaze turned back to the man and the Labrador. "Yes. He's recovered remarkably well, although Owen doesn't take him on rescue trips anymore. Mozart does shows like this to help raise awareness of the importance of Search and Rescue, and he's a great example of a well-trained dog for the puppy training lessons. He's like a bossy uncle to the pups. But Owen's training a new Lab now for rescue purposes."

"Tchaikovsky?"

Skye laughed. "Actually he's called Schubert. He's a black Lab."

"Aw. Great name for a dog. Although Bach would have been more appropriate, surely?"

"Too obvious, so Owen said." Skye latched the cup of her bra up under her T-shirt, lifted a now sleeping Harry into his carry seat, and clipped him in. "Looks as if they're ready to move on."

Owen and Ellie were walking back to her parents, Mozart following Ellie as if he'd been glued to her hip. She bent to whisper something in his ear, and he licked her face.

"Friends for life," Skye said, and smiled.

Georgia rose and went over to them. She made sure Ellie's parents knew where they were going, and thanked Owen once again. "I've put your Search and Rescue article up on the blog," she told him. "Hopefully it will give you a bit more exposure and might even see a few donations coming your way." Three Wise Men had already signed a generous check to the agency for his trouble, but she hoped she'd gain him some extra exposure and maybe some more funds too.

"That's great. I'm glad I could help," he said. "Hold out your hand."

Giving him a curious frown, Georgia did so. Owen turned it so her palm faced up, then said to Mozart, "High five." The Lab slapped his paw on Georgia's, and everyone laughed.

"I'll call you," Skye said, leaning forward to kiss her on the cheek, "and we'll go for coffee."

"Thanks. Bye Harry." Georgia ran a finger over the baby's downy head.

"Thank you for everything," Ellie's mum said. "We'll email you some of the photos we've taken."

"That would be great." Georgia would use them for the website and the newsletter she sent out every month.

The group went off together, Ellie super-excited at the thought of seeing all the puppies.

Georgia watched them go, swallowing down a sudden lump in her throat. It wasn't fair that some people seemed to sail through life with few major issues, while for kids like Ellie every step was a struggle.

Carpe diem, Georgia. Skye was right. Life was short, and Georgia had been surrounded by death and unhappiness for too long.

She tipped her face up to the sunlight, thinking about Matt King and his sexy smile, the way his muscular arms had tightened around her, and how much she wanted to kiss him.

Maybe she would go with him to Wellington. It would be fun to go to a posh party, and it didn't have to lead to anything.

But if it did, it might not be the worst thing in the world.

Chapter Six

"What did Matt mean when he said you should let him know about Friday?"

Georgia raised an eyebrow at her son. The Year Six graduation from primary school had just taken place, and they were sitting on the wall outside the school hall.

Noah had already dropped his certificate on the ground, and the corner had a footprint on it. Somehow, she didn't think he'd be interested in hanging it on the wall when he got home.

"Where did that question come from?" she queried, wondering why it had taken him a whole day to ask.

"I was just thinking about Matt, and then I remembered what he'd said before he left."

"Oh. Well. He's asked whether I'd like to go with him to Wellington on Friday for the Children's Book Awards ceremony. He's up for an award and he's a bit nervous going on his own."

Noah moved a stone around on the ground with his shoe. "Are you going?" He flicked the stone with his foot, and it skittered along the ground and hit the ankle of one of the mums standing talking in a group. She turned and glared at them. Georgia pulled an *eek* face and mouthed "Sorry." The woman rolled her eyes and turned away.

Georgia looked down at Noah, who'd lowered his gaze. She sighed, not wanting to make a big deal of it on the day of his graduation. "What am I going to do with you?"

"Sorry."

"Don't say it if you don't mean it."

"I do mean it."

"No you don't. And anyway, what's the point in apologizing to me? It was that lady you hit, not me. We talked about thinking of the consequences of our actions just this morning, didn't we?"

"I didn't know the stone would hit her."

"If you kick a stone, the laws of physics say it's likely to stop by coming into contact with something, and there are people in front of us. You should have been able to predict what might happen."

Noah said nothing, and Georgia suppressed a sigh and looked around the square. By the door to the hall, several students stood talking to some of the teachers. The students had all received awards for excellent behavior and achievement. Their parents stood with them, laughing and bathing in their reflected glory. How must that feel, she wondered?

"I'm sorry I'm not like them."

She turned her surprised gaze to her son. It was the first time he'd ever sounded remorseful.

"I don't want you to be like them," she said, and a little guiltily, because it wasn't a hundred percent true.

"You do. You wish I was smart like those kids."

"You are smart, Noah—all your teachers said that in your report. But achieving good grades is about application, as well as intelligence."

"I disappoint you," he said. Oddly, he looked near to tears. Perhaps the fact that this was his last day at primary school was affecting him more than they'd both expected, because she'd thought he'd be thrilled to leave.

She studied the other parents, who looked rather smug, as if they themselves had been awarded the certificates. She knew that many parents thought that children didn't know their own minds. They pushed them to play the piano or to do sports they hated or to work for several hours a night because they assumed the child would be grateful for it when they reached adulthood. But she'd never felt like that. She'd always felt resentful that her parents had pushed her so hard as a child, and she'd promised herself she'd never do that to Noah.

She looked back at her son. Maybe she should have been more forceful. Perhaps he would have been more responsible and better behaved if she'd been stricter. But Noah's problems went deeper than that. She'd impressed upon him the need for good manners, and therefore although he often got into trouble with his peers, he was never rude to his teachers. His issues were related to what had happened in Christchurch, and she would never know how he might have turned out if things had happened differently there.

She'd always tried to be honest with him, and she didn't see any reason to start lying to him now.

"There's no point you getting good grades or being well behaved for me," she said. "Would it make my life easier if I wasn't called into the principal's office every five minutes? Of course it would. It is embarrassing. I don't like the way he and the other teachers look at me as if I've done something wrong, when I feel I've done my best to be a good mum. It makes me feel bad, like I've let you down."

Noah stared at the ground, his face sullen. "It's not your fault."

"I'm responsible for your behavior—I'm the one who brought you up, so it is my fault. But I don't want you to think you disappoint me. What I am disappointed with is that you don't want to do better. You only get one chance at life. It's not that many years before you'll be leaving school and going off into the big wide world. It can be a scary place out there. There's nothing wrong with flipping burgers if it makes you happy, but you are a smart guy. You can do better than that, and I'm sure you'd like to get some kind of career that pays well and makes you happy."

He shrugged.

She rubbed his back. "It's my job to guide you while you're growing up, and to prepare you for when you're an adult, so you can look after yourself and provide for your own family, if you have one. And I don't feel as if I'm doing a very good job at the moment."

She put her arm around him. "But that doesn't mean you disappoint me. There are more important things in life than getting certificates. You might get into trouble, but I know that in here you're a good boy." She put her other hand over his heart. "You're not nasty. You're kind to kids who are less able than you—I watched you help that special needs girl up the steps in front of everyone—not all kids would have done that. I think you have a heart of gold in there, and that's what counts to me, not certificates."

Noah swallowed hard. "I don't mean to be bad."

"I know, sweetheart. Matt was telling me how difficult it is for boys of your age to control their anger. He sounds as if he was very similar to you."

"Really?"

"Yes. His sister died when he was ten, and it made him very angry. I think he understands how you're feeling, a little anyway."

Noah looked away, across the square to the trees. "I don't want to be like him."

"Like Matt?"

"No. Like Dad."

Georgia went still. Noah sat rigid beneath her arm, his spine stiff, his jaw clenched.

"I'm sorry," he said.

"It's okay."

"I just hate that half of me comes from him," he said, his voice low.

She swallowed hard. "I understand why you feel like that. But he was a wonderful man in many ways. I wouldn't have married him if I didn't think that."

He shrugged off her arm. "You married him because you were pregnant."

She struggled not to wince. "I know it must look like that, but I wouldn't have married him if I didn't like him. I wanted to be with him. I loved him. And he gave me you. I'll never, ever regret that."

Noah remained silent.

"I understand why you're angry with him and why you wish he wasn't your dad. But there are two things I want to say about that. First, it's because of him that you're so handsome." She smiled. Noah still didn't speak, but a ghost of a smile hovered on his lips. "And secondly," she continued, "you are your own person. You're not a carbon copy of him, or of me, for that matter. I know it's common to inherit characteristics from your parents, but you—and only you—have the power to control your own life. It's up to you to decide what kind of person you want to be when you grow up. And that's what I meant about being disappointed—not in you, but for you. I want you to *want* to do better at school. Does that make sense?"

He shrugged again, but she felt that maybe she'd gotten through to him, a little.

"I wish I didn't have to go to Grandma's," he said.

They'd moved up to Kerikeri shortly after Christmas the year before, but she'd promised her parents she'd return for Christmas this year. Initially, she'd missed her family and had looked forward to the idea of being all together.

Now, though, she was beginning to regret the decision. She knew she'd miss the gorgeous hot and sultry Northland weather, although

Christchurch could be lovely in the summer. And she'd also miss her little house and her garden. It had been instilled in her from childhood that Christmas was about family, and she was looking forward to seeing her parents and her sister, but she knew that after the initial hugs and exchange of pleasantries, she'd soon be wishing she was sitting on her deck looking at her roses. And her parents were always very strict with Noah. She'd used to think that was good for him, but if anything it seemed to make his behavior worse rather than better.

"At least Grandpa will take you fishing on his boat," she said, an activity that Noah enjoyed.

"Yeah, I guess."

Georgia looked around. Some families were heading off, and it didn't look as if anyone was desperate to talk to them. "Shall we go home?" she asked Noah. "We could call in at *Fantail's* and pick up something nice for lunch on the way?"

"Yeah," he said. He stood and glanced back over his shoulder at the school hall.

"You'll never have to go there again," she said. "Does that feel good?"

He nodded, his face brightening. Matt was right—high school would be good for him. Noah was ready for the challenge. She'd talk to him more over the summer break about it, and hopefully encourage him to raise his own expectations of his behavior and his learning.

"Come on then." She led the way toward their car.

"So are you going with Matt?" Noah asked.

"I'm still thinking about it," she said honestly. The day before, she'd decided she would, but when she'd laid in bed that night, doubts had set in, and she'd almost convinced herself not to go.

"You should," he said.

She smiled and pressed the button on her key to open the car door. "You like him, don't you?"

"Yeah, he's cool. I like the way he talks to you."

She raised her eyebrows as they got into the car. "What do you mean?"

Noah shut the door and plugged his seatbelt in. "He's nice to you. And he makes you smile. You never smiled like that with Dad."

Georgia put the key in the ignition and then turned to look at him. Although he didn't have Fintan's red hair, he did have the same lean, hungry look about him. How much of his father did Noah have inside him? Neither of them could be sure. She hated that she was always looking for signs of his character, warnings that Noah could be heading in the same direction.

Leaning forward, she put her arms around him and hugged him tightly. For a second he sat stiffly, and then he put his arms around her neck and returned the hug.

After a while, she moved back, started the car, and pulled away.

He's nice to you. And he makes you smile.

Her lips curved up, and she made a mental note to text Matt once she got home.

Chapter Seven

"I can't believe you own a plane and yet we're flying cattle class." Georgia lifted her hand luggage, moved forward a foot in the queue for the security check, and dropped the bag again.

Matt grinned. They'd already taken one flight from Kerikeri to Auckland, and now they were about to take another to Wellington. "It's being serviced this weekend, and anyway, I didn't think you were the sort of girl who'd be impressed by private jets."

"What on earth gave you that impression? By all means, attempt to impress me with your billions of dollars."

"I'll keep that in mind," he said wryly.

She rolled her eyes at him. "I don't know what it is with you three Kings. None of you knows how to spend money right."

"You were at Brock's place for that business meeting last month," he reminded her. "You can't say he doesn't know how to use his money to impress." Situated on Auckland's waterfront, the penthouse apartment was sumptuous and extravagant. Matt loved his house and wouldn't have exchanged it for his brother's in the city, but he could appreciate why Brock's place had cost so much.

Georgia shrugged. "Yeah. Well. It's about the only thing he's spent money on. And Charlie's even worse."

"I acknowledge that. Our accountant once joked that the only things Charlie used his credit card for were ready meals from New World and music for his iPod."

She chuckled, then gave him a curious look. "What's your house like?"

"Tiny," he said, picking up his bag as they shuffled forward again. "Barely room to swing a small cat."

"Really?"

"Nah." He smiled. "Maybe you and Noah will come over when you get back from Christchurch? I'll show you around."

"Sure." Her gaze rose to meet his. She had such gorgeous eyes. Sun flooded across the department lounge, turning her irises a beautiful amber. Her eyelashes were long and slightly curled, her skin flawless, her lips plump and pink and a little shiny. He guessed part of her glow came from makeup, but if she did use some, it certainly wasn't obvious.

His heart rate picked up at the thought of how it would feel to bend his head and touch his lips to hers. He'd barely been able to think of anything else since he'd sat next to her on the couch in her office and she'd cuddled up to him, although he'd done his best to put her to the back of his mind, certain she was going to refuse to go with him.

When she'd texted him the night before to ask whether the offer was still there, he'd been unable to stop a stupid smile breaking out on his face. He knew it didn't mean it would lead to anything. He'd been chasing her for long enough to know she wasn't going to be an easy conquest. But she was looking up at him now with warmth in her eyes that told him it was possible she was thinking about kissing him too.

Behind them, someone cleared his or her throat, and Matt glanced forward to realize the line had shuffled forward and they were holding everyone up.

"Sorry." He picked up his bag and they both walked forward, trying not to laugh.

He stopped by the x-ray machine and lifted his flight bag onto the counter.

"Do you have any large portable devices in there, sir?" one of the security guards queried. "Like a laptop or iPad?"

"A laptop," he said.

"Would you mind removing it please, sir?"

"Sure." He unzipped his bag and peeled apart the velcro strips that kept the laptop in place. While he was doing that, Georgia took her phone out of her pocket and placed it in the tray with her bag, then went through the metal detector ahead of him. It beeped, and the female security guard took her to one side.

"Do you have any metal items on you, ma'am?" the woman asked.

Georgia cleared her throat and glanced across at him, then looked back at the guard. "Last time I set it off, it was the underwire in my bra," she admitted. She looked back at Matt as if waiting for a rude comment. He just raised his eyebrows.

The guard waved her wand across Georgia's chest. Sure enough, it beeped.

"That's fine, ma'am, it's quite common," the guard said with a wink, and gestured for her to move on.

Matt chuckled, pulled out his laptop, and placed it with the bag in the tray. The male guard at the machine went to push it through the x-ray machine, then stopped and stared at it.

"Sir?"

Matt was about to walk through the metal detector, but he paused as the guard beckoned to him. "What?"

The guard looked at the tray. Matt looked with him.

Across the tray was a scatter of what looked like grains of marijuana. It had clearly come from his bag, because bits of it were stuck to the velcro strips.

He looked back up at the guard and said, "Ah. I can explain."

*

Georgia was very close to blushing from Matt's smirk at her troublesome bra, but the rising heat quickly vanished at the sight of him being directed to a table to one side. Another male guard joined the first, and they began to inspect his bag.

She went to walk over to him, but the guard who'd checked her bra stopped her with a, "Ma'am, I can't let you back through."

"Okay, sorry." Georgia circled around to the other side, behind where the guards were still checking other passengers' luggage through the x-ray. "What's up?" she called to Matt over the top of the small partition.

He was standing with his hands on his hips. Glancing at her, he ran a hand through his hair. He looked a mixture of amused and exasperated. "I packed a couple of your teabags, and one of them has split."

She stared at him. "You fucking idiot," she said without thinking, prompting a short laugh from both security guards. "Why didn't you put them in your main case?"

He glared at her with an *I know that now* kind of look, and she bit her lip to stop a hysterical giggle rising up. This was no laughing matter. Airport security took the possession of drugs very seriously, and one of the guards was already speaking into his radio.

"It's dried passionflower," she told them. "He's going to a big awards ceremony tonight and he's a bit nervous, so I gave him a box because they help anxiety." She gestured at his flight bag. "Have you found the split teabag?"

The first guard was in the process of unpacking the case. "Not yet."

She leaned on the barrier to watch. To her surprise, Matt had gone quite pale. She would have expected most men to react angrily, embarrassed at the attention. Was it possible he had more than the teabags in his case? It wasn't difficult to get hold of marijuana because it was grown right across the Northland.

She discarded the thought immediately. He might be a playboy, but she was certain he didn't do drugs.

"Do you know who he is?" she asked the guards.

The second one looked at his ticket. "Matthew King... Never heard of him."

However, the guard searching his bag looked up in surprise. "*The* Matt King? Who wrote the Ward Seven books?"

Matt blinked. "Yeah."

"Cool! My little girl loves those."

"A children's author?" the other asked.

"Yeah," the guard said. "I can tell you don't have kids. Every parent in New Zealand has one of his books at home." He smiled at Matt. "Cassie's favorite's *Humble the Hedgehog has a Headache.*"

Matt nodded, apparently speechless. Georgia smiled. "You can tell her there'll be a new character soon—Squish the Possum."

"Nice." The guard grinned and leaned forward in a semi-conspiratorial manner to his colleague. "He gives millions to kids' charities."

"Oh." The guard looked as if he was impressed but trying not to be. "I'm afraid that doesn't mean we can give you preferential treatment."

"Of course not," Georgia said, but she knew she'd established that he was a responsible guy and therefore not a likely contender for a drug smuggler.

The first man finally produced the offending item—a torn teabag. As he lifted it, several herbal grains fell out, identical to the ones in the tray.

"Okay," the guard said, "I'm sure this is entirely innocent, but I'm afraid we are still going to have to carry out our standard procedure for checking for drugs." As he finished speaking, a sniffer dog and his handler approached.

Matt stood back while the handler led the dog to the tray with the case. The German shepherd sniffed around the bag, but clearly he didn't find anything he'd been trained to search for, and eventually the handler led him away.

"Great," the security guard said. "We'll do a quick strip search and then you can go."

"Good grief," Matt said.

"Body cavity search?" Georgia suggested.

Matt put his hands on his hips again and gave her a hot, exasperated glare.

The guard cleared his throat, and she suspected he was hiding a smile. "That probably won't be necessary. If you'd come this way please, sir."

She watched Matt walk off with the guard, her smile fading as they disappeared into a room and the door closed. When it came to it, although he'd been an idiot to put the teabags in his case, she had given them to him. Was he going to be angry with her?

She waited nervously for him to come out. When the door eventually opened, she was relieved to see them laughing, the guard grinning at something Matt must have said. They walked back to the x-ray unit, and Matt was allowed to walk through the metal detector. Luckily, it didn't go off, and he collected his case and they set off for the gate.

Georgia glanced at him as they walked. "Are you okay?"

"All good," he said, and smiled.

"You're not angry with me?"

His eyebrows rose. "Why would I be angry with you?"

"I was your supplier for a start."

He laughed. "And I have to say you were right—the tea did help me relax, although it could also have been the glass of whisky I had after it. But no, it was my fault for being an idiot. I just didn't think."

"Well, I'm glad you're not cross. I am sorry I made the joke about the body cavity search though."

"That would not have been fun. The strip search was embarrassing enough." He rolled his eyes.

"I'm interested to know why the guard was laughing when you came out," she teased.

"It could have been at what he saw, but possibly because I told him if he wanted to search me like that again we'd have to get engaged."

"I'm glad you can find it funny."

He shrugged. "They're only doing their job."

"You looked quite worried at one point."

"My experience with figures in authority hasn't been great. Even if you're innocent, they somehow have a tendency to make you feel as if you've done something wrong. Luckily, the guard was fairly pleasant, otherwise it could have been a whole lot worse." He gave her a curious look. "Thanks for talking to them—I think that made a difference."

"You're welcome."

"You weren't worried I might have something else in my bag?"

She snorted. "Of course not. Just because you're a bit of a player doesn't mean you're irresponsible."

"A bit of a player?" He looked startled at her description. "I don't know whether to be amused, flattered, or insulted by that."

They slowed as they entered the flight lounge, and found two seats near the window. "You deny you're a womanizer?" Georgia said.

He leaned back in his chair and rested an ankle on the opposite knee. "Depends what you mean by that. Do I like women? Yes. Do I like sex? Yes. But do I consider myself a womanizer? Not really. That term has negative connotations for me, and I like to think I respect women."

She met his hazel-eyed gaze, a frisson running down her back. *Do I like sex? Yes.*

"I think you can respect women but still be a womanizer," she said, being deliberately provocative, wanting to find out more about his love life. "You've had four girlfriends this year, and that's only the ones I know of."

"You keeping tabs on me? Aw." He grinned.

She ignored that. "Let's just say you don't appear to be in it for the long haul."

"Maybe not. But there's no law that states there's a limit to how many women a guy can date in a year. And I have never, ever, cheated on a woman." His smile faded and his eyes held a touch of steel, telling her that he found the idea insulting.

Ooh, he was telling her off. It made her go all aquiver.

Chapter Eight

Matt puzzled over the feeling of hurt that arose within him at the thought that Georgia considered him a womanizer. He didn't like the word. It suggested he used and discarded women without a care, and that certainly wasn't the case.

Georgia was studying him thoughtfully. "So you're a serial monogamist?" she suggested.

He still didn't smile. "You say that like it's something dirty."

Her eyes sparkled. "Only if it's done right."

That made his lips curve up in spite of himself. "You little minx."

She rested her head on a hand and continued to look at him with interest. "I hurt your feelings, didn't I?"

"Maybe a little."

"I'm sorry. That wasn't my intention. I'm puzzled as to why you're upset."

"I just don't see why I'm the bad guy. It implies I talk women into sleeping with me against their will, or that I'm somehow devious and promise commitment to get sex. That's not the case. Far from it. Women like sex too, in my experience—in fact I think you'd be surprised how many of them come on to me. They enjoy having sexual freedom, and not many of them are looking for anything more than sex. I don't use the promise of a long term relationship as a carrot to get girls into bed. Maybe men used it as a technique in the Regency era, but today women are encouraged to be adventurous in the bedroom and to explore their sexuality. I'm happy to help them do that."

"I bet you are."

He glared at her. "Look, when I go to bed with a girl, I make sure she enjoys herself. Yeah, I've had a few partners, but I don't think that makes me a womanizer any more than it makes a girl a slut for having the same. Men don't expect their girl to be a virgin on her wedding night anymore. I don't care how many partners a woman's had, provided she protects herself against disease. I like girls who enjoy sex. Why would I want to sleep with a girl who's inexperienced? I'd much rather she knows her way around the bedroom so we can have some fun."

They studied each other for a moment. He couldn't read her expression, but he suspected she was upset or annoyed. He frowned, trying to work out what he'd said wrong.

"You imply that girls are never upset when you break up," Georgia said. "What about Tina, or Taylor, or Trinny, or whatever her name was? I bumped into her in Kerikeri a few months ago. She seemed right pissed off that you'd dumped her."

"Her name's Tanya. And I sincerely doubt she was pissed off. I think she was glad to see the back of me."

Georgia's eyes gleamed. "She did say you were insatiable."

"What can I say? I think it's a compliment to want to have sex with your partner as often as possible. She didn't agree."

She chuckled. Maybe she wasn't upset.

Normally, he didn't give a fuck what people thought of him or the way he lived his life. But for some reason it mattered to him what Georgia thought. "Am I completely missing the point?" he asked. "I thought that in the twenty-first century sex was about having fun. I thought women enjoyed the freedom to sleep with whomever they wanted, without it meaning they were labelled as easy."

To his surprise, her expression softened. "You're such a strange man. I never know what you're going to say next."

"I'm not advocating promiscuity," he pointed out, still not sure what she was thinking. "I don't think it's good to treat your body cheaply. One night stands can be exciting, but I think if that's all you have, there's something awry. But that's different to having fun. Don't you think?"

"I suppose."

He huffed an exasperated sigh. "You're such a closed book. Come on, tell me something about yourself. You've had one-night stands, right?"

She chewed her bottom lip, and he could see her debating whether to be honest with him. He said nothing, letting her take her time to think. She was such a puzzle. She fascinated him, and he was desperate to find out more about her. *Please*, he thought. *Please open up a little.*

She looked out of the window, across at the plane, where their luggage was currently being loaded. The sun turned her brown hair to shiny satin, and made her lips glisten. He wanted to kiss her. Fuck, he wanted to kiss her so much. He hadn't felt this much longing for a woman for ages, if ever. Why did he want her so badly?

Looking back up at him, she met his gaze for a long moment, and he saw something settle behind her eyes, like a leaf landing onto a river. She was going to confess something to him. His heart soared.

She leaned her chin on her hand. "I have had a one-night stand."

His eyebrows rose. "A? You mean only one?"

She continued to chew her bottom lip. Then she said, "And I got pregnant, and ended up marrying him."

He stared at her. "Oh."

She studied him a bit longer. "Fintan died four years ago, and I haven't slept with anyone since."

There was a long silence.

Eventually, he said, "You've only slept with one guy?"

"Yep."

"One."

"Yes."

"And you haven't had sex for four years?"

"Nope."

"Holy fuck."

She gave a short laugh. "Yeah. I can see how that would shock someone like you."

"Wow."

She looked away, her eyes distant, not seeing the view. "And my marriage was quite... troubled, is probably the best way to put it. Sex wasn't a major part of our relationship, at the end, anyway. Suffice to say, I'm not the most experienced girl you're likely to meet."

Her gaze came back to him, suddenly wary, and he realized that she thought his announcement of only being interested in experienced women meant she thought he wouldn't be interested in her.

His mind spun, and he blinked, speechless. Luckily, at that moment the call came for everyone to board the flight.

They stood and shouldered their carry-ons, and joined the queue.

Georgia scratched her nose, then glanced up at him. "Stop looking at me like that."

"I feel as if I've travelled back to the early nineteenth century. I should be asking you if you want to go to a soiree with me."

She laughed. Lowering her voice, she said, "Contrary to what you might think, not everyone in the world has a life that revolves around sex."

"And I feel so sorry for them."

"There are more important things to worry about."

"Really? I can't imagine what." Half-teasing, he looked down into her amber eyes. He'd spoken the truth when he'd said he preferred an experienced woman, but for some reason he couldn't fathom, the notion of Georgia being almost untouched gave him goose bumps. And she was looking at him not with the disinterest that her words implied, but with such longing and desire that he almost melted on the spot like a chocolate button placed in a hot oven.

Behind them, someone cleared their throat and then said, "You two again! Get a room, for crying out loud."

Matt glanced over his shoulder to see the same smiling older woman who'd been behind them while they were waiting for the x-ray machine. "Sorry," he said, laughing, and gestured for Georgia to precede him to the flight attendant who was waiting to scan their boarding passes.

"No worries," the woman said. "Oh to be young and in love again. Brings back memories."

Georgia let the flight attendant scan her boarding pass and waited for him. Her gaze rose to meet his, and they both gave a rueful smile as they headed for the plane.

"Sorry about that," he murmured. "I didn't think it was worth spending ten minutes explaining our situation."

"It's okay." She looked out of the window to where the sun streamed across the tarmac. "Beautiful day for flying."

"Gorgeous," he said, acknowledging that she wanted to change the subject. But he couldn't stop himself thinking about what she'd told him as they climbed the steps to the plane, found their seats, took what they needed from their carry-on bags, and then put them in the overhead compartment.

She'd only ever slept with one man, and sex hadn't been 'a major part' of their relationship, whatever that meant. She'd called her marriage 'troubled'. Obviously, she'd had a tough time.

It was clear that her husband had died around the time of the Christchurch earthquake in February 2011. Matt knew it had claimed many lives—maybe Georgia's husband was one of them? Or perhaps the timing was a coincidence, and he'd died from something like cancer, possibly after a few years of suffering. It would explain the trauma she'd been through. But it still didn't explain the way Noah had spoken about his father.

He offered Georgia the window seat and took the middle one of the three. He was just clipping in his belt when the older woman who'd been standing behind them discovered that her seat was the aisle one next to his.

He laughed. "Oh dear."

"Don't you love birds mind me," she said as she sat beside him. "Just pretend I'm not here."

He decided it wasn't fair to Georgia not to say something. "We're not a couple," he told the woman, "we're just good friends."

"Oh..." She clipped her belt in and her eyes met his with a twinkle. "Right."

He gave her a wry smile. Clearly she'd picked up that there was something between him and Georgia.

What that would turn out to be, he had no idea.

The flight was an hour long, and he didn't feel as if he could talk to Georgia intimately, so they kept their conversation light. She read her iPad, and he sat with his small travel sketchbook and doodled for a while, letting his mind wander as his pencil danced across the paper.

"Is that a character from your new book?"

He roused from his daydream some time later to see that Georgia had put down her iPad and was watching him draw. He examined what he'd done so far. He'd sketched a couple of scenes from the first chapter of his graphic novel, where the young hero visits Lake Taupo and discovers a *Taniwha* living in it—a supernatural Maori monster like a dragon. The boy's face was indistinct—he'd have to work on how to make the kid's expressions clear with a few simple pencil strokes, but he'd captured the boy's basic movements. "Yeah. His name's Rory."

"That's Noah's middle name."

"I know. He told me."

"Oh." Her eyebrows rose as she realized he'd named the character after her son. "That was nice of you."

Matt shrugged. "It's a cool name. The red hair will look good on the page."

"So do you have the story all planned out?"

"Not quite. I have some of the major plot points, the twists and turns, in my head. I hope the rest will come as I work on it."

She turned a little in the seat to look at the pad. Her shoulder pressed against him, the bare skin of her arm warm against his, strangely intimate because he'd never gotten this close to her, apart from the time he'd hugged her on the sofa.

"You smell nice," he said.

Her eyes rose to meet his, full of warmth. "So do you. I love that aftershave. What is it? I can smell myrrh and cardamom… it smells kind of… I don't know, Mediterranean."

"It's called Moroccan Myrrh," he said, amused. "How can you tell what's in it?"

"I took a course in aromatherapy as part of my study in controlling anxiety. It helps me separate the notes in aftershaves and perfumes."

"That's when you learned about the tea?"

"Yeah. A massage using essential oils can be great at reducing stress and tension."

His gaze slipped to her mouth. "I happen to be feeling very anxious right now."

She chuckled. "You poor thing. Maybe we'll have to see what we can do about that."

His gaze came back up to hers, and a tingle ran down his spine. She would never have said anything like that before. Her lips curved up, her expression warm and seductive. She wanted him, and for the first time since he'd known her, her eyes held the promise of sensual delights that made him long for the sun to set.

Chapter Nine

Georgia often forgot that the three King brothers had money. It was stupid really, because she worked for We Three Kings and knew perfectly well how much they funneled into charity work from their business. All three of them were incredibly generous and keen to help others, and she loved them all for that.

But in spite of Brock's magnificent apartment and the fact that they owned their own plane, they rarely showed signs of their wealth. Charlie was the worst, having no interest in money whatsoever, as far as she could see. Brock had finer tastes than the other two, but even he didn't throw his money around.

She was certain that the majority of women in the world would think she was crazy, but when she was with Matt, she always forgot he was a billionaire. He wore jeans and shirts rather than expensive suits, and although he drove a sports car, he'd chosen a gorgeous silver Aston Martin V8 Vantage and not a bright red flashy babe magnet. Granted, she hadn't seen his house, but she was sure that even if it was big, it wouldn't be dripping with gold and diamonds. He had the most up-to-date iPhone and an expensive laptop, but there was just something about him that was understated and sophisticated. He didn't seem to use his money to get women but relied on his natural talents, and she liked that.

Somehow, then, it was all the more shocking when they arrived at the hotel and checked in, and she discovered he'd booked them two top floor club suites.

Stunned into silence, she just stared at him as he signed in and collected their key cards, then picked up her case and followed him wordlessly to the elevator.

It was only when the doors closed and the elevator began to rise that she said, "Holy fuck, Matt. A club suite?"

His eyebrows rose. "What?"

"Seriously? You don't know why I'm nearly speechless?"

"Well, firstly, I can't imagine you ever being speechless, and secondly, you told me to impress you with my billions of dollars. I only do as I'm told." He winked at her.

She suppressed the shiver that ran down her back. "Yeah, right. I can't imagine you ever doing what you're told."

He grinned. "You'd be surprised."

Something in his expression told her he was talking about sex. Suddenly, she was very aware they were in an enclosed space. The deep, sexy scent of his aftershave invaded her senses, and his eyes turned hot and sultry. She had a vision of him dropping his bags and pushing her up against the mirrored wall. He'd kiss her until she was breathless, until she was senseless with lust, and she wouldn't be able to do anything about it.

She blinked. His lips were curving up. She'd been staring at him too long.

"You shouldn't look at me like that," he said.

But she couldn't tear her eyes away from his. He looked gorgeous today, young and fresh-faced in a checked shirt and jeans. His hair looked ruffled and unkempt as it always did, as if a girl had spent hours running her fingers through it, although she was certain he'd styled it to look like that on purpose. He wasn't aggressive or particularly macho, but something about him said he was a hundred percent male, and made all her lady bits clench.

He leaned on the wall above her shoulder, looking down at her, his eyelids at half-mast with lazy desire. He didn't touch her, but her body burned.

"I'm warning you," he said, his voice low and husky. "If you don't stop looking at me like that, I'm going to kiss you."

Her lips parted. More than anything in the world, more than she wanted food and drink or even air to breathe, she wanted him to kiss her.

The elevator pinged and the doors slid open.

"Damn it," he said, and laughed as he picked up his bags.

Swallowing hard, she did the same and followed him out.

He stopped outside her room, swiped her card, and opened the door for her. "Here you go, ma'am."

Still tingling at the heat that had flared between them, she slipped past him and went into the suite.

She walked forward a little and stopped in her tracks.

The place was huge and exquisitely decorated. The lounge had a dark leather suite and a glass table and chairs, and its windows overlooked the small capital. Vases of flowers decorated the tables, filling the room with a beautiful summery scent. Large, expensive-looking paintings hung on the walls, and she knew they'd be originals, not prints. A small kitchen appeared to house the sort of equipment she would have expected in a top restaurant. Rows of delicate fairy lights decorated the balcony outside, adding a festive touch.

She walked through and peered into the bathroom and saw spotless white tiles and sparkling chrome, with an obscenely large bath. Two people would be able to fit into that bath. She backed out hurriedly.

When she walked into the bedroom, her jaw actually dropped. The walk-in closet was almost the size of her own bedroom. A wonderful wooden dressing table stood against the wall, with a large oval mirror that made her want to sit in front of it, brush her hair a hundred times, and apply cold cream. But it was the bed that made her gasp. Glittering drapes surrounded a kingsize bed covered in a sumptuous duvet and plum-colored pillows. It looked like a bed from an illustration of *The Princess and the Pea*.

Heart racing, she walked out again. Matt had propped the door open with his suitcase and was standing in the living room, awaiting her reaction.

"I can't stay here," she said.

He frowned and looked around. "I thought it looked nice." His gaze came back to her, puzzled. "The best suite was already booked, unfortunately. Would you rather me try another hotel?"

She gaped at him. "Oh my God, you seriously think I've found fault with this place? Matt! It's like a bloody palace. I can't possibly stay here."

The puzzled look evaporated and turned to amusement. "Why?"

"It must have cost you a small fortune."

"I have no idea. I just asked for the two best suites they had available."

"Matt!"

His expression turned impatient. "What?"

"This would cost two weeks' rent!"

"Georgia, I asked you to come with me. I wouldn't expect you to pay. And it's not the same as Brock paying for Erin's room—you work for the company and this is a business arrangement. I hope it's a treat, but it's not a gift as such, and I don't expect anything in return."

"That's not the point. It's so extravagant! Another child could be helped with this money."

He stared at her for a moment. Then he dropped a shoulder and let his carry-on bag slide to the floor. Finally, he walked forward to stand before her. He put his hands on hips, which she was beginning to learn meant he was doing his best to hide a rising frustration.

"Brock works twelve hours a day nearly every day," he said. "Sometimes more."

She fought not to take a step back as he glared at her. "I know."

"He's on call every other weekend, and he's responsible for saving thousands of kids' lives."

"I know."

"Charlie's hardly ever out of the lab. All he does is think about how to help children."

"Matt…"

"I know I don't save lives," he said. "I'm well aware of that. I don't have those sorts of skills. I would never have made a doctor or a scientist—I don't have Charlie's brain or Brock's dedication."

It was gradually sinking in that she'd really upset him. "Oh God, that's not what I—"

"In the big scheme of things, creating a bunch of cartoon characters is very low on the list. Do you think I don't know that? Do you think I don't wonder whether I deserve my share of the money they insist I have?" Real pain shimmered in his eyes.

"Matt!" she said, horrified. "I'm not saying that at all. Your characters are a huge part of the reason why the Three Wise Men medical equipment has been so successful." She put a hand on his arm, relieved when he didn't pull away. "Come on, I've met hundreds of children over the past year, at the hospitals and through the Foundation, and they all adore your books—it's all they talk about. You're an essential part of the business, and it makes me angry to hear you put yourself down, and incredibly upset that you'd think I was talking about you!"

He frowned. "I thought you were saying I should have put the money to better use."

"Of course not! I'm always amazed at how much the three of you give away. Not only do you all help kids by making their lives easier with the equipment, but you help sick kids through the Foundation, you fund research, and don't think I don't know how much you donate anonymously to various charities—I have to process all the flipping checks!"

His frown remained, although he did slide his hands into his pockets.

"You work hard, and you have incredible talent," she said. "That's why you're up for this award tonight. You've done wonderful things with the gift God gave you—you've hardly frittered your life away. You thoroughly deserve every penny you get, and I wouldn't dream of criticizing you for spending a little on yourself, and having nice things. All I meant was that it's not my money, and I feel... I don't know... odd being in a place like this."

He looked around. "It's just a room."

"I know, but..."

"I didn't pay for it with my company card," he said. "I wouldn't do that. I paid for it with my own money." Then he looked alarmed. "That doesn't mean it's a gift from me, it is a business arrangement, and I wouldn't assume—"

Georgia took his face in her hands, reached up on tiptoes, and pressed her lips to his.

She felt him inhale sharply, and she moved back an inch, giving him the option to pull away if he wanted. Her heart thundered. If she'd read this wrong, she wouldn't have the courage to do it again. If Matt was upset with her, or didn't believe she hadn't meant to insult him, she might as well turn around and go home.

For a long moment, he didn't move. Both of them were breathing quickly. His breath whispered across her lips, and her skin tingled as hairs rose all over her body.

Don't pull away, she thought, waiting for some sign of what he was thinking. *Please don't pull away.* Only at that moment did she realize how much she liked him, and how much she wanted him.

Slowly, he pulled his hands out of his pockets. She waited, half-expecting him to push her away.

He didn't, though. He placed his hands on her hips, turned her, and moved forward, forcing her to back up a few steps. She met the wall behind her with a bump and a gasp, and slid her hands down to rest on his chest to steady herself.

Her heart hammered against her ribs, and as she looked up at him, words deserted her. He was so tall, his broad shoulders and wide chest filling her view, his aftershave invading her senses until all she could see, think, and feel, was him.

He brought his hand up to cup her cheek, and his gaze caressed her face, the look in his hazel eyes so intense and sexy that suddenly she couldn't breathe.

"Jesus, you're beautiful," he murmured. His low voice sent a shudder through her. He gave a short, helpless laugh as she shivered in his arms. And then he kissed her.

Georgia's fingers splayed on his chest, and her head spun as her senses tried to register everything she was feeling. The firmness of his muscles and the warmth of his skin through his shirt beneath her fingertips, and when she placed her palms on his ribs, his rapid heartbeat beneath her hand. The slight brush of his five o'clock shadow against her cheek. But most of all, the touch of his lips to hers, soft and dry. The kiss was light and innocent, but still so incredibly intimate after months of not touching him that her face burned and an involuntary sigh of pleasure escaped her.

Apparently seeing it as confirmation that this was what she wanted, Matt slid his hand into her hair to hold her head and moved closer, pinning her to the wall with his body. She gasped, and as her lips parted he brushed his tongue into her mouth and turned the dial up to eleven.

Georgia had never been kissed like it. Now she understood the phrase 'kissed senseless', because she was certain that when he stopped—if he stopped, because he was showing no signs of doing so at the moment—she wouldn't know which way was north and which was south.

His mouth moved across hers with a possessive passion she hadn't known existed, while his tongue teased and played with hers until she tingled all over. His left hand stayed in her hair while his right slid around her hip to hold her against him, but he didn't try to grope her breast or unbutton her jeans. Instead it was as if he put all his concentration into the kiss, which felt just as intimate as if he'd stripped her naked.

He wanted her—that was obvious from the impressive erection pressing against her mound, and the way his fingers dug into her hip and his hand tightened in her hair. But he didn't take advantage of her, and he didn't assume, and by the time he finally lifted his head to look down at her, it took all the willpower she possessed not to beg him to take her to bed.

Chapter Ten

It took Matt a few seconds of intense concentration to regain control.

Every red blood cell in his body was urging him to lift her up, carry her to the bed, and throw her onto it. To rip off her clothes, cover her warm skin in kisses, then part her legs and thrust home. His body burned for it. The erection straining at the stitching of his jeans throbbed, and he felt a deep, overriding hunger for the soft, tiny, beautiful woman in his arms.

He didn't, though. He gave himself a moment to cool down, conscious that her breaths were coming in gasps the same way his were, and then just kissed her gently. Georgia sighed, tilting her face up and closing her eyes, and he pressed his lips across hers from left to right, then back again, light, butterfly kisses to tell her he wanted more, but he wasn't going to take it right now.

When he finally lifted his head and moved back, her eyes looked distant and dreamy. He'd kissed off her lip gloss—he licked his own and tasted strawberry, nice—and her lips looked plump and rosy pink.

They studied each other for a moment, smiling, and then he gave a short laugh and ran a hand through his hair. "I'd better go." He turned to get his bags.

Georgia took a step forward. "You... you don't have to."

He turned back with a sigh. "I want to stay more than anything in the world, and I can't believe I'm saying this, but..." He took a deep breath and blew it out slowly, shakily.

Her lips curved up. "You're nervous."

"Yeah. I need to... I don't know... run a few miles or something." He gave a wry laugh.

"You sure you don't want to wear off some of that anxiety?"

"Jesus... I can't believe I've finally got you into a room and you're asking me that, and I'm turning you down." He moved closer to her again, and cupped her face with his hands. "I hope you know how much I want you right now. But when I do finally take you to bed, I want to give you a hundred percent of my concentration and not have to worry about the time. Does that make sense?"

She smiled and nodded.

He brushed his thumb across her bottom lip. "Kissing you is even better than I'd imagined. And I'd imagined it a lot."

"Me too," she whispered.

"Really?" He'd hoped she liked him, but she'd turned him down so many times he was surprised to hear her say it.

"Of course. You're sex on legs, Matt. Any woman would be mad not to find you attractive."

"Well, thank you." He briefly considered kissing her again, then sighed and dropped his hands. He'd meant what he said. When—if—he took her to bed, he wanted to have all the time in the world to fool around and nothing on his mind except giving her pleasure.

She looked at her watch. "It's five thirty. What time do we have to be downstairs?"

"I'll knock on your door just before seven."

"Okay."

He picked up his bags and then paused for a moment. "Thanks for coming with me."

"You're welcome. And I'm really sorry if I offended you earlier. That wasn't my intention at all. I'm very grateful for the opportunity to stay somewhere like this, and I really hope you win the award—you deserve it."

"Thanks." He gave her a smile and left.

His room was similar to Georgia's, and he didn't spend long looking around. He dumped his bags, extricated his suit and shirt from the carrier component of his case and hung it up, then turned on the shower. When the water was hot, he got in and soaked his hair and body, the warmth seeping into his bones.

While he soaped himself, he thought about their conversation. For a brief moment, he'd really thought she was criticizing him for spending money she didn't feel he'd earned. Now, he realized all she'd done was trigger the sensitive switch in his head that was always there. Deep down, he felt that he didn't deserve the money because, compared to his brothers, he thought he played an insignificant role in the business. He acknowledged the importance of the characters in making children feel comfortable with the equipment, but he knew he'd always feel that Brock and Charlie were the ones who were the most deserving.

He put his head under the spray and closed his eyes. He wasn't going to think about that now or he'd lose the courage to go to the ceremony. Instead, he thought about Georgia. How, when he'd panicked after he'd told her he'd paid for the room out of his own money, she immediately moved forward and kissed him.

Her lips were so soft, and her body had been too, when he'd pushed his against it. She was tiny, and he liked that. He would have enjoyed stripping her naked, then picking her up and wrapping her legs around his waist to take her right there against the wall. He imagined palming her generous breasts as he sank deep into her, thrusting until she clenched around him and cried out his name.

And... now he had a hard-on. He leaned on the tiles and blew out a long breath. Hopefully, she would still want to go to bed with him later, but it was possible she'd change her mind when she had some time to think about it. Either way, he was tense, pent-up, and anxious.

Taking himself in hand, he gave his erection a few long, slow strokes, imagining it was Georgia's fingers holding him. Maybe even her mouth closing around the tip, her lips sliding down the shaft. Jeez, that was a hot image, of her looking up at him with those sexy amber eyes as she sucked and licked him to a climax. His hand moved faster, harder. His daydream blossomed, his mind picturing her naked in the shower, kneeling before him, her pearly skin shimmering in the water. Her breasts glistening, the pink nipples swollen, her silky hair soaked, and her lips wet as they moved. She'd take him deep in her mouth, sucking hard, the sheer sight of her doing so enough to drive him to the edge. And just before he came, she would move back enough so he could watch each jet of silky fluid entering her mouth before she swallowed it down...

Oh... holy shit, that was fucking hot and he was going to...

His other hand tightened to a fist on the wall and he gasped as the exquisite pulses claimed him. His chest heaved and his eyes closed, and he cursed out loud multiple times until his body finally relaxed.

Jesus. She was going to be the death of him. He leaned his forehead on his arm. Perhaps he shouldn't have a sexual relationship with her. Because once he started something, he had the feeling he wouldn't want to leave her alone.

*

Georgia climbed onto the bed and lay back on the pillows, the drapes falling around her and enclosing her in a glittering fantasy world.

She covered her eyes with her hands, unable to believe she'd asked Matt to stay and he'd turned her down. She didn't know whether to feel embarrassed, humiliated, or touched at his honesty.

I hope you know how much I want you right now. He wouldn't have said that if he hadn't meant it. And it had been clear that he wanted her. Everything in his kiss—including the erection he'd sported—had told her that. But instead of throwing her onto the bed and taking advantage of the moment, he'd asked her to wait, presumably well aware that later on she might change her mind. How could she be anything but impressed by that?

This man had layers to him she hadn't expected. She'd thought him shallow, a playboy interested only in fast sex and good times. Possibly, she'd been right about the fast sex, but she was beginning to learn he was far from shallow. He'd been genuinely hurt when he'd thought she'd accused him of not deserving his money.

Georgia felt terrible when she thought about that. It was the last thing she would have said to him. He worked ceaselessly to better the lives of children. Making the world a better place wasn't always about curing cancer. Brightening someone's day with a smile or a kind deed could be as precious as gold if they were unhappy or lonely. She'd seen so many kids in the hospitals reassured by the Dixon the Dog or Carmel the Cat characters clipped to their nebulizers or drips. Children all over the country—and, she suspected, a growing portion of the world—adored his books and requested the stories every night before they went to sleep. It was a rare gift to be able to give comfort to another person through mere words on a page, and the thought would never have entered her head that he didn't deserve the recognition he got.

Feeling uncomfortable, she closed her eyes and thought instead about what had happened when she'd kissed him. The colors in his hazel eyes seemed to change according to his mood. She knew it was impossible and must be something to do with the light, but when she'd kissed him and then moved back, the irises had been a deep, warm brown with just a few flecks of green. And then he'd turned her, pushed her back against the wall, and kissed her properly.

Her body tingled with the memory, and she brushed her hands over her breasts, inhaling as she touched her nipples. She remembered the way he'd slipped his hand into her hair and tightened his fingers, a touch possessive—she liked that, and she knew he'd be the same in bed, taking charge, passionate and slightly forceful.

She moved a hand to her jeans, unbuttoned them, and slid her fingers beneath the elastic of her panties. She wasn't surprised to find herself swollen and wet. He'd done that to her, when he'd thrust his tongue into her mouth and kissed her into next week.

Georgia sighed and circled a finger over her clit, shivering with the pleasurable sensation. What would he look like without clothes? She knew he played rugby, ran, surfed—he'd be muscular and tanned. He had powerful arms and thighs, and he was much bigger than her. If he decided he wanted her, there wasn't much she'd be able to do about it.

Ooh.

She played with a nipple as her finger moved faster over her clit. She'd tell him firmly, "Not now Matt," but he'd just advance on her with that gleam in his eye, rip off her clothes, and push her onto the bed. She'd try to crawl away, but he'd capture her, flip her onto her back, and pull her toward him. He'd lean over her, clasping her wrists and pinning them above her head with one hand, so she was at his mercy. She'd struggle, of course, a bit, but he'd be too strong for her, and when he reached down and unzipped his jeans, she wouldn't be able to stop him pressing the tip of his erection into her folds.

Man, this was turning her on. She could see his hot eyes staring into hers, his victorious, smug smile as he held her down and then pushed his hips forward. *Ohhh...* that would feel good, to have a man inside her after all this time. And not just any man, but the gorgeous guy who made her heart race when he looked at her. He'd thrust hard, and she'd just have to lie there and take it, feeling him moving inside her, filling her up. He'd take his pleasure from her the way he wanted, and she'd be helpless to do anything but let him tease her to the edge, when her traitorous body would do his bidding and come at his command.

Her muscles began to tighten, and she gasped as everything tensed. The orgasm swept over her, swift and powerful, and she clenched inside in exquisite, strong pulses.

Finally, she fell back onto the pillows, exhausted and a little bewildered.

Jesus. Where had that come from? She'd never had that kind of fantasy before.

She stared up at the drapes, puzzled and a little embarrassed. Thank God he'd never know.

Rolling onto her side, she tugged a pillow down and hugged it. A smile crept onto her lips. She was in the capital, in an incredibly ostentatious suite, a gorgeous, sexy billionaire was staying next door, and there was more than a little possibility that she'd be having sex tonight.

Life could be a lot, lot worse.

Chapter Eleven

At just before seven, a knock came at the door. Georgia took a final look at herself in the mirror, brushed her dress down nervously, picked up her clutch bag, and opened the door.

Her eyes widened and her jaw dropped. Matt stood there in a black tuxedo. He wore a white shirt and a real bow tie, not one of those on elastic like her dad had bought for an office Christmas party one year. And... holy moly... the suit was a three piece with a waistcoat.

"Oh my God," she said.

"Holy fuck," he said in return.

She followed his gaze down to her dress. "What? Do I look okay?"

"Georgia... words fail me. I swear you are the most beautiful woman that's ever lived in the whole history of the world."

"Matt..." She pushed him shyly. Not wanting to show him up on his special night, she'd treated herself to a long black strapless gown. It was simple but elegant, and she wore her hair up in a chignon, with one thick strand curling by her cheek. A plain silver necklace and earrings completed the look.

He reached out and gently touched the curl. "You wore your hair like this to your interview."

"That's right. You remember."

"Of course I remember. I couldn't take my eyes off you then, and I can't take them off you now."

True to his words, he was looking at her as if she was something special, something precious, and it made heat flood to her cheeks for the first time since she'd known him.

He didn't mock her, though. Instead, he studied her blush with fascination, as if touched and pleased that he'd caused it. Then he leaned forward and touched his lips to her warm cheek.

Finally, he offered her his arm like an old-fashioned Hollywood movie star, Clark Gable, or David Niven. "Shall we?"

Saying nothing, feeling oddly breathless, she slid her hand underneath his arm, and they walked along the corridor to the elevator.

Now the initial shock had worn off, she could appreciate the cut and quality of his suit. It was a wool-and-mohair mix, if she wasn't mistaken, with grosgrain lapels, the peak shape of them telling her he hadn't bought it off the peg. He'd polished his shoes, and he wore a simple square in his pocket. Even his watch was classy, a circular, stylish analog with none of the buttons and fancy trappings she would have expected him to wear. And he wore cufflinks. Cufflinks! Time and again, this guy surprised her.

He looked down at her, catching her admiring him.

"You look good," she said.

He met her gaze, and they exchanged a long look. She thought about her fantasy, how she'd imagined him pinning her hands above her head and thrusting her to a climax, and her face grew warm again. Would her dream come true tonight? Or would something interfere to change either of their minds? She reminded herself that he was nervous about the ceremony—if he didn't win the award, he might not be in the mood for lovemaking later on.

The elevator dinged, breaking the spell, and they walked into the carriage. Part of her wondered if he'd kiss her once the doors had closed, but he leaned against the wall on the opposite side of her, and so she did the same, leaving several feet between them.

"I'd kiss you," he said after a few seconds of staring at her, "but your lipstick looks fantastic, and I don't want to smudge it."

She laughed and looked down at the toes of her high-heeled shoes that peeked out from beneath the dress. "We'll save it for later. Maybe."

"Yeah," he said.

She looked back up at him. "How are you feeling?"

He breathed in deeply, then blew it out. "Nervous. Unfortunately the security guard took the rest of your teabags or I would have had one."

"You don't look nervous, if that's any help. You look suave and sophisticated."

"Shows how looks can be deceiving."

"I'll say." She smiled.

He gestured to his clothes. "You like the James Bond suit?"

"I think we make quite a dashing pair, actually."

"Yeah." His eyes looked light brown and glimmered with emotion, but she couldn't decipher what it was.

"Good luck," she said.

"Thanks."

The elevator dinged, and the doors slid open.

They walked across the foyer to the main hall, and Georgia exclaimed with pleasure at the sight of the festive trimmings. The whole hall was decorated in red, green, and silver. White cloths covered the round tables that had been laid with sparkling silver cutlery and Christmassy centerpieces. Around the hall stood large cardboard standup figures of characters from the various children's books up for awards that evening.

"Matt, look!" She pointed to a huge Dixon the Dog standing along one wall.

"Nice." He grinned and looked genuinely pleased.

An awards assistant welcomed guests in the doorway, directing them to tables. She gestured to one at the side near the front, and Matt took Georgia's hand and led her over to it.

There were lots more people than she'd expected, and she felt breathless with nerves as they approached the table and she saw that six of the eight chairs were already taken. How must Matt be feeling, she wondered? But he looked anything but nervous as everyone introduced themselves and shook hands around the table.

She'd accompanied him countless times to hospitals, but of course whenever they met people he always wore a character costume and never said anything. The few times she'd been to a function with him, it hadn't been as his date, and she'd either been busy greeting other guests or organizing the event for We Three Kings, so she hadn't had the chance to see how he acted in this kind of environment.

Her heart warmed as she watched him talking and laughing, thanking those people who congratulated him for being a finalist, and generally putting everyone at ease. She would never have guessed he was anxious about the result tonight if she hadn't known him better. He wore a mask quite well, she thought, knowing she would never have expected him to be so sensitive about his money, or so worried about what people thought of him. How many other things had she gotten wrong?

An older woman with silver hair in a neat bob walked up to him and touched his arm. He turned and smiled, then bent to kiss her on the cheek.

"Georgia?" He held out his hand to bring her closer. "This is my agent, Jenny Long. Jenny, this is my friend, Georgia Banks. She works for We Three Kings and has kindly agreed to accompany me tonight so I don't look like a total loser."

"Oh, so nice to meet you," Georgia said, shaking her hand. "You must be so pleased that Matt's up for this award."

"Couldn't happen to a nicer guy." Jenny rubbed his arm. "I kept telling him he was a shoo-in for the picture book award, but he wouldn't have it."

"There's a long way to go yet," he said, prompting her to roll her eyes. "Oh stop it," he scolded. "I'm not counting any chickens until they're well and truly out of those shells."

Georgia smiled. "What do you think of his idea for the graphic novel?"

Matt's smile froze and his gaze slid to Jenny.

Her eyebrows rose. "Oh… what's this?"

"Shit," Georgia said. She sent him a despairing look. "I'm so sorry. I assumed she knew."

He put his arm around her waist, leaned forward, and kissed her forehead. "No worries. I was just keeping it to myself until I had something to show everyone." He proceeded to tell Jenny a little about the story. The older woman listened, but Georgia saw her gaze slide over to her and a smile appear on her lips, and she knew that Jenny had spotted his arm still around her. His hand was warm on her hip. It was a possessive gesture, as if he was telling everyone who might be watching that she was with him. It made her think of her fantasy, and then her cheeks grew hot all over again.

"I love the sound of it," Jenny said when he'd finished describing his idea. "Let me know when you feel you're well on the way, and I'll start approaching some publishers."

"Okay, great."

"Good luck."

"Thanks." He said goodbye to her and watched her go, then turned his gaze to Georgia.

"I'm so sorry," she whispered. "I hope I didn't put my foot in it."

"Don't worry about it. It's not a big deal."

She cleared her throat. "Your hand is still on my hip."

"I'm well aware of that. I'm letting the half a dozen guys around us, who haven't stopped staring at you, know that—for tonight at least—you're spoken for." His gaze was a tad challenging, as if he expected her to declare her indignation at his possessiveness.

Georgia was sure nobody was looking at her, and didn't care either way. She'd have eyes for nobody but Matt this evening. Normally, she would have been the first to tell a guy to keep his hands to himself. But tonight was filled with early Christmas magic, and the last thing she wanted was for him to leave her alone.

So she just gave a little shrug and nestled against him, and his lips curved up. "Come on," he said. "Time for dinner."

He held her chair for her as she sat, then took his place beside her.

After only five minutes, she realized she needn't have been nervous about the evening. The meal was wonderful, and the people around the table were thrilled to be there and happy to talk about books and their work, so there wasn't chance for any awkward silences to fall. Georgia sat next to an older Maori man who wrote action stories for teens, and she found out a lot about the publishing process that she was pleased to discover so she'd be able to be a bit more knowledgeable when talking to Matt. The man wanted to know all about Matt, and both he and his wife seemed genuinely touched when she told them some details about Matt's business.

"Our granddaughter has Cystic Fibrosis and she's been in and out of hospital," the woman said. "We've heard a lot about what We Three Kings has done for children, and Rangi just adores the Ward Seven books. She went onto the forum and left a question for Melchior, and she was thrilled when he gave her a big long answer and then sent her a signed copy of one of his books. She'll be so excited to know we were sitting on his table."

Georgia smiled and glanced across at Matt. He was listening to the woman beside him who was the head of a local small press, and they'd been discussing whether picture books would ever be as popular on the digital platforms as they were on paper. He looked as if he was concentrating, but as she continued to watch him, his hand reached for hers under the table and gave it a squeeze, so he was clearly aware of her.

She felt a sudden surge of pride for him. No matter whether he won the award tonight or not, he'd done such wonderful things with the gift he'd been given. It made her sad to think he considered himself less deserving than his brothers.

Waiters took the last plates away, refilled everyone's glasses with champagne, and then the presenter approached the microphone and announced the beginning of the award ceremony.

Matt's hand searched for hers again under the table, and she clutched it tightly. She flicked through the program as the presenter read his introduction. The Picture Book Awards would be announced halfway through, after the Young Adult, Non-Fiction, Junior Fiction, and Early Childhood awards. She scanned the nominees for the Picture Book Awards, spotting Matt's name, the third out of six. A smile spread across her face. She would save the program and scan it at work so she could put it onto the website.

After his award there were several others. To her shock, she saw that he was also nominated for an Illustration Award, a Librarian's Choice Award, and a Children's Choice Award. Was he aware? She nudged him and tapped the program. He leaned close and read it, then winked at her. He knew, and he hadn't told her. What a strange man he was. Clearly, the Picture Book Award was the one that was most important to him, but how odd that he'd kept the others to himself.

The evening progressed slowly, with occasional readings from the books, and much drama as winners were revealed and the authors took to the stage to accept the statue of a book sitting atop a stylized Maori *koru* or spiral, following which they were encouraged to give a speech.

Matt remained outwardly calm, but when it was time for his award, his hand tightened on hers under the table, and he fell quiet, clearly racked with nerves. As the presenter read out the nominees, she watched Matt close his eyes for a moment. Was he sending a prayer to his sister? Georgia squeezed his fingers, her heart racing. *Please let him win*, she begged Pippa, and indeed anyone else who might be listening. *Please, please let him win. He deserves it so much.*

"And the winner is…" The presenter slit open the envelope and extracted the slip of paper.

Chapter Twelve

The presenter paused for so long that Georgia thought she might pass out from holding her breath.

Then he smiled, looked straight at their table, and said, "Matt King for *Dixon's X-Ray Disaster.*"

Huge cheers went up across the hall. Georgia inhaled sharply and looked at Matt. The smile that he'd pinned on his face had faded, and he was staring at the screen behind the presenter that showed his name in huge letters and a copy of the cover of his book.

Georgia wanted to cry, but she just leaned forward and rubbed his arm. "Go on," she said. "You won, Matt. Go and get your award."

He turned and looked at her, and then the most gorgeous smile spread across his face. He glanced around the table and laughed at the sight of everyone clapping, pushing himself to his feet.

Then, to Georgia's shock, he bent and cupped her face, and gave her a long, hard kiss.

Her cheeks flamed, and when he finally pulled back, she knew she must be scarlet. He didn't say anything, just turned and walked toward the stage. She touched her hands to her face, conscious of a few people whistling and cheering, and caught Jenny's eye, not surprised to see the older woman smiling.

She watched Matt thread through the tables, stopping to give Jenny a kiss on the cheek before he approached the stage and climbed the steps to the podium. He shook hands with the presenter, accepted the award, and then walked up to the microphone.

The clapping died down as everyone waited for him to speak. He looked across the crowd, and then his lips curved up and he just said, "Wow."

Everyone cheered again, and he laughed. Georgia couldn't stop grinning. He looked like a young boy up there, full of excitement and joy, and so gorgeous in his suit. All across the room there would be young women fanning themselves as they looked at him.

And yet, if she played her cards right, he'd be coming back to her room tonight. She shivered and gulped a big mouthful of champagne. Dreams really did come true!

Matt ran a hand through his hair and blew out a long breath as the cheering died down again. "Thank you," he said, turning the trophy in his hands. "I can't tell you how much this means to me. I don't want to give a long speech because I know how dull they are, but equally I couldn't stand here and accept this award without saying a few words to those people who've made it possible. So quickly, a huge thank you to my publisher, and to my agent, Jenny Long, who was the first one to believe in me and take a chance on me." He waved at her, and she waved back, wiping under her eyes and then laughing as her husband put his arm around her.

"Thank you also to my parents for their encouragement and patience when I was younger," Matt continued. "I believe that success is very much related to both opportunity and support. I wasn't an easy teen, and I don't believe I would be standing here accepting this award if it wasn't for them."

Tears pricked Georgia's eyes, and she leaned on the table and covered her mouth. He was so sincere, and she could hear the emotion behind his words in the huskiness of his voice. That was why he enjoyed working with teenagers, she thought. He saw himself in each of them, and truly believed that help and guidance at that age could be the turning point in their lives.

"Thanks also to my brothers, Brock and Charlie," he said. "They've been absolutely amazing in their painstaking research into childhood diseases, and their development of medical equipment. I'm honored that they included me as one of the Three Wise Men, even though I was at the back of the queue when brains were given out." He laughed, and the audience went *Awww!* and laughed with him.

"I'd like to thank my sister, Pippa," he said. He paused for a moment and adjusted the position of the award on the podium. Georgia held her breath, wishing she could be standing beside him, holding his hand. He cleared his throat. "Pippa died when she was eight years old from an asthma attack, and she is the reason that we created the Three Wise Men, and why I write children's stories. Pip— wherever you are, this award is for you."

He picked the award up and kissed it, and everyone cheered and clapped.

He made as if he was going to leave the stage, then stopped, came back, and leaned toward the microphone. "Oh, one last thing. I want to say thank you to the gorgeous Georgia, who agreed to come with me tonight so I didn't look like Billy No Mates." He winked at her, sending everyone looking over at her. "She also saved me at the airport earlier, so I can sincerely say I wouldn't be here without her!" He blew her a kiss and left the stage to cheers and another round of clapping.

Already emotional from his words about Pippa, tears trickled down Georgia's hot cheeks, and she tried to wipe them away to no avail. As he walked back to the table, he saw her struggling to control them. When he reached her, he pulled her to her feet and wrapped his arms around her.

"Aw, don't," he whispered in her ear. "You'll make me cry."

She laughed and hugged him back. "Congratulations. You so deserve it. I'm so thrilled for you."

"Thank you." He kissed the top of her head. "I'm still taller than you even though you have heels on. How short are you, exactly?"

She pushed him away and thumped his arm, and he grinned. They took their seats again at the table. "Let's have a look at it, then," she said, and he passed her the statue. It was gorgeous, heavy and shiny, and she knew it would have pride of place on a shelf somewhere in his studio.

"It's amazing," she said, and gave it back to him. He smiled and passed it to the woman next to him who wanted a look, then winked at Georgia. Now, his eyes looked almost all green, filled with excitement and pleasure. She was so happy for him and was sure it would help give him confidence for when he started his graphic novel.

The rest of the evening passed in a blur of excitement, not in the least because Matt went on to win both the Children's Choice and the Illustration Awards. By the end of the evening, he had three trophies sitting in front of him, and a huge smile on his face.

The ceremony drew to a close, the lights lowered, the drinks started to flow, and the band took to the stage and started to play *Baby It's Cold Outside*.

Matt leaned back in his chair and looked at Georgia with a mischievous smile. "Please tell me you like dancing."

"I love dancing," she said, thrilled.

He stood and held out his hand.

She pushed herself to her feet, eyes wide. "What, now? We'll be the first on the floor."

"Yep. Everyone's staring at you anyway," he said, "so we might as well give them a good view."

Laughing, she took his hand and let him lead her to the dance floor. People clapped and cheered as they passed, and for the hundredth time that evening, Georgia's face flamed at the thought of being the center of attention. She didn't often dance in high heels— hopefully she wouldn't fall flat on her face!

She needn't have worried, though, because Matt didn't appear to have any intention of being more than an inch from her for more than a few seconds. As they reached the wooden square of dance floor in front of the band, he caught her left hand in his right and slipped an arm about her waist, and as they proceeded to dance, he held onto her as they circled around the floor. He could really move, and she soon forgot her inhibitions and threw herself into it, just enjoying the music, and loving every moment of being in his arms.

They danced to *I Wish it Could be Christmas Everyday*, *Merry Christmas Everyone*, and a dozen other Christmassy and non-festive songs, stopping only for a quick drink before they took to the floor again.

When the band started playing Bing's *White Christmas*, Matt finally pulled Georgia close and tightened his arm around her.

"Hello," he said. He was a little breathless, his cheeks pink and his hair damp around his temples. He'd ditched his jacket at some point, too hot to keep dancing in it, although he'd refrained from rolling up his shirt sleeves.

"I could eat you on a cracker," she said, running her left hand over his waistcoat. "You look gorgeous."

He chuckled, his gaze caressing her face. "Feel free."

She met his hazel eyes. They held as much promise as a sparkling Christmas parcel under the tree. His warm hand rested in the small of her back.

"Mmm," she said, feeling naughty. "Maybe I will."

His eyes took on a helpless look.

"What?" she asked, amused.

"Just remembering a daydream I had earlier." His sexy smile told her it had been more than a daydream. He'd been fantasizing about her.

"Oh, you too? Glad it wasn't just me." The words were out before she could stop them. Goodness! She had to stop drinking. The alcohol had released the safety catch on her speech filter.

His eyes widened, and his hand splayed just above the danger zone on her butt. "Oh…" he murmured, his eyes glowing. "Tell me more."

"You first," she said, although she was pretty certain she had an idea what his fantasy had been.

He laughed and kissed her temple. "Maybe later."

They were dancing closely now. The heat from his body seared through her, and her temple burned where his lips touched. He'd obviously shaved earlier because his jaw was smooth when it brushed against her cheek. As usual, his aftershave teased her senses, stirring up all kinds of sensations deep inside her.

"Do you know how sexy you look in that dress?" His gaze caressed her bare shoulder, lingering as if he wanted to place a kiss on it.

"Thank you."

"You have a great figure."

"Haven't I blushed enough this evening?"

"Hmm," he said, "about that. I don't think you've blushed in the whole year I've known you. For twelve months you've carefully avoided any intimacy between us. What's changed?"

"I don't know," she said. "I lead a very quiet life, and normally that's fine, that's what I've chosen. But I could do with some fun. Maybe it's because it's Christmas."

His lips brushed her temple again. "I'd be happy to provide some festive entertainment."

She laughed. "I'm sure you would."

The song finished, and Matt turned her and tipped her backward over his arm in a flamboyant end to the dance. She squealed as he lifted her up, conscious of cheers and claps from those watching.

"Thank God I've got a ton of tit tape on my boobs or I'd have been out of that bodice," she scolded him as he led her from the dance floor.

"That was the aim," he said, and grinned. They reached their table, and he hesitated and checked his watch. She peered over his arm at it. It was nearly eleven, and she sensed the evening was coming to an end, in the hall at least.

"Fancy going somewhere a bit quieter?" he asked. "To the bar for a drink?"

"That would be great."

So he collected his jacket, and she picked up her bag, and they said goodbye to everyone, then carried his three trophies between them across the foyer to the bar, which was a lot quieter and more peaceful than the busy hall.

Finding a cozy table in the corner, Georgia arranged his trophies in a row. "You'll need to put up an extra shelf for them all when you get home."

"Oh, they're going to have pride of place on the coffee table." He slid off his jacket and hung it over a chair. "What would you like to drink?"

She'd had a couple of glasses of champagne and didn't want any more. "What are you having?"

"Whisky, probably. I see they do a rare Bowmore here. I've got to try that."

"I'll have the same. I like a nice Islay malt."

"Sweet," he said, delighted. "I'll be back in a sec."

She slid onto the leather bench and let out a long, happy breath. Her heart raced at the thought of where the evening was heading. It had been so long since she'd been with a guy, and the idea of sleeping with Matt made her excited and nervous and panicky all at the same time.

Was she doing the right thing? There were so many reasons that it was a bad idea, but she was tired of always trying to do the right thing. Life was short, and she'd never wanted anything for Christmas more than she wanted Matt King in her bed.

She watched him pull out his phone and read a text while he waited for the barman to pour the drinks. His lips curved up and he glanced over at her, then typed something in before re-pocketing the phone. A few seconds later, her phone jingled in her bag. She pulled it out and saw he'd sent her a photo that Jenny had taken while they were dancing. It was a charming picture—they were both laughing, caught in mid twirl; her cheeks were pink and her dress was in a swirl around her, and Matt was holding her tightly, his hand in the small of her back.

She looked up at him, and he winked at her, then picked up the two glasses. Smiling, she slipped her phone back into her bag and watched him approach the table and slide onto the bench beside her.

He handed her the drink and held his up. She touched her glass to his. "Cheers, Matt, and congratulations."

"Cheers," he said. "Merry Christmas." His eyes glittered as he sipped the whisky. She honestly didn't think she'd ever seen a man as handsome as he looked tonight. And in a short while, it was very possible she'd be getting naked with him.

Holy moly.

Chapter Thirteen

Matt sipped his whisky, welcoming the burn of the expensive malt as he swallowed. He'd had a wonderful evening, and he was hopeful it wasn't over yet. Beside him, Georgia also sipped from her tumbler, tipping her head back and giving a satisfied *aaahh* as she swallowed.

His groin tightened in response, and he scolded it mentally. He didn't want to rush this moment. As much as he would have loved to pick her up in a fireman's lift and carry her to his room, there was also something tantalizing about drawing the moment out, like being really hungry and knowing a fillet steak was on the way, and nibbling at a plate of appetizers while you waited.

Besides which, he still wasn't a hundred percent convinced she wanted to go bed with him. He was about eighty percent sure—she'd dropped a lot of hints, and she was looking at him now with warmth in her eyes, but he extended his 'don't count your chickens until they're hatched' principle to all areas of his life to avoid disappointment.

"So," he teased, wanting to play, "about this daydream of yours… Feeling up to sharing details yet?"

She gave a girlish laugh, and he melted, just a little bit. It wasn't until tonight that he'd realized how serious she was a lot of the time. She had a wry sense of humor, but he didn't see her sexy smile often enough.

Clearly, she wasn't going to divulge her fantasy. He wondered what she'd daydreamed about. The thought of her lying on that luscious bed, sliding her hand into her panties as she pictured the two of them together got him all hot under the collar.

She looked stunning in the dress. She usually wore jeans and T-shirts to work, and although when they went to the hospital or to functions she occasionally wore a skirt, he'd never seen her in anything like the black dress. Although she was small, she had a gorgeous curvy figure, and with her hair up she looked like a movie star. He hoped she never took the dress off again. Although the idea of getting her naked also appealed to him.

The anxiety that had plagued him for the past week, which had morphed into nervous excitement throughout the evening, began to fade away. The bar was quiet, with carols playing in the background and the smell of cinnamon in the air, the lights low and intimate, and the fairy lights strung around the bar giving the night a magical feel. There were a few other people there, some couples talking softly, but everyone was lost in their own world. Matt liked this feeling of the approaching night, of the evening gradually fading to darkness, leaving just the two of them lit by the candle on the table.

"Thank you for coming with me tonight," he said. "I really appreciate it. It was much better than being on my own."

"Oh, I had a wonderful time." She gestured at his awards. "I wouldn't have missed it for the world."

He studied the trophies, feeling a swell of pleasure. He'd done Pippa proud. Okay, he wasn't saving lives, but even he couldn't ignore the hundreds of comments he'd received that evening about how much joy he brought to kids across the country.

He turned his gaze back to Georgia. She was leaning her head on her hand, half-turned toward him, looking relaxed and mischievous, exactly how he was feeling. He was far from drunk, but he was enjoying the mellow feeling that accompanied the couple of glasses of champagne and the excellent whisky.

Their bodies were almost touching, and he rested his arm on the back of the seat, almost—but not quite—around her. Her beautiful amber eyes studied him, alight with something. Desire? Excitement? He wasn't sure, but he hoped it boded well.

One of them was going to have to broach the subject at some point, and as he was the guy, he decided it was polite for him to be the brave one, even though he was more nervous about asking than he'd ever been before.

He took a deep breath. Oh well, what did he have to lose?

"So," he said. "Are you coming back to my room with me tonight?"

Her lips curved up. She lowered her gaze to her glass, swirled the liquid over the ice, and then took a sip. Her long lashes were dark against her pale cheek. Now, he could see that she'd applied a dark gray sparkly eyeshadow across her lids that glittered in the candlelight.

Was he going to have to talk her into it? He was willing to play the game if that was what she wanted.

"Come to bed with me," he murmured. He curled the long strand of hair at her temple around his finger like a piece of silky chocolate-colored ribbon. "Let me make love to you," he said, his gaze falling to her mouth with its beautiful plump lips and intriguing Cupid's bow. Jesus, he wanted to kiss her so much.

Georgia's breasts rose and fell rapidly in the tight bodice, but she still didn't say anything. He waited, letting her think about it, hoping she was picturing the same images as him. His lips on hers, his hands sliding up the black dress onto her bare skin. Her smaller, curvy body under his, his hands on her breasts, his mouth on her nipples, sucking, licking. Him sliding inside her until he carried them both away to blissful oblivion.

She lifted her gaze to his and moistened her lips with the tip of her tongue. Her pupils had dilated, but she said, "I shouldn't."

He ran the curl through his fingers. The slow, romantic refrain of *Have Yourself a Merry Little Christmas* filtered across the bar, and her eyes reflected the dancing candlelight, filled with longing.

Shouldn't wasn't the same as no. It was an invitation for discussion. She had doubts, but she was open to talking about them, and to being convinced.

He wasn't going to give up just yet.

*

Georgia felt as if the whole world was holding its breath.

She wanted the man sitting next to her more than anything, more than gold and diamonds, more than chocolate, which was saying something. But she couldn't just say yes. It wasn't that easy for her. *She* wasn't that easy. She needed to talk about it, but she wasn't sure whether he would have the patience.

She half expected him to huff a sigh, and to be exasperated that after a fun night she wasn't going to jump straight into his bed.

But he didn't look exasperated. He swirled the whisky in his glass over the ice, studying her thoughtfully. His eyes appeared a deep brown, warm and sensual, with no hint of irritation. Like her, he appeared to be enjoying this quiet moment, full of Christmassy magic.

"Why shouldn't you?" he asked.

She let out a long breath. He was prepared to discuss it, at least. "I work for you, for a start. And my job's important to me."

"You work for Brock, not for me."

She gave him a wry look. "I work for We Three Kings, of which you are one, in case you've forgotten."

He shrugged. "I have little to do with the business, as you well know. I'm a terrible businessman."

"You are. That's true."

He grinned. "There you go then. Next excuse."

She gave a short laugh and examined her glass. "I mean it, Matt. My job's important to me. I'd hate to jeopardize it for one night of... um..."

"Sizzling hot passion?"

Her gaze fell to his mouth. God, she wanted to kiss him. "Mmm."

"Why would going to bed with me jeopardize your job?"

She frowned. "Seriously?"

"Seriously." He looked puzzled. "The majority of people meet their partners through work, don't they?"

"Maybe, but that's not really what we're talking about here, is it?"

"Isn't it?"

"I've never had casual sex before. I have no doubt it'll be fantastic. But I don't know how I'll feel afterward and it makes me nervous."

He continued to look confused. "I'm not quite sure what you're getting at. We're both grownups, aren't we? If it doesn't work out, if you don't enjoy it, that's okay, I don't see why it would affect our working relationship."

"If I don't enjoy it... Jesus, Matt. That's not what I meant at all. Look, I like you. I mean... *really* like you. We're good friends, and I can't see how it wouldn't be awkward seeing you and knowing how good we were together, and not being able to do it again. Does that make sense?"

"Not really. If it's as good as I suspect it will be, why wouldn't we want to do it again?"

Now it was her turn to be baffled. "I thought we were talking about having a one-night stand? I know you're anti-commitment, and I assumed that if we—"

"I'm not anti-commitment."

Her eyebrows rose. "Pardon?"

"Just because I'm not in a relationship doesn't mean I'm anti-commitment. I just haven't met the right woman yet."

She blinked a few times. He looked perfectly serious.

He finished off his drink and put the glass on the table. "I think maybe we've got our wires crossed somewhere." Leaning back, he put his arm around her and moved closer until their bodies touched.

Sliding a knuckle beneath her chin, he lifted it and then lowered his lips to give her a light kiss. Then he lifted his head and smiled.

"Georgia, I've asked you out every week since you started work at the office. I fell for you the moment I walked into reception and saw you sitting there with your hair just like this, and your pantsuit, and your high heels. I admit I've been out with a few girls this year, but I honestly wasn't sure you'd ever go out with me. I don't mean to belittle the women I've been with, but it's been purely physical on both sides, and I've not led anyone on. I like sex. And I get a bit antsy when I haven't had it for a while."

He looked apologetic. She gave a short laugh. "Fair enough."

"I was so thrilled that you agreed to come with me tonight," he continued. "I don't expect you to go to bed with me. If you'd rather wait, that's okay. I'd be more than happy to go out on a few dates first. I have tried! If you want to come to bed with me, I'd be over the moon and the stars! But please don't think that one night is all I'm after. I've known you long enough to believe we'd be good together. Maybe we'd work out, maybe we wouldn't—there's no way of knowing. Either way, I hope we can remain friends."

She looked into his eyes, captivated by his words. This man continued to surprise her. "I thought you only wanted me because you couldn't have me," she said.

He shrugged. "Maybe that was the case in the beginning. I'm not afraid to admit it. But the more I've got to know you, the more my body hungers for yours." His eyes turned sultry, and he slid his hand against her cheek. "I want you, Georgia. So badly. I want to see what you look like beneath that shiny black satin. I want to cover your body with mine, to kiss you from head to toe, and to hear you sigh my name in the dark. I'll wait for you, if that's what you want. But I'm crazy about you, and if I don't have you tonight, I think I might go a little mad."

He gave such a look of helpless lust that she couldn't help but laugh.

"I don't want you to think that I don't understand the point of casual sex," she said, placing a hand on his arm. His biceps were hard and warm beneath his shirt. "I'm not saying I'm expecting anything. I just think it would be so sad if we weren't friends."

"We'll never not be friends, Georgia. I can't imagine life without you around."

He smiled, and it melted the last little piece of doubt in her mind. She wanted him, and he wanted her. Was there really anything else to talk about?

She finished off her whisky and placed the glass on the table. Then she picked up her clutch bag and one of the trophies. "Come on. Let's go to bed."

Chapter Fourteen

As they walked across the foyer to the elevators, Matt's heart picked up speed at the thought that Georgia had finally agreed to go to bed with him. Sex with a new partner was always a gamble, and she'd only been with her husband, so she was unlikely to be highly experienced. To his surprise though, he didn't care, because this wasn't all about bedroom gymnastics. More than anything, he just wanted to be alone with her, to spend time arousing her, and to watch her come, knowing he'd given her pleasure. The hunger was stronger than it had ever been before, and he puzzled on it as they pressed the button and waited for the doors to open.

The foyer was relatively busy, with the last few guests from the awards heading home or to their rooms, and the staff tidying up. He waited impatiently for the elevator to arrive, wanting to get her on her own, then gritted his teeth as at the last minute an elderly couple walked up and joined them in the carriage.

They stood to one side, making room for the couple, who talked in low voices as the doors shut and the elevator ascended.

Georgia looked up at him, trying not to laugh at his obvious impatience. He met her gaze and held it, heat rising within him at the thought that, in less than a minute, he'd be alone with her. Her eyes widened, and he knew she could see the raw desire in his eyes.

She lifted up on tiptoes and whispered in his ear. "I've changed my mind." The curve of her lips told him she was teasing him. "I think I'll go to bed on my own. Get a good night's sleep."

"Not an option," he murmured back. "Tonight, you belong to me."

She gave him a pretend affronted look and whispered again. "You sound as if I don't have a choice." Her gaze dared him to contradict her.

He bent so his mouth was by her ear. "Absolutely not. If you try to run away, I'll just tie you to the bed."

"Holy fuck." She whispered the words, but the fit of giggles that accompanied them wasn't so silent. He glanced across at the elderly couple, who were watching them with amusement. "Sorry," Georgia said, still laughing.

"No need to apologize," the woman said. "It's lovely to see two young people in love. Don't mind us."

Georgia examined the toes of her shoes, her cheeks flushing, clearly lost for words. Matt winked at the woman, put his arm around Georgia, and kissed the top of her head. He wasn't a hundred percent sure what it was like to be in love, and it was too early to discuss it with Georgia, but he was beginning to suspect it might feel like the butterflies he had in his stomach.

The elevator stopped and the couple got out, and the doors slid closed again.

Matt pushed himself off the wall. Georgia's eyes widened as he walked toward her. He was still carrying one of his awards in either hand, but that didn't mean he couldn't use the rest of his body. Putting his hands behind his back, crossing his wrists, he moved up close to her and lowered his head.

"You like the idea of me tying you to the bed?" he murmured, his lips just brushing hers.

"Sounds a bit like a dream come true." Her eyes danced with laughter.

He realized she was referring to the daydream she'd mentioned earlier. His heart rate sped up even more at the thought that maybe she was willing to have a little fun in the bedroom.

"I see." He touched his lips to hers, tingling all over. "We'll have to see what we can do about that."

"Mmm." She shivered and moistened her lips with the tip of her tongue, making the dark pink lipstick she'd reapplied before she left the bar glisten. His erection, which had been well on its way before they'd even entered the elevator, hardened to rock.

"What about your fantasy?" she whispered. "Are you going to share that with me?"

He chuckled and brushed his lips to hers again. "Maybe later."

"Oh, that bad was it?"

"Let's just say I have a very active imagination."

They were both breathing hard by now. Matt couldn't believe how turned on he was, and he hadn't even touched her yet.

The doors pinged, and he lifted his head. "Come on."

He strode out of the elevator and down the corridor, and Georgia followed him as quickly as she could on her high heels, laughing.

"Your place or mine?" she asked, breathless and pink-cheeked.

"Yours." He waited impatiently for her to swipe her keycard, then followed her in when she opened the door.

She walked through the living room to the breakfast bar and placed the trophy she was carrying on there, along with her handbag. Matt did the same, placing his two beside the first. He adjusted them so they were all in a line, loving the little swell of joy it gave him to look at them.

"Oh, look at that." Georgia had turned and was walking over to the windows, where she opened the sliding glass doors and stepped out onto the huge balcony.

Matt went with her, only then realizing what she'd exclaimed at. The view over the city was magnificent, lit up against the backdrop of the black velvet sky. Far above them, the nearly-full moon hung like a silver bauble.

"Wow." He moved behind her. The breeze was a little cool out here, and she shivered, so he slipped off his jacket and put it around her, then wrapped his arms around her waist.

"I feel as if I can see the whole world," Georgia whispered. Far below them, cars threaded through the streets, their headlights shining on office windows and doors, and traffic lights winked red and green, their own private Christmas show.

"Beautiful," he murmured, only half-referring to the view.

She turned in his arms and looked up at him, placing her hands on his chest. Her eyes shone in the moonlight, and her lips glistened.

Heat surged through him, and he lowered his lips and finally allowed himself to kiss her properly.

Georgia melted against him, and he sighed and gave himself over to the kiss. Her lips parted under his, and he slid his tongue into her mouth, tasting wine and whisky. He hardened even more when she whimpered and returned the kiss with enthusiasm, rising up on her toes to wrap her arms around his neck.

She was small and slim in his arms, although her full breasts pressed against his chest, begging for him to touch them. He restrained himself, though, wanting to take this slowly now he finally had her alone, wanting the delicious anticipation to last.

Georgia, however, appeared to have other ideas. She moved around until her bottom hit the table on the deck, broke the kiss briefly to hitch up her dress and lift herself up onto it, and then parted her legs and pulled him forward between them. Matt slid his hands beneath it and stroked up to her knees, then higher to discover the lace-topped thigh-highs she wore beneath.

"Mmm," he murmured with approval, continuing one hand up the outside of her silky thigh as he kissed her. His fingers met bare skin, so he realized she must be wearing a thong. His hand continued up… but he found no elastic at her hip or waist. No sign of any panties.

He moved his head back and raised his eyebrows. She gave a mischievous shrug.

"Please don't tell me you've been going commando all evening," he said.

"I didn't want a VPL."

He closed his eyes. "Thank you for not telling me earlier. I wouldn't have been able to concentrate."

She laughed, then inhaled sharply as he moved his hand over her thigh and between her legs. He stroked the triangular area there and found only soft, silky, shaved skin.

Somewhere in his brain, a gasket blew.

"Holy fuck, Georgia…" He dropped to his haunches before her and pushed her knees apart.

She gasped. "What are you doing?"

"I have to taste you." Carefully, he removed first one high-heeled shoe, then the other, placing them to one side. He smoothed both hands up the inside of her thighs to the top where they were bare above the stockings.

"Matt!" She squealed. "Someone could see us!"

"They'd have to have binoculars, and good luck to them if they have. I hope they enjoy it as much as I'm going to." He placed a hand either side of her folds and parted them, groaning at the sight of her glistening flesh.

"You can't… not here… oh no…" Her speech faded away as he pressed kisses on the baby-soft skin either side of her folds. "Oh my God…"

He pushed her dress further up her legs. She had a couple of moles on her hip, just above the crease of her thigh, and he brushed his thumb across them. They were small, barely bigger than the end of a pencil. The one on the top was perfectly circular. The one underneath was a circle with a tiny tail.

He stared at them. They weren't moles. It was a tattoo, and he recognized the symbol.

Suddenly, it all made sense. What had happened all those years ago back in Christchurch. Why she'd left. Why Noah was such trouble. And why she hadn't dated anyone else since. It all slotted into place like cogs fitting together, and it crashed over him like a wave washing away the barrier that had stood between them since he'd known her.

This wasn't the time or the place to discuss it, though. He'd talk to her later, when they were in bed, and hopefully she'd finally feel able to open up and discuss it with him.

But the knowledge left him with a powerful sweep of emotion, of respect and admiration for her, and he resolved to make her feel loved and wanted that night, until she had no doubt of his feelings for her.

It had only taken him seconds to come to that conclusion, and before she could comment on why he'd stopped, he ran his tongue up the triangle of pale skin, amazed at its silkiness. Jesus, that was so fucking hot. A primal growl came from somewhere deep in his throat, and he buried his mouth in her.

"Ohhh…" She collapsed back onto her elbows with a long moan.

Matt tipped forward onto his knees, closed his eyes, and slid his tongue into her folds. She was already swollen, and moisture coated his tongue as he slipped it deep inside her, as far as he could reach. Georgia exclaimed, and he felt her fingers sink into his hair, but he couldn't have stopped even if she'd wanted him to. Luckily, that didn't appear to be the case—her hand clenched, but she didn't push him away, and he took that as a sign that he should carry on.

He licked up through her folds and explored with his fingers, pressing either side of her clit to expose it, and then covering it with his mouth and sucking gently. Her thighs loosened and she dropped her knees wide, and he growled his approval and slid two fingers inside her while he continued to suck.

She was obviously as keyed up as he was, because it was less than a minute before she started trembling, her breath coming in ragged gasps. "Matt," she whispered, "stop."

He ignored her and concentrated on her clit, swirling his tongue over the swollen bud.

"Oh God, you've got to stop or I'll come…"

In reply, he curled the fingers inside her toward him and increased the pressure of his tongue, and she cried out as her orgasm swept over her.

He groaned as she clenched, the pulses strong and powerful around his fingers. Jesus, that was going to feel good when he was inside her. He wanted to make her come again and again so she squeezed his erection like that.

She squealed, loud enough to make him laugh even while he was still licking her. When she finally collapsed back, he pushed up from his knees and leaned over her.

"Nice?" he queried.

"It was all right," she said, still gasping, looking up at the moon.

"Next time, can you be a bit louder? Someone over by the airport is complaining they couldn't hear you."

She sat up, blushing furiously and tugging down her dress. "It's your fault. Fancy doing that out in the open."

He laughed and slid his hands underneath her, lifting her up and wrapping her legs around his waist. "We're hardly in the open, and I was joking. Although apparently someone's rung in and claimed there was an earthquake. A seven-point-five, apparently."

"Matt!" She buried her face in his neck.

"So you're telling me the earth didn't move?" Chuckling, he bent carefully to pick up her shoes, then took her inside. He closed the sliding doors, and carried her through to the bedroom. There, he lowered her feet to the floor. He tossed his wallet from his pocket onto the bedside table, and pulled her against him.

"You're so tiny." He nuzzled her neck, satisfied he'd given her pleasure. "You weigh practically nothing."

She slipped off his jacket and hung it over a chair, then came back and placed her hands on his chest. He lifted her chin with a finger, and they exchanged a long, lingering kiss.

When he eventually pulled back, she wrinkled her nose. "I can smell myself."

"Lovely, isn't it? I'm never going to wash again."

She gave a short laugh and ran her fingers over his buttons. "I'm sorry about the noise. I can't help it."

"Honey, scream all you like. It turns me on, big time."

"Oh. Okay." She nibbled her bottom lip. "Am I allowed to get you naked now?" She looked up, her expression hot, pleading. "Please?"

He kissed her. "Feel free. I'm having the time of my life. And I'm all yours."

Chapter Fifteen

I'm all yours.

Georgia sucked her bottom lip, hoping she wasn't drooling. He lowered his hands and held them out to his sides, palms up, offering himself to her, giving her permission to do whatever she wanted.

"It feels like Christmas morning." She tugged his black tie undone.

"I'll put a red bow around it if you like." He grinned and moved his hands behind his back, apparently enjoying watching her undress him.

She chuckled and slid the tie out from under his collar, then tossed it on the dressing table. "That won't be necessary, but thank you for the offer." Her heart raced, and she moistened her lips as she unbuttoned his waistcoat. "Seems a shame to take it off, in a way."

"I'm happy to leave it on if you want."

"No, no... I want to see you." She finished the last button, pushed it off his shoulders, and took it from him to hang over the chair.

She came back and placed her hands on his chest, enjoying the anticipation of removing each piece of clothing and revealing more of him as she went. He didn't seem in any hurry, waiting patiently for her, his eyes holding a gentleness she hadn't expected.

"You're so different than I thought you'd be," she said, trying to undo the top button of his shirt. The collar was snug rather than tight, but she didn't want to put pressure on his Adam's apple.

"Here." He brought his hands up to help her out, lifting his chin to undo it, then replaced his hands behind his back. "How, different?"

"Nicer." She pressed the next button through the hole, revealing a triangle of tanned flesh behind it, and the dip in the hollow of his throat that made her want to touch her lips there.

He tipped his head to the side. "You didn't think I was nice before?"

"Yes. But you're softer than I thought."

"I'm not sure that's the description I'm looking for at the moment."

She laughed, more than conscious of the impressive erection he was sporting beneath his black trousers. "That's not what I meant. You have more… heart than I thought you'd have."

She glanced up, and caught her breath at the look in his eyes. Tenderness and genuine affection lay within them, and her fingers paused on the button as he lowered his head and kissed her.

Closing her eyes, she let his lips move across hers, slow and sensual, feeling like a glass of champagne, bubbles of excitement, nerves, and pleasure rising within her and giving her tingles all over.

He lifted his head, and she dropped her gaze to his chest, continuing with the buttons, very slowly popping them through the holes.

"I want this to last forever," she whispered, wishing there were more buttons on the shirt.

He rested his hands on her hips and nuzzled her ear. "My stamina's good, although I don't know it's that good. But I know what you mean."

Sighing as he ran his tongue around her ear, she reached the final button, and pushed the shirt open. "Oh…" She placed her palms on his defined muscles, then brushed over the gorgeous scattering of hair to where it trailed happily down beneath his belt. She ran a finger along the edge of his trousers, loving his flat stomach, desperate to see what lay beneath, but not wanting to rush it.

Lifting a hand, he offered his shirt sleeve to her. She'd noticed earlier that his cufflinks were silver artist's palettes with a tiny silver brush and, after removing one, she examined it more closely. "These are gorgeous. Who gave them to you?"

"A girl." He smiled.

"Oh. Sorry. I didn't mean to pry."

He kissed her forehead. "They were from Fleur—Brock's late wife. It seemed appropriate to wear them tonight, I felt."

Georgia placed the cufflinks to one side and rested her hands back on his chest. She leaned forward and kissed his breastbone, just under the hollow of his throat. It made her sad to think that his life had been touched with such loss. First Pippa, then Fleur… And yet events like that had shaped him and made him the man he was.

He shivered at the press of her lips, and she moved back and pushed the shirt off his shoulders. He let it drop to the floor, then rested his hands on her hips again.

"Ooh." She ran her fingers up his arms, feeling his biceps and the powerful muscles of his shoulders and neck. "You're a fine figure of a man, Matt."

"Thank you, but I'm getting jealous." He slid his arms around her to the zip at the back of her dress. "May I?"

She gave a little nod. He slid the zip down until it reached the small of her back, slowly enough for her to know that he was enjoying this gradual reveal too. The bodice was boned to help it stay up, but she'd applied a couple of strips of fashion tape to the edge to try to dissuade herself from tugging it up all night. She peeled the tape carefully from the curve of her breasts, and the bodice came away.

The dress floated down her body to the floor in a whisper of satin, leaving her standing there in just her black thigh-highs.

Matt tipped his head to the side to run his gaze down her body, inhaled deeply, and then blew out a long breath. When his gaze came back to hers, it held enough heat to send her nipples peaking, and suddenly the desire to go slowly was overridden by the deep, dark urge to get him naked.

He toed off his shoes while she fumbled at his belt and then undid the button of his trousers. She tried not to laugh when the zip practically undid itself because his erection sprang out.

"Stop smirking," he said as he flicked off his socks and stepped out of his trousers.

That only made her laugh more, and the giggles didn't stop when he picked her up and tossed her onto the bed. She bounced, but had no time to prepare herself, because he placed his hands behind her knees and tugged her toward him, then climbed on top of her.

"Ooh." All the breath rushed out of her. "You're squashing me."

"Don't care." He kissed her, hot and hard, and Georgia wrapped her arms around his waist, enjoying the feel of his warm, bare skin beneath her fingers. His erection was hard against her mound through his silky boxers, and she adored his weight on top of her, pressing her into the mattress.

He plunged his tongue into her mouth, any notion of gentleness or taking his time vanishing as he claimed the kiss. Georgia senses spun, and she dug her nails into his shoulders and scraped them lightly down his back, either side of his spine.

"*Aaahh...*" He lifted his head and studied her, his eyes now the dark brown of melted chocolate, full of delight. Slowly, he rocked his hips, stroking his erection against her mound.

Georgia slid her hands down his back to his boxers, slipped her fingers beneath the elastic, and cupped the firm muscles of his butt. Wow. She was handling Matt King's ass. She really had died and gone to heaven.

Digging her fingers in, she met each movement of his hips with a rock of her own, keeping her gaze locked on his.

His eyes took on a lazy, sexy sparkle, and he kissed her again, grazing his teeth on her lip before kissing around her jaw to her ear, where he nipped her lobe.

"Ouch." It made her twitch and tighten her legs around him, and sensual shivers rippled through her body.

He chuckled and kissed down her neck, his tongue lacing across her skin. "Oh Georgia... You're so fucking hot. I think I'm going to melt."

Raising his hand to her breast, he cupped it, presenting the nipple for his mouth. He admired it for a moment, bringing heat to her face, and then he closed his mouth over it and sucked.

"Oh..."

He teased it to a peak with his lips and tongue, then swapped to the other one and did the same, played with the sensitive tips until she was writhing beneath him. Jesus. She was going to come again if he carried on like this.

"Matt." He ignored her, so she sank a hand into his hair and tugged. "Stop."

He raised his head and laughed, lifted off her, and rolled onto his back. After removing his boxers, he reached for his wallet on the bedside table and extracted a condom. Georgia sat up and watched, fascinated, as he rolled it onto his erection. Then he held her arm and tugged. Caught off balance, she fell forward onto his chest with a squeal. He grabbed her knee, and in one swift move pulled her astride him.

She pushed herself up to a sitting position. "You know some smooth moves." Her hair had come loose, so she released the clip holding up the chignon and let it unfurl over her shoulder, then tossed the clip onto the bedside table.

Matt's eyes lit up. He wrapped the brown ringlet around his hand once, then again, and continued to do so, forcing her to lean forward until her mouth was close to his.

"Ouch," she said. "You're so bossy."

"You can always tell me to stop." He moved his other arm around her waist and shifted her so the tip of his erection pressed against her folds.

"I have a strange feeling that wouldn't work," she said wryly, almost breathless with desire.

He looked into her eyes and pushed his hips up, sliding a fraction of an inch into her. "Probably not." His lips curved up and his eyes shone with a wickedness that made her heart hammer against her ribs.

She'd thought he'd be good in bed, and she'd expected him to have a few tricks of the trade up his sleeve. She'd hoped for an orgasm, or two if she was lucky. But she hadn't expected him to be this… naughty.

She felt like a child who'd been staring at the window of the department store all year, and who'd awoken on Christmas Day to find she'd gotten the toy she'd longed for.

Oh dear. Her heart was in serious trouble.

Her wariness must have shown in her eyes, because he hesitated and blinked a couple of times. Then he released her hair and rested his hands on her waist. "You want to stop?"

She paused, mischievously leaving him to worry for a few seconds. Then, in answer, she pushed down her hips, letting him slide right inside her.

"Aaahhh…" He closed his eyes.

"Aw." She kissed his bottom lip and tugged it with her teeth, then pushed herself upright. Slowly, she rocked her hips, driving him in and out. "Poor Matt," she said, pouting at him. "All worried he wouldn't get his end away. You looked so sad."

He opened his eyes and met her gaze, his look so full of helplessness that she laughed with sheer pleasure, enjoying this sudden power over him. Tipping back her head, she sank her hands into her hair, reveling in the feel of him inside her. His hands rested on her breasts, and she arched her back, pushing them toward him, rewarded when he took her nipples between his thumbs and forefingers and tugged. He did so once, twice, then the third time a tad harder, and she moaned, clamping around him.

He laughed and slid a hand into her hair. "Oh boy, are we going to have some fun." Sliding an arm around her waist, he held her tightly and lifted up.

One second she was on top of him, the next she was underneath him. Shocked, she placed both hands on his chest, but he captured them in his own and pinned them above her head.

It was so close to her fantasy that she gave a little whimper and said, "Oh no."

He pushed his hips forward, burying himself inside her, so deep she thought for a moment he'd spear her to the bed.

"Relax, Georgia," he said, circling his hips and grinding against her. "Come on, half an inch more. You can take it."

She groaned and let go of the last little piece of resistance, letting her thighs drop open, and he gave a satisfied grunt, moved back, and then slid in right to the hilt.

"Balls deep," he said. "Nice."

Any indignant retort she would have given was muffled by his mouth as he kissed her, and she sighed. His tongue slid sexily against her own, the kiss hungry and demanding. She flexed her fingers in his, but he didn't release her hands, and when he finally lifted up and began to thrust, she could only lie there and watch him take his pleasure from her. It was exactly the way he'd taken her in her dream, only this time he was real, and smelled good, and his hard, masculine body made her melt. She could never have imagined the weight of him on top of her, the heat in his eyes, and the incredible sensation of him sliding deep inside, filling her up.

Wrapping her legs around his waist, she closed her eyes and concentrated on the muscles that were beginning to tense, but he nibbled her earlobe and whispered, "Open your eyes."

She did so, frustrated, wanting to focus on the approach of her orgasm, but he slowed the pace of his hips, lowered down onto his elbows, and pinned both of her hands there with one of his own. He slid the other hand under her bottom, holding her tightly as he thrust into her.

Georgia realized that she didn't have to concentrate on making her orgasm happen, because he would make sure it arrived when he was ready. He was totally in command of her desire. She hadn't expected that, and when he looked into her eyes, she could only stare up at him with the longing she'd felt all her life for a man like this.

He kissed her in between thrusts, hot, hungry, wet kisses that made her ache, and before long she was moaning against his mouth with each movement of his hips.

"Yeah," he said, "come on," and he lifted up again and thrust harder and faster.

She couldn't fight the orgasm, couldn't do anything but surrender to it. She lost herself, spinning out of control, and cried out as the intense pulses swept over her, beautiful and so strong they were almost painful.

Matt stiffened, and his mouth clamped on hers as he gave short, fierce thrusts with each spasm of his muscles, his climax seeming to go on forever, leaving her limp and exhausted by the time he finally collapsed on top of her.

Holy hell. She couldn't move, couldn't do anything but lie there with the hunk of the century pinning her to the mattress. "Matt." She tugged her hands weakly, but he still didn't move. "Oh Jeez." Now she knew what Trinny, or Taylor, had been on about. A girl would never be able to put up with this every night. He'd literally sex her to death.

But what a way to go.

Chapter Sixteen

Matt lifted his head and looked into a gorgeous pair of amber eyes.

"Wow," he said.

"I'll second that." Georgia's face was flushed, her hair rumpled, her mouth swollen from his kisses. "What Trinny said kind of makes sense now."

"Tanya," he said with a chuckle. "And is that a complaint?"

"No." She gave a little shake of her head. "No. Absolutely not. You're a dream come true."

He touched his lips to hers, and they exchanged a long, gentle kiss.

"Mind you," she said when he eventually lifted his head. "I'm glad your empty room is next door. You nearly thrust the bed through the wall."

"Your enthusiasm egged me on," he teased, withdrawing and moving beside her. He disposed of the condom, unable to stop a laugh as her already pink face turned red.

She rubbed her nose. "Was I really loud?"

"Honey, you are by far the most vocal girl I've been with."

"Jesus."

"I love it." He pulled her into his arms and nuzzled her ear. "It fires me up."

"Like you need that," she mumbled.

He laughed and kissed her, adoring the feel of her soft body pressed against his.

Knowing that she hadn't been with anyone for a long time, he'd expected her to be nervous and hesitant, and had thought he'd have to rein himself in. In actual fact the opposite had occurred, and in the end he'd just let go and thoroughly enjoyed himself.

He wanted to ask if he could see her again, but he knew there was something they had to get out of the way first.

Part of him didn't want to broach the subject because he worried she'd be angry with him for interfering. But equally, if they had any chance of having a relationship, she was going to have to open up to him.

So they kissed for a while until their bodies had relaxed, and then he got them both a bottle of water from the fridge while she nipped to the bathroom.

When she came out, he handed her a bottle and they both drank a good half. Then he finally knew it was time and slid his arm around her waist and pulled her close.

"You should know now that I want to do this again," he said.

Her lips curved up. "I might need a few minutes."

He grinned. "I meant in the future. I'd like to see you again. To date you properly. To get to know you. But there's something I need to talk to you about first."

Her eyes widened. "Okay."

"Shall we get into bed?"

She nodded, and they climbed under the covers and he pulled her into his arms.

"What is it?" she asked.

He ran a hand down her ribs, into the dip of her waist, and over her hip. There he paused, and touched his finger to the tattoo.

She glanced down at it, then back up at him. "It's just a couple of moles."

"They're not moles. It's a tattoo."

She shrugged. "It doesn't mean anything. It's just two circles."

"It's a semicolon."

"So I like grammar," she said. "So what?"

"A semicolon is used when a person could have ended a sentence but chose not to."

She stared at him.

"It's used by people who've dealt with depression, suicide, and mental illness," he said gently. "Georgia, did your husband take his own life?"

She continued to stare at him. After about ten seconds, her lips parted, her chest heaved, and he realized she was struggling to breathe.

"All right," he said calmly, sitting up and taking her into his arms. He rubbed her back and kissed her hair. "It's okay, I'm here."

"Matt…" She gasped, quivering in his arms. "I'm sorry…"

"It's okay. You can talk to me. Just breathe. Come on, slowly, in and out, right deep in your belly."

She continued to shake, but he put a hand above her solar plexus and told her to breathe in until his hand rose, then out again as if she was blowing through a straw, making the out breath longer than the in breath. They counted her breaths together, up to ten, then again, then once more, until she was breathing more normally, and her shaking had subsided.

"God, I'm so sorry." She ran a hand through her hair. "Every time I think I've conquered my anxiety, it comes back and slaps me in the face."

"It was the shock, that's all. I'm sorry to do it like that, but I couldn't just ignore the tattoo once I'd seen it."

She looked up at him, her eyes glistening like wet amber. "How did you know what it meant?"

"I run art workshops occasionally through the hospital's youth mental health services. One of the teenagers did a piece of work based around the semicolon, and she explained what it meant."

Georgia nodded and leaned back against the pillows. He kept his arm around her, though, and held her hand, hoping it would encourage her to open up to him.

"I rarely talk about Fintan," she said. "I just find it too upsetting. It's one reason I moved from Christchurch. It's easier to be around people who don't know me, and who are less likely to ask questions."

"I understand. And you don't have to talk about it if you don't want to. But I'd like to know what happened."

She looked down at their hands, studying their linked fingers. Her lips twisted wryly. "Are you sure you want to know? It's not a fun story."

He lifted his hand, bringing hers with it, and kissed her knuckles. "I want to know."

She watched him lower their hands back to the duvet and brushed her thumb across his. "Okay. Well, I went to an all-girls boarding school, but there was a boys' school next to it, and they brought us together a lot for sports and social functions. I was really unhappy at the school, miserable because I felt unwanted by my parents, and lonely. I met Fintan at the swimming pools the school used, and I started meeting up with him. It was easy to sneak out. He was a year older than me, but we were both young and stupid. I'd just turned sixteen when I fell pregnant."

"That can't have been easy."

"It was awful. My parents pulled me out of school to have Noah. Fintan was allowed to finish his Level 3 studies, but our parents insisted we get married. Neither of us argued because, well, we had Noah, and we did like each other, and we weren't particularly rebellious, just unhappy. So we decided to go for it and make the best of what had happened."

She leaned over to fetch her water bottle, took a long drink, then carried on. "When I was eighteen, my parents looked after Noah so I could go back to school. They're quite wealthy, and they paid for me to go to university and get a business degree. They were determined that having a baby wouldn't be the end of my life. But it wasn't so easy for Fintan."

"His parents didn't support him?"

"His father died when he was young. His mother hooked up with another guy who just hated Fintan, and pretty much threw him out when he got me pregnant. Fintan was quite sporty and he wanted to be a sports physio. I told him that once I got my degree, I'd hopefully earn enough to support him while he went to uni to get the qualifications he needed. He got a job working in the local sports shop, but after I qualified, I just couldn't get him motivated to go back to studying."

"He suffered from depression?"

"Yes. I know more about it now, but I was pretty clueless back then. I thought he was unhappy with me—that it was my fault. We used to have terrible arguments. He'd yell at me that I'd ruined his life by getting pregnant, then he'd feel guilty and collapse into a black hole of gloom, and nothing would be able to get him out of it."

Matt stroked her back, feeling her anguish rolling off her in waves. "That must have been hard for you."

"He was good with Noah, don't get me wrong, and I know he couldn't help it, but yes, it was very hard. And then the earthquake happened."

"Jeez."

"Yeah. Our flat was right on top of it. Luckily, we weren't at home when it happened. It was still bad—we were five minutes away, shopping, and I can't tell you how terrifying it was. Noah was with us, and everything started falling from the shelves, and then a whole shelf toppled. Fintan managed to grab Noah just before he was crushed beneath it."

"Fucking hell."

"We escaped by the skin of our teeth, only to find that our home had been destroyed. The shock and the trauma was just too much for him, I guess. We went to my parents' house, and he couldn't stop crying. My parents were so worried they called the doctor in, and he gave Fintan some pills and wanted to hospitalize him, but he refused. I was exhausted and didn't register how bad he was. You get to the stage where you're just trying to hold it together, you know?"

Matt nodded, although he knew she'd half-forgotten he was there.

She gazed off into the distance, but he had a feeling she wasn't seeing the moon over the city, but instead some other scene. "It was only two days later that I woke up in the morning and he wasn't in bed. I went into the bathroom..." She stopped talking and covered her mouth.

Matt held her tightly and kissed her hair. "It's okay."

"He was in the bath, with a razor..." She dissolved into tears.

"It's all right." He put his other arm around her and pulled her tightly against him. "I'm so sorry."

She spoke in a squeak. "I still dream about it. I hate him for doing it, Matt. I know he was sick, and that by that stage he couldn't think about anything but himself, but I hate him for doing that to me, and to Noah. What if Noah had been the one who'd found him?"

Matt went cold. "God, don't."

She dashed her tears away. "Those first six months were hellish. Noah was all over the place. He's calmed down a lot since then, but he gets so angry, at his dad and at the world. I thought coming up here would help to get him away from the memories, have a fresh start, but you can never really begin again, can you? All the worries and the troubles just come with you. He's not a bad kid, and he wants to be good, but he fears he's going to be like Fintan. I can see why it frightens him."

"That poor kid." He leaned forward and propped the pillows up a bit, then lay back, bringing her with him. She curled up next to him, leaning on his chest. For a while they didn't speak. Everything she'd told him settled into his brain like silt on the bottom of a river.

When he'd seen her tattoo, he'd guessed what had happened, and knew it must have had a traumatic effect on her, but the truth was so much worse. He had nothing but admiration for her, though. In spite of everything life had dealt her, she'd done her best to rise above her problems. She'd moved across the country and tried to start a new life. She'd looked after her son on her own, and had coped with the boy's behavioral issues as best she could.

"When did you get the tattoo done?" he asked, brushing his fingers over her hip.

"Last Christmas, I decided I needed to do something drastic. It had been just under three years since the earthquake, and I was unhappy in Christchurch. Too many bad memories, and I felt that Noah needed a change. Time was moving on, but I didn't feel we were putting the tragedy behind us. I've had moments where I've felt terribly low, close to ending it all myself. Plus, although I love my parents, I needed some time apart from them. They always treat Noah like a delinquent, and don't seem to make any allowances for him for what's happened."

She touched the semicolon on her skin. "So I moved to the Northland, almost as far away as I could get without leaving the country. A few weeks later, I had the tattoo done to remind myself that there is always an option. That we always have a choice." She smiled up at him, wiping her face. "You're the only person who knows I have it."

"I'm so glad you came here and started working for us."

"Me too. I love my job. That's why I was so wary about dating you."

He cupped her face and stroked his thumb across her cheek. "And what about now? Have you changed your mind? Or are we going to see each other again?"

Chapter Seventeen

Georgia looked up into Matt's eyes. They seemed to have returned to standard hazel now, brown flecked with green, and they were full of warmth and admiration.

Was he offering her a relationship? She was so surprised she was speechless for a moment. She'd been so convinced he was a womanizer who didn't want to be tied down that she couldn't believe he'd be interested in dating seriously, let alone her, of all people, someone with a traumatic past who clearly had issues.

"Are you sure that's what you want?" She wasn't certain how to put her doubt into words. She knew she'd hurt his feelings a couple of times with her assumptions. Her heart might just be able to cope with a one-night stand, although she knew that even if she never saw him again, the memory of him on top of her, thrusting her into next week, would take a long time to dispel. But if she started seeing him properly, and then he got bored with her and dumped her the way he broke up with all his girlfriends… She might never recover.

He brushed a hand down her back. "I'm crazy about you. I've been crazy about you since I first saw you. Being with you tonight, making love with you, and then having you finally open up to me… it's made me realize I'd like more."

"More?"

He shrugged.

She pushed herself up a little and turned to face him. It felt important to lay all her cards on the table at this point. "You're saying you want more sex?" she clarified.

"Well, yes please. To start with anyway."

They studied each other quietly. She wasn't quite sure what he was offering. He wanted to sleep with her again, which was flattering. But was he talking about a relationship?

She sucked her bottom lip. "I'm not sure. Noah and I… we've had such a rough time. We're just getting on an even keel, and I don't know that I should rock the boat by indulging in some kind of fling."

She hesitated, not wanting to come down all heavy on him, but then again Noah liked Matt, and she didn't want him getting excited at the thought of having him around, only to have Matt dump her in a few weeks.

"That's fair." He reached for his bottle of water, took a few swallows, screwed the lid back on, and replaced it on the table. He studied her for a moment. Then his lips curved up and his eyes took on a wicked glint. "Okay. I have a proposal for you."

"Jeez."

"Not that kind of proposal," he said wryly, echoing the words he'd said to her in her office, which was only a few days ago but felt like another lifetime. "There are twelve days until Christmas Eve, when you leave for your parents, right?"

She calculated in her head. "Yes."

"Come and stay with me." He kissed her nose. "For twelve days. And twelve nights."

"The Twelve Shags of Christmas?"

That made him laugh. "If you like. It'll be fun."

She chewed her bottom lip. "Stay with you at your house?"

"Yes." He tucked an arm under his head, and ran the fingers of his other hand along her spine. "And I don't mean in the spare room."

"I might never walk again."

"If you can, I'm not doing it right."

They both laughed.

She kissed his chest. "Are you sure? You have no idea how grumpy I can be. Or how awful I look in the morning."

"Okay, now I'm having second thoughts." He smiled and ran his fingers through her hair. "It's not just about getting you into bed. We can go out to dinner. Go to the cinema, or the theatre. Just get to know each other better, the way I've wanted to since I first met you."

Still she hesitated. His smile faded and he cupped her face. "Are you worried about Noah?"

"Amongst other things."

"Noah being away is partly the reason I suggested you coming over—not because I don't want to see him, but because it doesn't complicate things, initially anyway. We can concentrate on each other. And then when you get back from Christchurch, you can decide whether you want to tell him about me."

He was suggesting they might continue seeing each other afterward, then. Her throat tightened. "Okay. I'll come and stay with you."

He leaned across to turn off the bedside light. The room faded into the night, the fairy lights around the balcony giving it a silvery Christmas glow.

"Come here," he said, turning her so her back was to his chest, and curling around her. "I'm so glad you came with me tonight."

"Me too. I wasn't sure I'd done the right thing." And she still wasn't a hundred percent sure this would end the way she hoped, but she did recognize that she had to take a step out of her comfort zone and take a chance if she was ever going to be happy with a man again.

"Goodnight, sweetheart." He kissed her ear. "Sleep well. I'll wait as long as I can before I wake you up, but I can't guarantee it'll be morning."

She shivered at the thought of him wanting her so badly that he couldn't wait until the sun rose. "Goodnight."

His body was warm against hers, his slow breathing comforting in the darkness, although she had the feeling from the way he continued to trace patterns on her back and hips that she fell asleep long before he did.

*

In actual fact, when Matt finally awoke, it was morning. It had taken him a long time to get off to sleep, and a result he'd slept soundly, waking only when the room began to lighten.

He stretched out a hand to find the bed empty, the sheets cool.

Sitting up, he looked around, fearing Georgia had left in the night. To his relief, she stood in one of the hotel's white toweling dressing gowns out on the deck, leaning on the railing. The sun was just rising, flooding the room with light, and as he got out of bed he saw that the tops of the buildings looked as if they were gold-plated, the sun bouncing off glass and metal, nearly blinding him.

He visited the bathroom, then came out and padded across the plush carpet to the sliding doors. She'd closed them, and he slid them open, letting the fresh morning air spill into the room.

She turned as he stepped onto the deck, and her eyes widened.

"You're not wearing any clothes," she pointed out.

"If you want to complain, you'll have to fill in a form at the reception desk." He walked up behind her and put his arms around her. "Morning."

He'd wondered briefly whether the reason she was standing out there was because she'd come to the decision that she didn't want to see him again, but as he hugged her, she tipped her head to one side to let him kiss her neck and murmured, "Morning."

"You want to come back to bed?" he asked.

"In a minute. It's so beautiful out here."

He leaned his chin on her shoulder and looked down with her at the city below. "Mm. I like early mornings, watching the city wake up. It makes me want to grab a pencil and draw it."

"Do you do much drawing of things other than your characters, like landscapes and still life?"

He laughed. "You could say that."

"What's so funny?"

"You'll understand when you come to my house." He pulled her bathrobe away from her shoulder and touched his lips to her skin. "You're still coming to stay with me?"

She gave a long sigh as he kissed up her neck. "Yes," she said. "I'll stay."

Relief and pleasure flooded him, and he slid a hand inside the robe onto her warm skin. "I'm glad."

She leaned back against him and closed her eyes, and Matt took that as a sign that she wanted to play.

Tugging on the tie, he loosened it and pulled the sides of her robe apart, exposing her body to the morning sun.

"Matt!" Her eyes flew open and she tried to push his hands away. "It's broad daylight."

"It's not even six a.m. yet, and nobody can see us."

"Even so. It feels... decadent..." Her voice trailed off, and she closed her eyes again as he smoothed his hands down to her thighs, then back up her body to her breasts.

"Yeah, you're such a wicked girl." He looked down—her creamy skin glowed in the sunlight, and her nipples had tightened in the cool morning breeze. "You're so fucking beautiful," he said, cupping her breasts and brushing his thumbs over her nipples.

She sucked her bottom lip and tipped her head back on his shoulder, arching her back and pushing her breasts into his hands. "Mmm... that's nice."

He stroked her for a while, caressing her skin from her thighs up her body to her breasts while he kissed her neck, nuzzled her ear, and whispered in her ear all the things he'd dreamed about doing to her and with her since they'd met. He continued until she was sighing loudly and pushing back against the erection that was now hard against her bottom through the bathrobe.

Unable to bear it any longer, he turned her in his arms to face him, moved her around so she was leaning against the table, and pressed his lips to hers. Too aroused for gentle pecks, he poured all his desire into the kiss. She moaned and opened her mouth to him, meeting each thrust of his tongue with one of her own.

Fired up now, Matt lifted her onto the table and pushed her onto her back, tossed both sides of the robe wide to expose all of her to his gaze, and bent and fastened his mouth onto her nipple. She gasped, sliding a hand into his hair and tightening her fingers. He swapped from one nipple to the other, watching them pucker to tight beads.

Moving back, he kissed down between her breasts to her stomach, then lower, the way he had the night before, only this time the shafts of sunlight that fell across her meant that when he pushed her knees wide, every inch of her was exposed to his gaze. He groaned as he saw her glistening and swollen, and he slid two fingers straight inside her, causing her to buck and moan as she pushed against his hand.

Closing his mouth over her clit, he swirled his tongue across it, but only a few times before he pushed up to his feet again. He didn't want to make her come this time—he was too keyed up, too ready for her, and gave her a quick, hard kiss before saying in a husky voice, "I'll just grab a condom."

"Wait." She caught his arm. "Just so you know, I have a Mirena coil fitted. I had one after I had Noah—and it was so convenient that I've kept it. So... if you don't want to use a condom... if you think it's safe... I don't mind."

He leaned over her and looked into her eyes. "You're sure? I'm clean, I swear. I've always used condoms."

"I'm sure."

Keeping his gaze fixed on hers, his heart racing, he pushed the tip of his erection into her folds, then slid inside her.

"Fuck." The sensation of being without a barrier, skin on skin, was so exquisite that he had to fight not to come immediately like a sixteen-year-old, his whole body tensing as he struggled for control.

"Easy, tiger." She smiled and stretched her arms above her head, still in her bathrobe, purring like a cat. "Take your time."

He leaned on the table on either side of her ribs, pulled back until he was almost out of her, then slid forward again slowly. She was slick and hot, and the sensation was like nothing he'd felt before. Moving back again, he brushed a hand down her body and over her bare, shaved skin, then pulled out of her and slid the tip of his erection up through her folds and over her clit.

"You're so smooth," he murmured, watching as he slid back inside her. "It's such a turn-on."

"Glad I could be of service." She wrapped her legs around his waist, smiling up at him as he leaned over her.

He looked into her eyes while he thrust, slowing down rather than speeding up this time, enjoying the sensation of being teased to the edge by her beautiful, warm body.

"I hope you have some serious stamina, because I intend to make the most of you over the next twelve days." He leaned down to kiss her.

She rocked her hips to meet his, giving him a drowsy look of desire when he lifted up. "You talk like I'm a sexual plaything, there for your amusement."

"Yep." He plunged in and out of her slick flesh, conscious of the approach of his climax, way off in the distance. "I intend to have my wicked way with you whenever I want, and there's nothing you can do about it."

She gave a helpless whimper. "Oh dear."

He covered one nipple with his mouth, then the other, sucking until she moaned beneath him. "In fact," he whispered as he kissed back up to her ear, "maybe I'll cuff you to the bed for a few weeks and leave you there, chained up, ready for when I feel the need for loving."

"Which is, like, all the time," she said, panting.

He laughed and kissed her hungrily. "Yeah, especially when you're around."

It was no good, he couldn't stave off his orgasm any longer. The sweet sensation of being enveloped by her warm, wet body was just too sensual, and every stroke of his hips took him a step closer to heaven.

His hands tightened to fists on the table, and he fought to hold it back, but Georgia slid a hand into hair, pulled his head down for a kiss, and whispered, "Let go."

So he did, conscious of every tiny muscle tightening in turn inside him, feeling warmth spreading up as his body jerked and spilled inside her.

She watched him with fascination, apparently enjoying his pleasure, before sliding her hand between them as his climax ended and circling her fingers over her clit. It only took her a few seconds, and then she came too, tightening around him and making him gasp with the strength of the pulses, her cries of pleasure filling the air.

Eventually, her eyelids fluttered open, and she smiled lazily. "Your eyes have gone brown again."

"Sorry?"

"They change. It must be the light." She stretched beneath him. "Was I noisy again?"

"Always. I love it."

"I'm really sorry. I'm not aware of it when I do it."

"Don't apologize." He kissed her. "I love your enthusiasm."

He was crazy about this girl. He wanted to be with her all the time, to hold her close, to make love to her as often as he could, and to keep her safe. It was practically prehistoric, but he couldn't help it. He loved her, and he had twelve days to show it, and he was going to prove to her that his motives were pure.

Chapter Eighteen

After landing at Kerikeri airport, Georgia let Matt take her home to pick up a few things before they drove to Opua. There they boarded the car ferry for Russell, where he lived.

"Did you know that Russell was originally called Kororareka?" he asked her as they leaned on the side of the ferry, looking down into the water.

"I didn't, no."

"It means sweet penguin."

"Oh! Have you ever seen any?"

"Penguins? Yes, once, when I went out on a boat trip through the Hole in the Rock. We'll have to go—most times you get to see dolphins, and occasionally penguins, seals, and orcas."

"I'd love to do that."

"It's a date," he said, and smiled.

Georgia bumped shoulders with him, and he put his arm around her. She snuggled up, excited and a little nervous about the prospect of spending almost two weeks with him. It had been a long time since she'd lived with anyone, and she'd grown used to her independence. To getting up and going to bed when she wanted, eating what she liked, or going out for a walk without having to please anyone else. Being in a relationship meant giving up a certain degree of freedom, and while the benefits usually outweighed the downsides, she knew it would take time to adjust.

Matt appeared to be sincere in his feelings for her, but it wouldn't be until they settled into each other's company that she would discover what he was really like. She didn't care if he left socks on the floor or the toilet seat up—those kinds of things didn't bother her. But while she enjoyed his company, she had yet to see if he was the type of man who was possessive in a relationship. He acted possessive in bed, and she liked that, but she wouldn't like it if he demanded her attention all the time, or refused to let her do her own thing. And she didn't know him well enough to understand whether it was still the chase that was keeping him interested, and if maybe his desire would wane once they were together all the time.

It didn't show much sign of waning yet, she thought, as he stood behind her and wrapped her in his arms. In spite of being in public, he was nuzzling her ear and sucking on the lobe.

"Stop it." She wriggled in his arms, but he just laughed and kissed her cheek. "Tell me about your house," she said, trying to distract him.

He rested his chin on her shoulder, and they watched a couple of gannets swooping into the water for fish. "It's very... me. I hope you like it." He sounded nervous.

She looked over her shoulder at him in surprise. "Of course I'll like it. Why wouldn't I?"

"I'm not big on furniture."

"Does it have a bed?"

"Yes, Georgia, it has a bed. That was one item I did insist on."

"And somewhere to sit and maybe watch TV?"

"Yeah..."

"Then don't worry about it. I love it already."

He didn't say anything, though, and she pondered on that as they made their way back to their car and got in. Why was he worried? She didn't have any idea what the place would be like. Was he very scruffy? Would it be like a bachelor pad, made for inviting girls back to, with subdued lighting and Barry White on repeat on his iPod? She couldn't imagine why he was concerned about her seeing it.

The ferry bumped gently against the land and the tailgate lowered to allow the cars to leave. Matt started the engine and headed along the main road to the town.

Georgia had been there a couple of times when she'd first moved to the Northland, and she'd written the blurb about the area for the Three Wise Men website. The Bay of Islands encompassed 144 islands and what were sometimes called the boutique towns of Opua, Russell, Paihia, and Kerikeri a little further inland. It gave a hint of paradise, full of beaches and water activities, and with the most history of any part of New Zealand, housing the country's oldest stone building, the Stone Store in Kerikeri. Although Christchurch was often hot in summer, she loved the sub-tropical weather of the Northland, and was looking forward to her first full summer there. Shame she was going to have to break it by going back to the south island halfway through. Not for the first time she wished she'd made a different decision. Still, too late now—Noah was there, and her parents would be disappointed if she didn't spend the festive week with her family.

Pushing the thought of it to the back of her mind because she knew she'd start feeling anxious, she looked out of the window eagerly for the first sign of Matt's house.

He drove along the winding path through the bush, past all the lush palms, before taking a turn onto a quieter road that led along a hill overlooking the bay. Georgia's eyes widened at the view of the glittering Pacific, and then she stared outright as he signaled and turned off onto a drive. He parked in front of a long, low, whitewashed house with a terracotta roof.

"Is this it?"

"This is it." He got out, and she followed him, trying to remember not to let her jaw sag.

She lifted her bag from the back and he retrieved his suitcase and the box containing his trophies. He led the way to the front door, opened it, and stepped back to let her precede him.

Georgia left her bag by the front door and walked slowly through the house. It was mostly open plan, with high ceilings, white walls to the left and right, and glass to the front and, as he'd said, very little furniture. The living room had a sumptuous leather sofa in front of a huge wall-mounted TV with a Playstation, and a chrome-and-glass coffee table piled with books. She glanced at them as she passed—mainly art books, but also astronomy, history, architecture, and cooking, something she wouldn't have expected. The kitchen was clean and modern.

"I feel like I'm in a cathedral," she said, walking slowly through to the hallway she could see on the other side. To her left, the windows led onto a huge deck that overlooked the bush and the town of Russell, framed with the Pacific in the background. It gave her a feeling of light and space, but it wasn't particularly... homely. It didn't look as if he spent a lot of time there.

Matt said nothing, leading the way along the hall to the bedroom and placing his suitcase on the bed. Like the living room, it had a high ceiling and little furniture, the bare minimum a guy who lived on his own needed, just a large bed with a white duvet and pillows.

There were no signs of any women, she thought with relief, half-expecting to see pairs of panties and used lipsticks all over the place.

"Why all the white?" she asked. "I'd expected to see your paintings everywhere."

"It's restful, after working with color all day. And it seems kind of egotistical to hang one's own paintings in the house."

"I suppose." She wasn't sure if she agreed, but she accepted the hand he held out and let him lead her further along the hall. There were three other, spare bedrooms, and an impressive bathroom with a large bath easily able to fit two people.

Still he didn't say anything, though, and she followed him along to a closed white door. To her surprise, he took out a key and unlocked it. Why was a door locked in his own house?

He paused with his hand on it to look at her, and an impish light filled his eyes, turning them a bright green. Then he opened the door and let her walk through.

Georgia's jaw dropped for the second time as she walked into his studio. Suddenly, she understood what he meant about the living room being restful, because this place was full of color.

Like the main part of the house, it had high ceilings and white walls. He walked across to the front wall that was covered with long blinds and pressed a button, and the blinds lifted electronically to reveal that the whole wall was made of glass. Sunlight spilled into the room as if someone had knocked over a huge pot of melted butter.

This was obviously where he spent most of his time. To the right was a large architect's table, and she could see proofs of Squish the Possum laid out on there, so that was obviously where he did most of his Ward Seven work. Next to it was an old-fashioned desk with a laptop, sheaves of notes, and a couple of old coffee mugs—that was where he did his writing. There was another, more comfortable looking sofa in the corner with a smaller TV, a place for him to relax in between projects, and she guessed from the blanket on it that sometimes he even slept there.

To the front of the room, near the windows to catch the best light, were at least six easels with a variety of different pieces of work half-finished on them. And all around them were canvases. Leaning against the wall, ten or twenty in rows, some covered with cloths to protect them from the strong New Zealand sunshine, others hanging on the walls to provide splashes of color against the white.

She walked slowly around to look at them. She recognized the brushwork from his Ward Seven books, which she loved, but it was only now that she realized what a talented artist he was. Some of the canvases bore abstracts, exploring bright colors and shapes. There were a few of objects like bottles and fruit, and a couple of landscapes. But most of them were of people. Faces and postures, showing movement and action. There were some detailed paintings investigating the layers of color in a person's face. An old gentleman, smiling and wrinkled. A few of his parents, whom she'd met a couple of times at functions—his father's handsome face with Matt's distinctive hazel eyes, his mother's pretty smile and her hair that Matt had taken hours to paint with hundreds of different shades of gray and silver. Lots of faces of both men and women she didn't recognize, including several of children. He had a real talent for capturing expression.

She stopped by one canvas on the wall and caught her breath. It was a painting of Brock, his gaze far away. It featured his head and shoulders, his hair only fleetingly captured, focusing on his expression, which was quite clearly grief—Matt had captured the shine in his eyes, the sorrow in his features.

"My God," she said, and glanced over her shoulder at him. "Has he seen this?"

He shook his head. "Don't tell him. I took a photo the day Fleur died." He looked wary, as if half-expecting her to criticize him for invading Brock's privacy. But she knew why he'd done it. He needed to understand how to express a range of feelings. Now she knew why he liked to study her face so intently. Emotion fascinated him, and he obviously felt an urge to capture it on canvas and paper.

She stopped by a canvas of a young girl. Like the one he'd done of Brock, this was a detailed painting. This time the girl looked right out of the canvas, her mischievous face filled with light and life.

"Is this Pippa?" she asked softly.

"Yeah." He stopped beside her, and she saw that he was carrying one of the trophies he'd won. He placed it on the shelf further along, adjusted it slightly, then stepped back and shoved his hands in his pockets.

She stroked his arm and continued on. Heaps of large sketch books littered the many tables that were up against the walls. She glanced over at him, and he nodded, so she flicked through a few.

They contained hundreds of sketches, mainly just in pencil, a few in watercolor. More people, faces, expressions, and lots of movement, people walking, running, climbing, his bold strokes capturing the shape of muscles and the angle of limbs. There were also many drawings of animals: dogs, cats, giraffes, elephants—everything was there, big bold sketches, again capturing shape and movement without too much detail.

"I watch a lot of the Discovery channel," he said.

Smiling she traced her fingers along the outline of a leopard, noting the way he'd caught the bunch of muscles in the big cat's hips, the fluidity of its movements. "Do you sell many?"

"Sometimes. Most of them are just sketches. I rotate them on the walls so they don't get faded, and I can study them, see what works in different lighting."

Leaving the sketchbooks, she walked to the next painting. The beautiful woman in it gazed off to her right, her dark hair curling over her shoulder. She had bright blue eyes and she was laughing. The painting was filled with affection and love.

Matt came to stand beside her again, looking up at it with her.

"Who is she?" she whispered.

"It's Fleur."

"Oh." She hadn't expected that. She remembered the cufflinks he'd worn that Brock's late wife had given him, and turned to him with a curious frown. "Were you in love with her?"

"Not in that way. I was seventeen when Brock started dating her. She only ever had eyes for him. I guess I might have had a bit of a crush on her when I was young. I envied them their relationship, their closeness. But we got on really well, more like brother and sister. She used to tease me a lot—I always thought that Pippa might have grown up to be like her."

And he'd lost her too. Were these paintings an attempt to capture his past? And to keep the people he'd lost, or was afraid of losing?

Georgia turned to him and slid her arms around his waist, touched that he'd allowed her this glimpse into his world. "I half-expected to find the room full of nudes of beautiful women," she teased.

"Ah, they're all locked in the cupboard."

She laughed. "Seriously. You obviously love observing the way the body moves. You've never painted any of the women you've brought in here?"

He kissed her nose. "I've never brought a woman in here."

Her eyes widened. "You're kidding me."

"No. You're the first. I always keep the door locked."

"Why?"

He glanced around. "I don't know. This place is… private. I don't want anyone intruding."

But he'd brought her here. And he'd let her see his paintings.

Wrapping her arms around his neck, the warm sun streaming across her back, Georgia closed her eyes and kissed him.

Chapter Nineteen

When he'd first unlocked the door to his studio, Matt had felt a flicker of unease at the idea of finally letting someone into his private space. He kept the blinds down when he wasn't working so the sunlight didn't fade the paintings, and therefore even if guests went onto the deck, they couldn't see into the room. In the past, girls had occasionally asked to see where he'd worked, but he'd always changed the subject and generally they'd taken the hint and hadn't asked again.

He wasn't sure why he'd let Georgia see it. He would have said because it was the first time he'd asked any girl to stay longer than overnight, and that was certainly part of the reason. It would look—and feel—odd if she stayed with him until Christmas Eve and he kept part of the house locked.

But it wasn't just that. Georgia wasn't a stranger, and she wasn't a one-night stand. He'd known her for nearly a year, and he'd thought of her as a friend before he thought of her as a lover, and that was new for him. For the first time ever, he wanted to share the part of himself that he normally kept locked away. It felt odd to open up to someone, but he discovered that it wasn't as scary as he'd thought, and in fact there was something nice about watching her admiring and asking him questions about his work.

So he kissed her back, beginning to relax at last, and loving how easygoing she was. He didn't feel the need to impress her, and although it remained to be seen how comfortable they were with each other around the house, he was looking forward to spending time with her.

Georgia pulled back and checked her watch. "It's nearly one o'clock."

"Are you hungry?"

"A bit."

"I thought we could eat out tonight," he said. "There's a great restaurant in town that does fantastic seafood."

"Sounds lovely."

"Shall we just have a sandwich now then?"

"Mmm. Come on."

He took her hand and led her back to the kitchen, and they spent some time making themselves some lunch. She checked out his cupboards and fridge, and they ended up choosing baked ham and salad. Georgia made the sandwiches while Matt made a fresh fruit smoothie, and then they took it all onto the deck to eat while they sat and chatted and looked out at the view.

Afterward, uncertain what she liked to do at home in her spare time, Matt asked her if she wanted to go out for a walk.

"Maybe later," she said. "I thought you might want to spend some time in your studio?"

His eyebrows rose. He'd been itching to start work on his graphic novel, but he'd thought he'd have to wait until she went to work on Monday. "Um... Are you sure?"

"Of course. I've brought my iPad and fancy a read. And maybe a doze. You've worn me out." She grinned.

"Well, okay. Are you going to bed?"

"No, no, I'll stay here." She pointed to the cushioned lounger on the deck.

He hesitated. "You can use the sofa in the studio, if you like."

She studied his face for a moment. Then she smiled. "All right. But if you feel I'm intruding and you can't concentrate, just say so. I'd be happy to lie out here."

"Okay."

So they went into the studio, and Georgia took her iPad and stretched out on the sofa, while Matt sat at his architect's table and fumbled around for a while sorting out paper and pencils and making himself comfortable.

It was strange, having someone else in the room with him, and for a while he was too self-conscious to work, wondering if she was bored or was expecting him to take her out. But after a while he glanced over to see the iPad lying on her stomach and her eyes closed. He smiled slowly, his gaze caressing her face, her parted lips, her shiny hair spread out on the cushion. He liked having her there. He was happy being alone, but having her there made him feel... complete.

Stifling a snort, he rolled his eyes and turned his attention to his drawing pad. *Seriously dude. Concentrate.*

He began sketching, drawing a series of boxes on the page similar to the ones he'd made on the plane, this time elaborating on the chapters, working out the pacing of the story and where the twists and turns would go.

After that, he put the page to one side and broke the first chapter down into the number of pages he thought would be suitable, and planned out what he wanted to happen in each scene of the chapter. Then he began sketching the first scene, where Rory got bored on holiday in Taupo and went off to explore the lake.

Sometime later, part of him was aware that Georgia had roused, and he gave her a kiss when she came over to ask if he wanted a cup of coffee and said yes he would, as his back was getting stiff sitting in the same position, and he'd long ago learned to move around frequently. While they drank their coffee, they took a walk outside. The strip of land around the house contained palms and flowering shrubs, and Georgia pointed some of them out to him, naming the plants and telling him a little about them.

"I might have a tinker out here," she said when they'd finished their coffee. "Do you mind?"

"Of course not." He kissed her and left her to it, taking their cups back to the kitchen, then returning to the studio, where he spent another couple of hours working on his book.

In the beginning, it didn't flow and the drawings didn't look right, but he was used to this period of trial and error, and he just removed the page and binned it before starting again, sketching until he eventually grew satisfied with the character's basic body shape. It would be useful if Noah would pose for him at some point, and he decided he would leave the facial features until later, when he was happy with the storyline and had the foundation of the scenes planned.

Deep in thought, in his own little world, he roused eventually at the sound of Georgia's voice in the distance.

He stood and stretched, listening to her singing an old Beatles' song, *Revolution*, if he wasn't mistaken. He walked to the window, catching sight of her at the edge of the deck, working on a large rose bush. She'd found one of his baseball caps somewhere and had pulled it on to protect her from the sun, and she was dancing a little to the tune while she clipped and pruned.

She looked happy and extremely beautiful. He caressed her with his gaze for a while, enjoying the anticipation of the time he knew would come later, when he would take her to bed, remove her clothes, and hold her warm, soft body against him. He'd thought it would be invasive having her in the house, but it wasn't, it was oddly comforting, and he would miss her when she went to work.

Smiling, he opened the sliding doors and stepped out onto the deck. She looked up, surprised, and straightened as he walked over to her.

"Sorry, did I disturb you?" she asked. "I think I was singing."

"You were, and very lovely it was too." He put his arms around her and, unmindful of the bits of leaves stuck to her top and the smear of dirt across her nose, kissed her.

"Mmm." She turned and put her arms around his neck and kissed him back. "Nice," she said when he eventually lifted his head.

"I'm hungry," he advised. "Shall we catch an early dinner?"

"Ooh yes. I'll freshen up and get changed."

They went inside and Georgia carried her bag into the bedroom. Matt made some space in the walk-in closet for her to hang up her clothes, and moved some of his T-shirts aside so she had a few shelves too. She rid herself of the leaves and dirt and changed into a pretty summer dress, while he pulled on a clean shirt over his jeans.

She took ten minutes to ring Noah, walking out onto the deck while she did so. He didn't like to follow, not wanting her to think he was trying to eavesdrop. He doubted that she was mentioning to Noah where she was and who she was with. Strangely, the thought made him a little sad. He liked Noah, and he thought that the boy probably wouldn't be averse to Georgia spending some time with him.

When she'd finished, they drove down to the restaurant on the waterfront, which happened to be part of the oldest hotel in New Zealand.

"How is Noah?" he asked as they parked and got out of the car. The sun glittered on the ocean, and the warm evening had encouraged plenty of people out. The smell of cooked food mingled with the sound of the music in the air as they walked across to the restaurant.

"Usual," Georgia replied. She didn't elaborate, and Matt didn't press her. Maybe she'd tell him more later.

They ordered a seafood platter and nibbled their way through pan-friend scallops with lime and coriander, bowls of green-lipped muscles, salmon bites, prawn kebabs, salt-and-pepper squid rings, and fish pieces in tempura batter, while they sipped a glass of Pinot Gris and talked.

As they moved on to dessert, Georgia asked him how his book was progressing, and he described his work process, and the story he'd come up with so far. She made a couple of suggestions, and one of them solved a plot dilemma he'd had, which made him smile.

"What are you smirking at?" She was finishing off a bowl of locally-made mint-choc-chip ice cream, scraping out the last flakes of chocolate with her spoon.

"I'm not smirking, I'm smiling. I'm having a nice time."

She sucked the spoon, then licked her lips. "Did you not expect that?"

He thought about it, not wanting to sound arrogant or insulting, but feeling the need to be honest. "I knew I'd enjoy being with you. I wasn't sure about having someone in the house. You know what it's like—you've lived on your own for a long time. You get used to your own company. You develop quirks and get set in your ways. And I wasn't sure whether there was space in that for someone else. But I think there might be."

She put down the spoon and leaned on the table, meeting his gaze, and they studied each other quietly for a moment. He felt as if they were settling together, like two circles of different colored paint on a palette that were touching, merging, and finally blending into another color brighter than the first.

A dab of chocolate sat on her bottom lip. He licked his thumb, leaned forward, and brushed at it until it was gone. Her lips curved up, and then she drew his thumb into her mouth. She sucked, and his groin tightened in response, his heart rate increasing.

"Maybe we should go home," he said, his voice husky.

She released his thumb and nodded, her eyes gleaming.

He paid the bill, and they returned to the car and drove the short distance back up the hill to the house.

"We'll have to get you some Christmas decorations," Georgia said as they made their way in. "If you'd like," she added as an afterthought.

"I'd like. I just hadn't thought about it. Guys don't tend to bother with stuff like that." He closed the door behind him and pulled her into his arms for a long kiss. Just the memory of the way she'd run her tongue across the pad of his thumb was enough to make his erection magically appear again.

But Georgia pushed him away and said, "Not yet. I want you to do something for me first."

He let her go, throwing his keys on the table and following her into the room. The sun was setting, and the sparkles on the Pacific in the distance were a Christmas decoration of their own. The sky was a beautiful blend of orange, red, and purple—he'd have trouble recreating that on a palette, although he'd love to try.

He turned his attention to Georgia, though, more important things on his mind at the moment than painting, which was saying something. "What can I do for you?"

"I want you to sketch me." Her nose wrinkled. "Like one of your French girls."

He chuckled at the quote from *Titanic*. "Seriously?"

"Seriously. You know. Nude. I want to see what I look like through your eyes."

He nodded slowly, his lips curving up. "All right."

She slipped off her jacket. "Where do you want me?"

"Oh, everywhere. But I'll sketch you in the studio." Suddenly, he wanted her in there, naked, like a Paleolithic man dragging his woman back to his cave.

Laughing, she toed off her sandals and left the room, her bare feet making no noise on the floor. Matt watched her go, already hard as a rock at the thought of her stripping off. But he made himself calm down and poured them both a glass of wine from the fridge before following her through to the studio.

It was on the east side of the house, and although north facing, was filled with shadows, so Georgia had switched on the lamp above his architect's table, and it spilled yellow light across the floor and the sofa where she lay.

He stopped and stared, catching his breath at the sight of her lying there, naked, head propped on a hand, her silky brown hair spread out behind her, her creamy skin glowing in the light from the lamp.

"Wow." He placed the glasses of wine on the table to the side. "You expect me to work under these conditions?"

She grinned but didn't move, and he sighed, found a fresh pad and a newly-sharpened 4B pencil, and pulled a stool opposite her.

"Tell me how you want me to lie," she said.

"That's not bad. But put one foot on the floor. Open your legs."

She gave him a wry look. "Really?"

"I'm the artist. I'm paying you well for this."

"No you're not."

"Do as you're told anyway. I might as well enjoy the view."

Giggling, she shifted a bit more onto her back, then opened her legs, exposing every inch of her to his hot gaze. She lifted one arm above her head, her round, full breasts glowing in the lamplight, the nipples relaxed and soft, calling to him to suck them.

He swallowed hard. "This might have backfired on me, actually."

"I don't care. No stopping until you're done."

He blew out a breath and settled on the stool. "Wow, you're bossy."

"Yep. You'd better get used to it."

Chuckling, he put the pencil to the paper and began to sketch.

☐

Chapter Twenty

Georgia relaxed back into the sofa as Matt's smile gradually faded and he lost himself in his drawing. Lying like this, she was able to watch him work, which was a treat in itself. His dark hair flopped over his forehead, which creased a little as he concentrated, his pencil flying across the page.

Every now and again, he looked up and observed her, his hot gaze caressing her body, lingering on her breasts and between her legs. Desire glimmered in his eyes, but each time he returned to the paper and continued to sketch. He wanted her, but he was enjoying the anticipation of the moment to come.

It was nice to be able to study him for a while without feeling as if she was intruding. The way his shirt sleeves stretched across his biceps and shoulders as his arm moved. The triangle of tanned skin where his top button was open, and the hollow of his throat that glistened with moisture because of the warm room. The way the denim of his jeans stretched across the powerful muscles of his thighs. He'd kicked off his Converses and his feet were bare, giving him a sexy edge, hinting at the bare skin she'd be seeing soon, when she finally undressed him.

Where would they make love tonight? In that big bed of his? She knew he'd shared it with other women, but it didn't bother her. He hadn't brought any other girl into his studio. That was what mattered.

She couldn't wait to feel his mouth on hers, his warm skin beneath her fingertips. Her heart began to race, and mischievousness surged through her. Lazily, she trailed her hand down her body, over her breasts, imagining it was his hand, stroking, teasing. He glanced up, and his pencil poised on the paper as he watched her cup her breast and run a thumb over her nipple. It was soft, but it puckered as she touched the sensitive tip, and she played with it for a moment until it was hard in her fingers.

Matt's gaze lifted to hers, and he gave her a hot, exasperated smile before returning his eyes to the paper.

Turned on now, she moved her hand to her other breast and did the same, teasing the nipple, inhaling as he glanced up to watch before looking back at his sketch. How far could she push him before he gave in?

Sliding her hand down her body, she stroked her thighs, then ran light fingers up the insides. Matt continued to sketch, but his breathing had grown faster, and his gaze repeatedly flicked up to her, his smile fading and being replaced by dark desire as she continued to arouse herself.

She moved her hand between her legs and stroked the bare skin there, enjoying the shivery sensation it gave her, before sliding her middle finger down. Gathering some moisture, she smoothed it through the swelling folds to the top, and circled her finger over her clit.

Still, he didn't move, although his stares at her became longer, with more time between the strokes of his pencil while he watched her. So, he was going to sit there until she made herself come? Whatever the customer wants… Her face heated a little under his intense gaze, but she closed her eyes and lifted her other hand to her breast while she continued to arouse herself.

The knowledge that he was watching her only added to her arousal, and it wasn't long before she was slick and swollen. Her hand moved faster, her other fingers teasing her nipple, and she sucked her bottom lip, knowing it wouldn't be long before her muscles would tighten and her climax would sweep her away.

"For fuck's sake."

His sudden words and the slap of his pad onto the floor in the stillness of the room made her jump, but she didn't have time to react because he was dropping to his knees before her, his fingers fumbling at the buttons of his shirt as he hastened to remove it.

She laughed, still stroking herself as he tore the shirt off, and she murmured with approval at the sight of his tanned flesh shining in the lamplight, his muscles rippling as he moved forward and placed a hand beneath each of her knees. He tugged, and she squealed as she slid down the sofa. He unzipped his jeans, freed his erections from his boxers, and then he was inside her in one smooth, easy thrust.

Moaning, she arched her back, delight spreading through her at the sensation of being stretched and filled to the brim.

"Fuck," he said again, and she opened her eyes to see him looking down at her, his gaze hot, his eyes now deep brown and his pupils dilated.

She hooked her leg around his hips, tilting up to meet him. "Hard and fast," she whispered. "I can't wait."

"If you insist." He was obviously struggling to hold back too, and he set up a fast pace, thrusting hard, his hips meeting her bottom and thighs with a smack as he plunged deeply into her.

He kissed her, and she opened her mouth to him, exchanging a long, wet, hungry kiss, welcoming the slide of his tongue against hers, aroused by the sensation of being invaded, as well as his obvious desire for her.

Sliding her arms around him, she stroked down his back, loving the feel of his muscles tightening and loosening with each movement. She moved her hands beneath his jeans and the elastic of his boxers onto the muscles of his ass and pulled him toward her, encouraging him to thrust harder. He obliged, grinding against her clit with her push of his hips, and it was only minutes before she felt the spread of warmth deep inside that announced the imminent arrival of her orgasm.

"Yeah," he said, obviously sensing it too, and she gave into it and clamped around him, crying out with each strong pulse as he continued to thrust until his own climax claimed him. He stopped moving, turned to stone, and the two of them locked together for a long moment. Georgia opened her eyes to see him watching her with such love and affection that it almost made her weep.

It seemed like forever before her orgasm ended, and even then, as he gave little thrusts of his hips, she felt delicious aftershocks spread through her, beautiful and pleasurable.

Matt kissed her, gentle this time, his lips caressing hers before he eventually withdrew. Lifting her, he turned her until she lay on top of him on the sofa, and she rested her head on his chest and reveled in the afterglow.

"That was nice," she murmured.

"That was fast," he corrected. "Sorry. But that's what happens when you lie there like a strumpet and play with yourself in front of a hot blooded Neanderthal."

She laughed and kissed his chest. "Did I destroy your concentration?"

"Just a bit." He smiled and tucked her hair behind her ear, obviously far from upset.

"Can I look at the sketch now?"

An impish smile curved his lips. "Sure."

She reached down for the pad where he'd dropped it on the floor, pulled it toward her, and flipped it over.

It was a beautiful sketch, capturing her perfectly, making her look—she thought with some surprise—rather beautiful, with a happy smile on her face and a sparkle in her eyes that she hadn't known was there.

She looked up at him. He grinned.

"You only drew my face," she said.

"Yeah."

"I lay there naked and spread out for you, and you only drew me from the shoulders up."

He shrugged. "Don't worry. I enjoyed the view."

"Matt!"

"What?" He took the pad from her, tossed it onto the floor, and wrapped her in his arms. "One day, maybe I'll capture you on paper, but for now you are for my eyes only." He kissed her, long and lingering, and she melted against him.

"Shall we go to bed?" she murmured.

"In a minute. Look at the view."

She turned her head to look at the window, seeing that the last rays of the sun had coated the tops of the bush with a reddish-gold. The studio was cast into shadows, making her feel as if the light from the lamp had created a tiny world for them where nobody could touch them.

It made her both happy and sad at the same time. She missed Noah, but she'd spoken to her mother in Christchurch who'd told her he was being difficult, and when she'd eventually spoken to him, he'd announced that he hated being there and wanted to come home, and then he'd hung up on her.

Was it terrible that she was enjoying a few days apart from him? That she was enjoying just being Georgia, and spending time concentrating on herself for a while after so long worrying about him? Her loyalties were torn in two, and she sighed, feeling Matt's hand brush down her spine as she did so. Somehow, she thought, he understood, and that brought a smile to her lips.

She wasn't a bad mother just because she needed a few days to herself. Soon she'd be with her son and they could start thinking about the following year and how they were going to try to make things better for him. But for now, she would concentrate on herself and on the gorgeous man lying beneath her, and all her other worries could wait.

*

Sunday was possibly the best day Georgia had ever spent in the whole of her life.

From the moment she opened her eyes, it was apparent the weather was going to be kind to them. Morning sun streamed through the open curtains across the bed, coating the naked body of the man lying next to her in gold, making him look like a gold-plated statue of a Greek god.

He lay sprawled on his front, facing her with his arms wrapped around a pillow, his hips and legs tangled in the sheet they'd pulled on in the night because they were too hot in the duvet.

Georgia lay there for ages watching him, resisting the urge to touch him as long as she could. He looked younger in sleep, his face free of worry lines, his creative mind quiet for once. He'd put himself down when he'd told her that his brothers had been given the brains in the family. Maybe it was true that he didn't have the particular talents needed to make a doctor or a scientist, but that didn't mean he wasn't intelligent. He thought in a different way, that was all.

Brock was a Sudoku—he thought in black and white and straight lines, and fitted numbers into boxes to solve puzzles. Charlie was a chess set, always thinking one step ahead, his smart brain doing its best to map out patterns and make sense of the world.

Matt was like the Spirograph she'd had as a child. He saw in spirals and loops, and in rainbow colors. The three Kings were all different and yet also very similar. They used their gifts to help their fellow man, and ultimately that was what made them all special.

He's too secretive and private. He doesn't let anyone in. Trinny—or was it Toni? Georgia could never remember—had said that about him. He'd never let any of his girlfriends into his studio. And yet he'd taken Georgia in there. Had let her watch him work.

The death of his sister, and then of Brock's wife, whom he'd obviously been fond of, must have shaken him to the core. Until now, he'd been wary of letting anyone get close to him, maybe fearing that if he let them in, it would hurt more when he eventually lost them. But he'd told her all about those he'd lost, had shown her his paintings. He'd let her in—into his studio, into his life. Would he let her into his heart too? Only time would tell.

Unable to keep her hands to herself any longer, she trailed a finger over his shoulder and down his spine to where the sheet lay across his hips. Impishly, she slid her finger down to the swell of his buttocks, and lower, investigating as far as she dared before she brought her hand back up his spine and lifted her gaze to his face. Her heart missed a beat—his eyes were open, lazy and warm, watching her.

"Enjoying yourself?" he asked.

"Mmm." She traced the muscles of his shoulders and back, stroking and exploring, and he closed his eyes again, finding pleasure in being admired, being wanted.

She stroked him for a long time, until his breathing deepened and his eyes opened again. Then she leaned close to him and murmured, "Turn over."

He did so, lying on his back and tucking his arms under his head, stretching in the morning sun. Georgia spent some time exploring the muscles of his chest, his ribs, the hair that petered out to a trail. Then she closed her fingers around his erection and explored that too, enjoying the way he swelled in her hand, discovering each ridge and vein beneath the thin layer of skin that moved as she stroked him.

When he could stand it no more, he pulled her on top of him, and they made love slowly in the sunlight. They took time to arouse each other, to explore, drawing out each other's pleasure the way they hadn't had the patience to do the night before. Sitting on top, she rode him as if she had all the time in the world, and Matt seemed content to let her, admiring her as she moved, trailing his hands across her skin, cupping her breasts, and holding her hips so he could push up and bury himself in her.

By the end, every cell and nerve ending in Georgia's body was on fire, burning for him. When her orgasm finally arrived, it was a blessed relief and a tiny disappointment too, because she wanted the morning to go on forever, the two of them to remain like this while the clock's hands ticked around and the seasons passed outside.

And as she continued to rock her hips and she watched Matt's climax sweep over him, his brow creasing and his lips parting with his groans of pleasure, she knew that, although it had only been days, it didn't matter. She was in love, probably had been since the day of her interview, and all that mattered now was whether by the end of their twelve days he felt the same, and wanted to prolong the Christmas magic into the New Year.

Chapter Twenty-One

The rest of Sunday passed as pleasurably—almost—as the first hour. They had breakfast in bed, Georgia reading out the news headlines from her iPad while Matt drank his coffee, and then they showered together, wanting to make the most of their time, and enjoying the opportunity to slide slippery hands over each other's naked skin.

After that, they went for a walk in the bright sunshine, taking the wide, cultivated path through the bush to the picnic spot further along that overlooked the bay. While they walked, fantails flittered in the air, cicadas sang in the bushes, and tuis called from the treetops, the sounds of summer, filling Matt with a lightness of heart he'd come to associate with Georgia being around.

As they walked, he asked her about Fintan, curious about her relationship with him. It became apparent as she gradually told him more details that their marriage had run into trouble when Fintan had felt unable to talk about his depression.

"He would shut himself away for hours," she said, looking at her feet as they crunched through the dead leaves and broken twigs. "Just lock himself in the bathroom, or go out and not say where he was going."

"That must have been hard."

"It was." She looked up at Matt then, her amber eyes like polished mahogany in the sunlight that streamed through the trees. "I don't want you to think that means I have to be glued to your side the whole time. I do think being with someone is about sharing—good and bad things. But I've grown to value my independence too over the years, and maybe now I understand a bit more what he went through, and why he felt the need to deal with it himself."

"Did he go to a counsellor?"

"Yes, lots over the years, and he took a variety of pills, but I think he saw both things as a weakness of character. He thought if he was strong he should be able to cope with his worries on his own." Her hand strayed to her hip, as Matt had noticed it sometimes did absently, when she thought about her husband. "I don't think the counsellor helped, anyway. All she did was dredge up the same negative feelings and remind him why he was depressed in the first place."

Matt was holding her hand, and he ran his thumb across her knuckles, remembering what she'd said about Noah seeing a therapist. "I get the feeling you don't have a very high opinion of counsellors."

"I'm sure they are helpful for some people. But they didn't help Fintan, and they haven't helped Noah."

"If it helps, I know someone up here who's very good. I'm sure she would be able to help Noah, if you wanted to try again."

She looked up at him. "You see a counsellor?"

"Not so much nowadays. I did when I was younger. After Pippa died, my parents decided they needed extra help. I hated it, at first. I was angry and rebellious, and resentful that this woman thought she could help me when she was so much older and clearly knew nothing about the problems I had." He smiled.

Georgia slipped her arm around him, and he placed his around her shoulders. "I can't imagine you angry and rebellious," she said. "You seem so placid and relaxed now."

"I suppose to some extent I don't rant and rail against life anymore. When you're a kid, you think you're the center of the universe, but I came to accept that Pippa wasn't taken away to punish me. It was a big step."

"Did Fleur dying make things worse again?"

"Oddly, no. I was sad, of course. Terribly sad, and it was awful watching Brock's heart break. But after that, I began to see my place in the world, tiny and insignificant, and I realized it was pointless to try to swim against the current. Since then I've just gone with the flow, and it's been a lot easier."

"Do you think you've come to terms with it? Or have you just sealed yourself away from the world to protect yourself? Physically, in the house, and emotionally?"

He said nothing for a while, thinking about her words. Barbara, his therapist, had said much the same in the past—that rather than dealing with his issues, he just removed himself from situations where he might open himself up to being hurt. But he didn't know any other way to be. Loving someone meant accepting the possibility that he might lose them. It had been easier to hide behind real and imaginary walls, lock the doors, and throw away the key.

"Sorry," Georgia said. "I didn't mean to pry."

"It's okay. You're right. I'm better than I was, and I'm a lot happier now. But it's probably why I'm still single."

"It might sound incredibly selfish, but I'm glad you are." She smiled.

He smiled back, lowering his lips to kiss her. He had no doubt that Georgia had discovered the key to the padlock around his heart. As yet, he wasn't sure where it was going to lead, but he resolved not to think about it now. It was a beautiful summer day, he had a gorgeous woman in his arms, and he wasn't going to think past spending the day with her and having fun. The furthest into the future he'd let himself imagine was the moment when they would slide into bed tonight and he'd be able to let her spirit him away to the blissful place where nothing mattered except her warm, soft body pressed against his.

*

After their walk, they drove down to Russell for an ice cream and a walk along the sea front, followed by a visit to the old church that still bore the bullet holes from the Maori Wars. Then they returned to the house to relax for a few hours before going out to dinner again, this time taking the ferry to the mainland and driving to Paihia, where Matt had booked a table at the restaurant that did the best barbecue ribs in the Northland.

The day ended with them returning to the house and watching a movie in the living room before sliding into bed together. Still full from their dinner—Georgia had surprised him by eating every one of the huge mound of ribs he'd piled onto her plate as well as half a ton of coleslaw and a mountain of French fries, and then they'd shared a huge chocolate sundae—and tired from the fresh air, they kissed and talked for a while, then mutually agreed to cuddle up and let sleep settle its blanket over them.

Matt held her in his arms and felt her gradually relax against him as she dozed. In the dark sky, two stars shone side by side, the brightest possibly Sirius, twinkling away like the star from the Nativity, which reminded him it was nearly Christmas. He'd have to get Georgia something. He wasn't sure what yet, but he had a little time before she was due to go away.

The stars made him think of Pippa and Fleur. When Fleur had died, one of his first thoughts was that at least Pippa wouldn't be alone anymore. He wasn't a religious man particularly, but he liked the idea of them looking after each other, watching over him as he went about his daily life. Would they have liked Georgia? He couldn't imagine they wouldn't have. No doubt they would have been good friends, if they'd all been alive today.

Swallowing hard, he closed his eyes and concentrated on the feel of Georgia in his arms, the softness of her skin and the smell of her hair where she'd tucked her head under his chin. And then he fell asleep.

*

On Monday, Georgia returned to work. Matt drove her to her house where she picked up her car, then left her with a kiss and a promise to call her at lunchtime.

She missed him, and she filled any spare minutes in her day with daydreams of him lying naked in her arms, his mouth on hers, imagining what delights they were going to get up to in the evening. But even though she would rather have been with him all the time, she loved her job, and she threw herself into the organization of the Christmas events that the We Three Kings Foundation had planned with renewed enthusiasm, enjoying the opportunity to plan some final wishes for sick kids whose parents would no doubt find the festive season difficult.

The rest of the week passed the same way, and somehow it made the evenings sweeter, returning to his house to find him happy after a full day's work in his studio. Cooking and eating together, or sometimes going out for dinner. Visiting the cinema one night, the theater another, or coming back home to watch movies and then going to bed together. Spending hours exploring each other's bodies, and learning how to pleasure each other.

Her relationship with Fintan had been complicated, and although when they'd first been together sex had been often and good, as they'd neared the last years of their relationship and his depression had become an issue, their sex life had been the first thing to suffer. His libido had vanished, and by the end, sex had become so tied up with feelings of frustration and guilt that she'd lost the joy in sharing her body with someone.

Knowing Matt's reputation, Georgia had assumed that lovemaking with him would be fast and furious, and lots of it. And that was certainly the case, to some extent. Matt's hunger for her seemed insatiable, and a day didn't go by without him reaching for her at night, or in the early hours of the morning, or whenever else the urge struck him.

But it was the quality of his lovemaking more than the quantity that surprised and overwhelmed her. She'd expected him to know his way around the female body. She hadn't expected the sheer joy he took in pleasuring her, and his deeply sensual nature that led him to constantly find different ways to make love to her.

Rather than it always being about the end product—the race to the finish line, like a fast food meal—lovemaking with Matt was like a medieval banquet, with numerous courses intended to tease the palate and do more than just fill the stomach. She soon lost her inhibitions as he encouraged her to try new positions, to make love outdoors, to experiment, and to generally associate sex with fun and excitement, something she'd lost a long time ago.

The days ticked by in a blur of passion and pleasure, and then it was the weekend again. Saturday they spent at the Jazz and Blues Festival in Paihia, visiting the local bars where bands were hanging out, drinking and eating, and generally having a whale of a time. But Sunday they spent at home, sitting out in the sunshine, talking, reading, dozing, and continuing their exploration of other, both physical and emotional.

Monday, Georgia was back at work, and she began to feel a rising sense of unease at the thought that there were only a few days left before she had to leave to fly down to Christchurch. She spoke to Noah every evening, and she was well aware he was extremely unhappy being without her down there. Anna Banks repeatedly told her that he was sullen and difficult, and Georgia struggled with guilt at leaving him there when she was having such a fantastic time with Matt. She'd thought Noah might enjoy the change of scenery, going fishing, and being apart from her when he seemed so angry with her a lot of the time, but the opposite seemed to have happened, and she'd only made him angrier because he felt she'd abandoned him.

There wasn't much she could do about it, though, so she got on with things as best she could. Her contract with We Three Kings gave her a generous amount of holiday, but even so she didn't want to use it all up in one go, and she wouldn't have dreamed of playing on her relationship with Matt to ask for more time off. So Noah would have to wait, and until then she'd make the most of the time she had with Matt and put her other issues to the back of her mind.

Chapter Twenty-Two

Around Monday lunchtime, while she was eating her sandwiches at her desk, Georgia's phone rang.

She picked it up, wondering if it was Matt, her eyebrows rising as she saw the name Skye Hall on the screen. She and Skye had swapped numbers when they'd met at the domain, but it was the first time she'd heard from her.

"Hello?" she said.

"Georgia?"

"Yes, Skye? Nice to hear from you."

"I'm so sorry I haven't rung before now, I swear when you have a baby the fabric of time distorts itself. I can barely manage to get dressed by midday."

Georgia laughed. "How is Harry?"

"He's great, although I have to say I am absolutely loving the fact that my mother has him for an *entire night.*"

"I see. Owen in for a good evening, is he?" Georgia teased.

"If by that you mean we're going to watch TV and fall asleep in front of it, probably." Skye chuckled. "I was wondering if you're free after work? I thought maybe we could catch up over a coffee."

Georgia nibbled her bottom lip. "At any other time I'd have said yes, but actually... You remember me talking about Matt King?"

"The Highlander?"

"Yeah. Well, I'm off to Christchurch on Wednesday, but until then we're sort of... having a thing for a few days."

"Ooh. Hot sex. I remember it well."

"Aw. It'll get better after the first eighteen years."

"Georgia!" Skye sighed. "Look, feel free to say no—I'll understand completely if you want to keep the gorgeous billionaire to yourself, but you don't fancy going out for dinner, the four of us?"

Taken aback, Georgia wasn't quite sure what to say. "Oh, um..."

"It's just that I see my sisters and their friends and partners up in Doubtless Bay quite a lot, but Owen and I don't socialize much in

Kerikeri as a couple, and it would be nice to go out with friends who were ours, you know?"

"I'm touched that you'd think of me, thank you."

"It's okay, you can say no. I wouldn't have asked, but it's our first evening without Harry, and I have this feeling that if we go out on our own we're just going to sit and talk about him all evening, you know?"

Georgia smiled. "I'll have to check with Matt, but it's a definite yes from me. Can I call him and ring you back?"

"Of course!" Skye sounded delighted. "Speak to you in a bit."

Georgia hung up and stared at the phone for a moment. Her stomach did a strange flip. For some reason, suggesting going out on a foursome felt like a big step. Why was that? It didn't mean anything. But maybe it was because in doing so, it meant they were a couple. She wasn't sure how he would feel about that. They'd been out together locally and he hadn't been shy to show affection in front of others. But so far they hadn't discussed what was going to happen after she left for Christmas. She hoped he'd want to see her again when she came back, but she wasn't sure, and for some strange reason she felt as if this was a test.

She dialed Matt's number, heart racing. They'd taken to calling each other at lunchtime, but sometimes he took a while to answer if he was in the studio and covered in paint.

This time, though, he answered relatively quickly. "Hey gorgeous. How's the wonderful arse of the most beautiful girl in Christendom?"

"Matthew King, this is Georgia's mother. I just called by to see Georgia and happened to pick up her phone..."

He snorted. "Don't full name me. And how is your beautiful butt anyway?"

"Matt..." She suppressed a memory of his hands roaming over her backside the night before doing all kinds of unmentionable things, and tried to concentrate. "Look, I understand if you want to say no, but I've just had a call from a friend—well she's an acquaintance at the moment, but I'm hoping she'll grow to be a friend—and she was wondering, well I was wondering..."

"Spit it out, sweetheart," he said, amused.

She blew out a breath. "I don't suppose you fancy going out to dinner with her and her husband tonight? They have a baby but her mother's looking after him for the evening, and I think it might take their minds off leaving him, you know? She's really nice, and he's a dog handler for Search and Rescue."

"Sounds great," he said.

"Oh. Really?"

"You thought I'd say no?"

"I wasn't sure if it was a bit... formal. You don't have to worry. It doesn't mean anything."

He went quiet for a moment. Then he said, "No, of course not. What time?"

"I've got to ring her back. What shall I say, six? I think sleep's an issue for them and I'm guessing that they're not going to want to be out late."

"Sounds great. In Kerikeri?"

"Yeah. How about The Italian?"

"Mmm yeah. I fancy one of their pizzas."

"Okay. Shall I come to you first?"

"Sure. Why don't we get a taxi? Then we can both have a glass of wine."

Normally she would never have paid for a taxi all the way from Russell to Kerikeri, but she said "All right." There were some benefits to dating a billionaire.

He didn't say anything, and she hesitated. "Matt, I haven't upset you, have I?"

"Of course not. I'm in the middle of something, that's all. You know what I'm like. I get distracted."

"Oh okay, sorry to have disturbed you. See you around five?"

He said goodbye and hung up.

Georgia placed the phone slowly on the desk and looked at it for a moment. She knew she'd said something to upset him. What had she said? *You don't have to worry. It doesn't mean anything.* She'd been trying to make it clear that she wasn't putting pressure on him. But maybe he'd taken it as meaning she wasn't interested in taking things further.

Well, there wasn't anything she could do about it now. She'd talk to him later when they got home. It was about time they discussed what would happen after Christmas, and that might be the perfect time.

Picking up her phone, she dialed Skye's number to tell her they were good to go.

*

"Schubert?" Matt laughed. "For a Labrador? I love it."

Owen grinned and helped himself to some more garlic bread. "Yeah, it fits him really well."

"How's Mozart with him?" Georgia dipped her bread in the olive oil and then the salt before chewing it dreamily.

"Like an old uncle. Gives him the occasional cuff around the ear to keep him in his place."

Georgia grinned, her gaze flicking across to Matt, who was busy cutting up the mozzarella and bacon bread so Skye could have another piece. They were sitting outside under the covered outdoor area, and it was a balmy evening, the cicadas loud in the trees behind them. Although it wasn't yet dark, tea lights on the tables and tinsel around the bar gave it a Christmassy feel. It was strange to think it was Christmas Eve in three days. She'd be down in Christchurch by then, hundreds of miles away from Matt.

She wasn't going to think about that now though. "How are the dogs with Harry? Are they good with him?"

"They're wonderful," Skye said. As she wouldn't be breastfeeding until the next morning, she'd allowed herself a glass of wine as a special treat. "Very protective of him, Mozart especially."

"I read about you two in the paper," Matt said to Owen. "When you rescued the lawyer's boy. It was some story. I'm glad Mozart made it through."

"Yeah, me too." Owen smiled.

"I've been thinking," Matt said, "about doing a special one-off Ward Seven book where one of the characters, Carmel maybe, goes missing in the hospital and Dixon has to help find her, with the proceeds going to Search and Rescue. What do you think?"

Owen stared at him in delight. "That would be wonderful."

"We could have a kind of joint launch to bring some exposure for the cause, have dogs there, do a little show. Georgia's good with that sort of thing, and she could coordinate it all."

"It's a great idea," she said, finding his hand under the table, pleased that he and Owen seemed to be hitting it off.

Her gaze met Skye's as the two guys started talking about what events they could have on the day. Skye winked at her as she bit into a piece of bread, clearly as pleased as she was. How nice to find a friend. For the first time since she'd moved to the Northland,

Georgia felt like a local rather than an outsider, like she might actually be able to make a real life for herself there.

Would it include Matt? His hand was warm on hers, and he squeezed her fingers as if he'd read her mind. *Please let him want to see me again*, she begged the stars in Orion's belt that had popped out in the darkening sky to the east. She didn't know what she'd do if, when she brought up the subject, he made it clear it was over.

The waiter came to collect their empty plates, and she swallowed hard and pushed the thought away. Maybe she wouldn't bring up the subject tonight after all. It would be a shame to spoil the last two nights they had left.

The evening progressed pleasantly, all four of them getting on as if they'd known each other forever. Skye told them about the *Treats to Tempt You* coffee and chocolate shop where she'd worked until she'd gotten pregnant with Harry, and made them promise to pay it a visit before Christmas to try the Christmas Pudding truffles her sister made every year.

Owen asked about the awards Matt had won, and Matt told him about the ceremony, and how he came up with his ideas for his books. And Georgia watched him, loving just looking at his handsome face, and wanting to stand up and yell to all the other diners, *He's with me! Look at how gorgeous my date is!*

Georgia's carbonara was heavenly and Matt polished off his pizza, then they shared a portion of Tiramisu before finishing off with coffee. She'd had a couple of glasses of wine, but Georgia couldn't help but indulge in a special coffee, loving the rich cream floating in a layer above the coffee laced with Cointreau. Finally it was time to go, and they paid the bill, then walked slowly back to the carpark, where Matt and Georgia were going to pick up a taxi.

Matt and Owen walked a little in front, talking again about Matt's idea for a Search and Rescue book. Georgia hung back with Skye, feeling a little hazy, watching as the other girl took out her phone to check for messages.

"All good?" Georgia asked.

Skye gave a relieved smile. "Yeah. Sorry. I must look neurotic, constantly checking my phone."

"Actually I think you've done amazingly well tonight, considering it's your first evening out."

"I miss him," Skye admitted as they crossed the road. "And I desperately need to express some milk! My boobs are like concrete-filled balloons. But it's been good to be just me and Owen again. It reminds you how good things are, you know?"

Georgia smiled. "Yeah."

Skye glanced at the two guys walking in front of them, and lowered her voice. "So what's the deal with Matt then? Is it a long term thing?"

"I... don't know. We'll find out soon I guess."

"Do you want to continue seeing him?"

Georgia watched him saying something to Owen, illustrating his words with hands, as he tended to do. "Yeah," she said. "I'd like that very much. But I know he's not the commitment type."

"No guy is until they meet the right girl."

Georgia laughed. "I suppose. But I'm sort of prepared for him to say 'that's it.'"

"He doesn't look at you as if he wants it to be over."

"Well that's a nice thing to say. But like you said when I said to you that I'd never gone with a guy just for sex, you said it could be good to have a fling and remove the pressure about it having to mean something, and to enjoy the moment, and I wonder whether that's why we're having such a good time—because he thinks there's no need to commit."

Skye raised an eyebrow. "Well, yeah. It's possible. But when I said I'd had a fling, you know I was talking about Owen, right?"

Georgia stared at her. "Oh."

"Yeah. Started as a one-night stand. Now look at us. Maternity bras, nappies, and sex where you can barely keep your eyes open before you fall asleep." She smiled though, her eyes filled with such affection that Georgia knew it was far from being a complaint.

"Ah. I didn't realize that."

Skye put her arm around her. "He looks at you as if you're a priceless Monet he didn't expect to find in a junk shop. Maybe he's scared of commitment, and you never know if someone's fears will get in the way of their better judgement, but I swear, Georgia, he's crazy about you. It's written all over his face."

Georgia's cheeks burned. "Thank you."

Skye laughed. "I'm so glad we went out tonight. I've had such fun, and Owen really likes Matt. I hope we can do it again, maybe after Christmas."

"Yeah, me too."

The guys had stopped walking, and Skye said, "Here's our car," and hugged her, then kissed Matt on the cheek. Owen did the same to Georgia, and shook hands with Matt, and they got into the car with a wave and a promise to meet again soon.

Georgia slipped her hand into Matt's, and they walked back to the main road where they'd told the taxi they'd be waiting. The cab pulled up within minutes, and they got into the back and snuggled up as it headed off for the coast.

Chapter Twenty-Three

Georgia hiccupped.

"Are you drunk?" Matt asked suspiciously.

"Nope." She shook her head. "No!" She rubbed her nose. "Well maybe a tiny bit. Tipsy. Merry. Not drunk."

He chuckled. "Fair enough. As long as you're *compos mentis.*" He bent his head and nuzzled her ear. "That Tiramisu has got me in the mood."

She sighed, her hot breath on his cheek sending tingles through him. "You're always in the mood."

"True. When you're around."

She was wearing a black mini skirt and a blouse that matched the color of her eyes. Her legs were bare, and he slid a hand up one, pushing her knees apart so he could stroke up the silky skin of her inner thigh.

"Matt!" She pushed at him, glancing at the driver, but the man was singing loudly to the Wizzard song playing on his iPod with his eyes on the road, and besides, Matt had paid him four times the going rate to take them all the way to Russell, so he thought the guy wouldn't mind looking the other way.

He parted her thighs, slid his fingers beneath the elastic of panties, and in the same smooth movement, stroked across her folds.

She shivered. "Ooh."

He nibbled her earlobe. "Do you want me to tell you what I'm going to do to you when I get you home?"

"No."

He ignored her. "I'm going to strip you naked except for this gorgeous little skirt, bend you over the kitchen table, and take you hard."

She moaned, and the driver glanced at them in the rear-view mirror before returning his gaze to the road, a smile on his lips.

Matt laughed and withdrew his hand. It would have been fun making her come in the back of the taxi, but there was no way she'd have been able to keep quiet, and he didn't fancy giving the driver a private sex show.

"Come here." He pulled her into his arms and kissed her hair.

She curled up on the seat and snuggled against him. "I'm so glad you're not angry with me."

He rested his lips on her hair. He hadn't been angry. But her words, *You don't have to worry... It doesn't mean anything*, had been a kind of a wake-up call, a eureka moment for him.

She thought he wasn't interested in anything serious. She was assuming he was going to let her go on Wednesday and then not call her again. That it would all be over once she left for Christchurch.

He'd sat at the architect's desk with a blank sheet of paper and had spent thirty minutes drawing with his mind elsewhere, only to realize when he eventually focused and came back to reality that his sketch featured an image that had obviously come from his subconscious to symbolize his situation—a picture from an old nursery rhyme, *Sing a Song of Sixpence*.

It was something he'd discussed with Barbara, his therapist, ages ago, only a year or two after Pippa had died. She'd said he was developing a thick skin and that it hid his feelings. "Like the pie in the nursery rhyme," he'd said to her. "With all the birds underneath it." It had come out of nowhere, and it had made her laugh.

"Yes, Matt," she'd said softly. "Just like the pie. And you have to cut that crust and let all the birds out."

Sitting in his studio, he'd looked at his drawing of the King in his counting house, counting out his money, the enormous pie resting on the table next to him. And, lowering his pencil, he'd cut open the crust and drawn birds escaping from it, ten, then twenty, then a hundred, filling the page with fluttering wings that he'd then colored in with pencils.

He couldn't keep himself locked away forever. It might feel safe, but it was like living in monochrome, and he was desperate to fill his life with color. And Georgia brought all the shades of the rainbow into his world. He loved her—he knew that now. They might not have been sleeping together for long, but he'd fallen for her the day he'd seen her in reception, swinging one leg in that gorgeous suit, the curl of hair around her cheek. He'd taken her into his studio, he'd opened the door to her physically and metaphorically, and he'd let her into his heart. And he didn't want to lose her.

They remained quiet as the taxi wound along the coast road to Opua, and they boarded the ferry just as it was about to leave. Georgia was humming along to the Elton John Christmas song playing on the driver's iPod, her voice vibrating through his chest.

Matt looked out of the window at the stars reflecting on the water like a string of fairy lights. Now wasn't the time to talk about what the future held, because they'd had a few drinks, and he wanted to make decisions in the sunlight, sober, sitting across the table from her, so he could see all the emotions on her face and know that when she said yes to him—if she said yes—she meant it.

But he couldn't hold it all in until the morning. There were some things he needed to know, questions to ask, things to say that were bursting to get out of him.

The ferry bumped against the landing dock, and the ramp lowered to let the cars off. They'd be home soon.

He kissed her hair again. "Georgia?"

"Mmm?" She tipped her head back, her pupils large in the semi-darkness, making her eyes look black.

Suddenly, he couldn't think what to say. His brain felt like scrambled eggs, and the right words wouldn't form. What if she said no? That she'd only wanted to see him for sex, and wasn't interested in anything more serious? When they'd first gotten together, she'd said, *I don't want you to think that I don't understand the point of casual sex.* Was that all this was?

She pushed herself back, her eyes widening. "Is this it?"

"What?"

She swallowed. "Are you about to tell me it's all over?"

He stared at her. "No! Of course not. I was about to ask you if you think you'd ever want to have more children."

She blinked. Then, to his surprise, she burst out laughing.

His lips curved up. "What's so funny?"

"I don't know." Giggles pealed from her, loud enough and infectious enough to make the driver chuckle in the front.

Matt pursed his lips, not sure whether to be amused or insulted. She saw his face and attempted to rein the giggles in, but it was hopeless, and soon she was convulsed in gales of laughter, tears leaking from her eyes.

He met the driver's eyes in the rear view mirror, rolled his own, and blew out a breath. Then he looked back at her. He had to admit that Georgia laughing was the most beautiful thing he'd ever seen or heard. He wanted to make her do this all day every day, until her sad thoughts had fled her mind and her life was filled with sunshine.

He needed to talk to her, but the best thing to do would be to put her to bed and wait until the morning when their heads were clear. Pulling her against him, he kissed her, and she threw her arms around his neck and kissed him back. Her body still shook with laughter, but her kiss was genuine, her arms tight around him.

"Sorry to interrupt, but is this it?"

Matt raised his head to see that the driver was slowing as he approached the house. "Yes, thanks, if you could just turn off and pull up out the front."

The driver did so and stopped the car. Matt paid him the fee and gave him the generous tip he'd promised, and they got out into the balmy evening as the taxi pulled away.

Georgia twirled in a circle, her arms in the air, then stopped to look at the twinkling lights of Paihia across the water. "What a gorgeous evening. I love this house, Matt. It feels like I'm on top of the world."

He smiled and unlocked the door, then stood back to let her pass. "I'm glad you like it."

"I like you." She kissed him, hard, yanking his head down to hers and delving her tongue into his mouth, then danced away into the house. "Music!" she said. "We need music."

Matt closed the door and followed her in, his heart racing from the kiss. She'd bought some fairy lights for him and had strung them around the wall of the living room, and she flicked them on, scolding him when he went to put the main light on. Going over to where he'd left his iPod in the dock with the speakers, she took it out, flicked through the music on her phone, and slid it onto the dock. Wham's *Last Christmas* started playing.

Matt rolled his eyes. "Seriously?"

"It's Christmassy," she protested, dancing through to the kitchen.

"You need water," he said. Pulling a bottle out of the fridge, he handed it to her. She drank half of it in one go, then wiped her mouth, her eyes coming back to his, hot and suggestive.

He perched on the edge of the bar stool and leaned back on the breakfast bar, watching her with a smile. "Are you okay?"

"Yeah, I'm great." She swayed around the bar to him and kicked off her shoes. He sighed—she knew he loved her being barefoot. Winking at him, she began to give him a lap dance. When he put his hands on her hips, she knocked them away and tutted. "You can't handle the merchandize, sir."

Giving her a wry look, he leaned back against the bar. "What's got into you?"

"You." She moved slowly in front of him, sensual and sexy. "You make me hot." She lifted her hair off her neck, winding her hips.

He gave a short laugh. "*I* make *you* hot?" He blew out a breath as she moved closer, dancing right up to him. She brushed her lips against his, provocative and tempting, before moving back and wriggling again.

"What's the matter, Matt?" She began to undo the buttons of her blouse. "Am I turning you on?"

"What do you think?" He didn't bother to hide the erection that stretched the seams of his jeans.

"Mmm." Her gaze caressed it, and heat spread through him as her eyelids lowered to half-mast and she ran her tongue over her top lip.

"You're playing a dangerous game," he said, his heart racing. "I told you in the car what I was going to do to you tonight."

"Nuh-uh." She reached the bottom button and pushed the blouse off her shoulders, daring him to contradict her. "No touching. You're only going to watch me." Turning her back to him, she eased the blouse down her arms.

He ran his tongue over his teeth and huffed a sigh. Lowering her arms, she let the blouse drop to the floor, then turned back to him. She wore a black lacy bra, the demi-cups outlining her beautiful breasts. Sinking her hands into her hair, she danced in front of him to the Christmas music, pressing her breasts close to his face before moving back and grinning impishly.

Matt raised an eyebrow, then gave a silent groan as she put her hands behind her back and unclipped her bra. She caught the cups in both hands and let the straps slip off her shoulders before sliding her arms through them. Keeping the cups pressed to her breasts, she turned around and presented her naked back to him, still moving her hips.

Unable to stop himself, he reached out and ran a finger down her spine. She shivered, then turned around. "Naughty boy. What did I say?"

"It's only a matter of time," he pointed out. "Every second that goes past, you're getting yourself deeper into trouble."

"Promises, promises." She licked her lips. "You're going to have to catch me first." Taking hold of the bra, she pulled it away from her breasts and dropped it to the floor.

Matt's gaze rested on the creamy globes, his hands itching to cup them as she lifted her hands to her hair again, exposing the soft skin under her arms. She danced like that for a while, then lowered her hands to slide up the tiny skirt. Hooking her fingers into the elastic of her panties, she pulled them down her legs, stepped out of them, and threw them at him.

He caught them, pressed them to his nose, and inhaled deeply, keeping his gaze locked on hers. Georgia's jaw dropped. "You're incorrigible," she said, dissolving into giggles again.

Putting the panties down, he rose from the seat and reached out for her. "Come here."

She moved back, though, her eyes dancing. "No touching."

Matt had had enough. His blood had reached boiling point, and if he wasn't inside her within ten seconds, he was going to embarrass himself. He marched toward her, but she dodged around the dining table, squealing. Turning, she went to run away, but he was too quick for her.

Catching her around the waist, he turned her and pushed her forward against the table. "That's it," he announced. "I'm going to fuck you from behind now." He bent her over it, lifted her skirt, and smacked her butt.

She squealed, then giggled, folding her arms beneath her, and gasped as he nudged her legs open and slipped a hand under her.

"Oh..." He stroked her firmly, his fingers sliding through her already moist folds. "You're ready for me. You're such a naughty girl."

She wriggled and laughed, then caught her breath as he moved his erection beneath her. "Oh God..."

By now, all thoughts had fled his mind, and all he felt was overwhelming desire for this beautiful creature. He moved the tip of his erection into her, then held her hips and thrust home.

"*Aaahhh…*" She lowered her head and rested her forehead on the table. "Matt."

"Sorry, but this is what you get when you drive a man insane with lust." He pulled almost out of her, then slid back in, groaning at the sweet sensation. "Fuck, Georgia."

She moaned and lifted her knee onto the edge of the table to give him better access, and he swore again as he plunged into her soft flesh, driving deeply.

He could easily have come then, but he slowed down, cursing under his breath. This wasn't how he'd meant for the evening to go. He'd teased her that he'd take her like this, and over the past ten days he'd discovered that she enjoyed sex hard and fast as much as he did. But this wasn't what he wanted tonight.

Slowly, he withdrew from her. She swore and her knees buckled, but he caught her, lifted her into his arms, and took her through to the bedroom.

Chapter Twenty-Four

Georgia was far from being drunk, but she'd had enough to blur the world around the edges and jumble her thoughts. Part of her brain wanted to think about what Matt had said in the car, that when she'd asked him if this was it, he'd mumbled something about having kids. Kids! But she couldn't focus all the while he was kissing her, and she resolved to file it away to puzzle over later, when the fog had cleared.

What did remain was a glow inside her at his vehement rejection of her query about whether they were over. *No! Of course not.* He wasn't thinking about breaking up with her. He wanted to see her again.

In the background, as Matt carried her through to the bedroom, she heard the song in the living room change to one of Enya's haunting Christmas melodies, and she shivered as he lowered her onto her back on the bed.

He paused to undo his shirt and slip it off, and stripped off his jeans and boxers. Finally, he tugged her mini skirt down her legs and dropped it on the floor, then climbed on top of her and stretched out, pressing her into the mattress.

Georgia welcomed his weight, wrapping her legs around his hips and opening her mouth to his kiss. She sank her hands into his hair, trying to show him how much she wanted him, and was rewarded when he shifted on top of her and pressed the tip of his erection into her folds. To her surprise, he lifted his head to look at her, and stared into her eyes as he slowly penetrated her.

She groaned and closed her eyes, but he kissed her nose and whispered, "Open." She did so, wondering why he wanted her to look at him, but all he did was smile and begin to thrust slowly, almost pulling out before pushing forward and burying himself deep inside her.

When she'd danced around him, she'd meant to drive him to the point where he couldn't wait any longer. It had surprised her when he'd stopped, but she'd thought he just wanted to be more comfortable, and that once they were on the bed he'd take her hard and fast. And she would have been happy with that.

But the mood had changed from fun and playful to darkly sensual, the music stroking across her nerve endings, teasing her as much as Matt's warm hands on her skin and the soft press of his lips on hers. What was with him? Over the past ten days, she'd learned that he could make love in a myriad of different ways. They both liked it fun and a little rough, but he'd also been slow and sexy, especially in the mornings, taking the time to arouse her until she was begging him to let her come.

This time was different, though. He was looking at her with such affection in his eyes that it made her melt. He kissed her in between thrusts, stopping each time she lifted her hips to meet his, and capturing her hands when she tried to dig her fingers into his butt to pull it toward her.

"Slowly," he scolded, and she gave in and let him move at his own pace, the passion building between them like a log fire being stoked rather than blasting straight to sizzling the way it usually did.

"What's got into you?" she whispered, stretching out beneath him.

He kissed her, taking time to move his lips across hers, the light touches of his tongue sending shivers through her. "I want to savor you," he murmured back, circling his hips to make sure he was as deep as he could go. He paused, and she groaned at the feeling of him hot and hard, all the way up.

"Matt..." She couldn't last much longer like this.

He touched his nose to hers, moving slowly. "I love you."

She blinked. "What?"

He kissed her. "I love you." He smiled at her bemused expression, sliding a hand down to wrap her thigh around his hips to change the angle of his thrust.

"Oh." Her brain wouldn't work. Had he really just said that? She tried to focus, but he was grinding right against her clit, and tension was building inside her.

"Yes," he said, slowing down. "Come for me."

She closed her eyes as the orgasm crept over her. Usually they were fast and furious, seven or eight seconds of intense pleasure like a hot blast from a blowtorch. This time, though, it was longer and more gradual. She felt the slow sweep of pleasure that led up to its arrival, the tightening of every little muscle, and then the individual dips and clenches of her womb that made her gasp out loud. Matt kissed her as if he wanted to drink in her pleasure, staying still, and she gave a long, low, "*Mmmmmm*," of pleasure as the pulses gradually subsided to leave her floating on a cloud of bliss.

Her eyelids fluttered open, and she looked up at him, blinking. He smiled, kissed her, and then started moving again.

He'd just said *I love you*. She slid her arms around him and felt tears prick her eyes as he closed his and frowned, his breathing becoming ragged as his climax approached. He was so beautiful, handsome and strong, and she felt no qualms as she reached up to kiss him and whispered, "I love you too."

His lips curved up and he went to say something, but it was too late, and he just half-laughed, half-groaned as his body hardened to rock and he shuddered into her. Georgia bit her lip hard, but was unable to stop the tears tumbling over her lashes and down her cheeks.

Gradually, his breathing levelled out, and his eyes opened. He blinked a few times, then his lips twisted and he kissed her wet cheeks. "Aw. Don't cry."

She fought to control her emotion, too blurred to make sense of what she was feeling right now, and just let him kiss her while their bodies relaxed and the intensity of the moment faded.

Matt glanced at the doorway, and she sniffed and lifted her head. "What is it?"

"Your phone's ringing. I thought I heard it earlier, actually, but I got... distracted." He looked back at her and smiled. "I'll get it for you." He withdrew and pushed himself up.

"No, it's okay," she began, wanting to keep him in her arms, but he was already standing, and he waved a hand at her to say it was no problem and left the room to fetch her bag.

Feeling bereft, she reached for a tissue, then pushed herself back against the pillows and wrapped her arms around her knees. He came back in with her bag and the half-drunk bottle of water, and handed the bag to her before climbing back onto the bed. "It stopped as I picked it up," he said, unscrewing the lid of the water and taking a swallow.

She retrieved the phone from her bag. Three missed calls from her parents' house in Christchurch.

"Late for them to call," Matt said. She spoke to them every evening, but usually just after dinner. If Noah rang her himself, he tended to call from his mobile.

She sighed. The last thing she wanted to do right now was talk to her mother, but Anna would only keep ringing until Georgia finally answered. "I hope there's nothing wrong. Do you mind if I call?" she asked.

"Of course not. You want me to go?"

"No." She cupped his face and lowered her lips to his for a long moment before saying, "We need to talk."

"Yeah." He smiled. "No hurry."

"I suppose not." She hesitated, then dialed her parents' number. Best to get this out of the way, and then she could relax, cuddle up to Matt, and really think about what he'd said.

She lifted the phone to her ear and waited for them to answer.

"Hello?"

"Hi Mum," she said. "Sorry I missed you."

"I've rung three times, Georgia."

"I know. I was away from my phone and didn't hear the first two. Is everything okay?"

"No, it's not." Anna's voice was flinty hard. "Your son got himself in trouble this afternoon."

Georgia's heart sank. "Oh no. What happened?"

"He tried to steal a packet of cigarettes from a man's pocket in a shop. The guy caught him, and the owner called the police. The police officer brought him home an hour ago."

Georgia closed her eyes and covered her face with a hand. This was a new one. Noah had never stolen before. And to steal cigarettes…

"Mum, I'm so sorry you had to deal with that."

"I swear, Georgia, I felt about two inches high when the officer was telling us what had happened."

"What did the police officer say?"

"Luckily, Noah appeared to show some remorse. The owner of the shop and the customer were lenient because of his age, and they're not going to press charges. But it's not good enough, Georgia. Something has to be done."

"I know." She felt Matt rub her back as she fought against angry tears.

"You've let him run wild. I can't believe a grandson of mine has been caught stealing. Stealing! And smoking!"

Georgia gritted her teeth. She couldn't deny that Noah was difficult because he was, and his behavior appeared to be escalating, which wasn't good. But her mother's implication that she'd 'let' him run wild hurt. "All right," she said as calmly as she could, "let's not overreact."

"Overreact? Smoking's one thing. But he broke one of the Ten Commandments. That might not mean much to you, but it means something to me. You told me that moving away was what he needed, and I agreed to it because I trusted that, as his mother, you might know better than I what was best for him. Clearly, I was wrong."

I agreed to it. Georgia bristled at the implication that she'd only been able to move away because her mother had given her permission.

But there was no point in yelling, or fighting with her. Anna had a backbone of steel and firmly believed she was right in everything she did. She'd instilled in both her daughters from an early age that they should always respect their elders, and Georgia hated confrontation so much that she knew she wasn't strong enough to argue.

That didn't mean she was going to let her mother trample over her, though. "Can I speak to Noah, please," she said.

"No," Anna said. "I've sent him to bed without his dinner, and he can stay there for the rest of the night."

"What is this, Jane Eyre?" Georgia snapped. "You can't not feed him. He's your grandson, for crying out loud."

"My house, my rules. You want to make the decisions? You come here and talk to him yourself."

Georgia's anger melted away, to be replaced by an icy calm. "I will. I'll get the first available flight in the morning."

"Fine." Anna hung up.

Georgia lowered the phone to the bed and swallowed hard. Part of her wanted to throw her phone across the room and break it into pieces, but that would solve nothing and would only mean she wouldn't have access to Noah at all.

"What happened?" Matt asked.

"Noah was caught stealing cigarettes in a shop, and a police officer took him home."

He blew out a breath. "Shit."

"Yeah. And my mother's going Dickensian on him. She's sent him to bed without his dinner. What the fuck?"

"Jeez."

She sank a hand into her hair. "She wouldn't let me talk to him."

"Can you ring him on his mobile?"

She looked at the phone. "Oh, yes, of course." She dialed Noah's number and put the phone to her ear.

It rang for so long that she was certain he wasn't going to pick up. But finally he answered dully, "Hello?"

"It's me."

"Oh," he said. "Hi."

She let out a long, slow breath. "Grandma just rang me and told me what's happened."

Noah said nothing.

"Cigarettes?" Georgia said. "Stealing? Really?"

"I'm sorry," he said.

"Don't say it unless you mean it. Otherwise it's a pointless phrase. Why did you do it?"

He didn't reply, but she could almost hear his shrug.

"I don't know what to say," she said helplessly. "I thought we were getting somewhere, and now this?" Against her will, her throat tightened. It was just before Christmas, and she was supposed to be spending the week with her parents.

"I miss you," Noah said.

That tipped her over the edge, and she burst into tears.

Chapter Twenty-Five

Matt sighed as Georgia started crying. He leaned over and pulled another tissue from the box on the bedside table and gave it to her.

"Hold on," she mumbled into the phone. She placed it on the bed and blew her nose, then picked up the phone. But the tears refused to stop, and he could see her struggling to control her emotions.

Pushing himself up against the headboard, he held out his hand. She stared at it for a moment, the tissue pressed to her nose. Then her eyes met his, a beautiful, shiny amber, like circles of polished wood left out in the rain. Finally, she handed him the phone.

Matt held it up to his ear. "Noah?"

"Yeah?"

"It's Matt King here."

"Oh. Hey, Matt."

"Hey, dude. I'm just going to chat for a bit. Don't worry, your mum's okay. She just needs a minute or two to compose herself."

"Are you both at the office?"

"No. We've been out for dinner with some friends." He didn't like lying to the boy, but he didn't want to divulge their relationship in case Georgia wanted to keep it a secret for some reason. And besides, they'd just had dinner with friends, so he was telling the truth. "I hear you've had a rough day."

Noah was quiet for a moment. Then he muttered, "Yeah."

"Sorry to hear that. Want to tell me what happened?" He made himself comfortable on the pillows. Georgia had stopped crying, but to his surprise, she didn't ask for the phone back. Instead, she curled up next to him and rested her head on his chest. He put his arm around her and kissed her hair.

"I took some cigarettes out of a guy's pocket, but he caught me." Noah's voice was sullen. "You gonna yell at me now?"

"No. Not my place to do that. I'd like to know why you did it, though. How long have you been smoking?"

A scratching sound came down the phone. Matt had a vision of the boy sitting at a desk, engraving the surface with a compass or a pair of scissors.

"I don't smoke," Noah said eventually. "I was going to give them to someone."

"A mate?"

"Yeah. Someone I used to go to school with before I moved to Kerikeri."

"Why did you steal them for him?"

"Didn't have any money."

"I meant, what was he going to give you in return?"

"He said if I got him ciggies, he'd let me in his gang."

"Ah. That makes sense, and I can see why you'd want to help out your mate and be friends with him again. But it was quite a risk to steal for him, wasn't it? When you're only down there for another week or so?"

"Grandma says we'll be moving back in the New Year."

Matt didn't react to that, but his arm tightened around Georgia. Was this Georgia's plan? She'd made no mention of her return to Christchurch being permanent.

"Right. Is that what you want?"

"Don't care," Noah said.

"Really?"

"It don't matter what I want. Nobody asks me."

"I'm asking you."

"Well... I hate it here." The words burst out of the boy like projectile vomit. "I fucking hate it." He stopped with a gasp that Matt thought was probably a strangled sob.

His stomach twisted with pity. He knew how it felt to be that miserable and torn up inside. "It's all right, Noah."

"She sent me down here. She don't care what happens to me."

Matt lifted his arm from around Georgia, rose from the bed, and walked over to the window. "That's not true," he said. "She loves you very much, and she's worried about you."

"So why did she send me away? She didn't even bother to look upset. She couldn't wait for me to go."

Matt looked across the deck, past the bush to the glittering lights of Russell. "Is that why you took the cigarettes? To punish her for sending you away?"

"I dunno." Noah gave a snotty sniff. "Maybe."

"That was dumb," Matt said wryly. "You should have just sent her a rude text. You know if you type the number 58008 and turn your phone upside down, it looks like the word boobs?"

Noah gave a half-laugh, half-sob.

"Try it," Matt said. "I'll text you my number and you can text me back."

A slurpy sound followed like a wet nose being wiped on a sleeve. "Okay."

"Sorry to hear you haven't had dinner."

"It's all right. I had a KFC bucket before I got caught. I'm not hungry."

"Only the one bucket to yourself? Lightweight. I would have managed at least two at your age."

Noah gave a short, hoarse laugh.

Matt smiled. "All right. Well look, it sounds as if your mum will be flying down to see you tomorrow. You need to be honest with her and tell her what you're feeling, okay?"

"Are you coming with her?"

Matt hesitated. "Ah… that wasn't the plan. I expect she'll stay down there now for Christmas."

"Please," Noah said. "It's going to be awful. Grandma's being such a dragon. And Mum goes weird when she's here. She speaks politely but it's like she's trying to talk through her teeth."

Matt frowned and glanced over his shoulder at Georgia. She was drinking out of his water bottle, still watching him.

He turned back to the view. "I'll talk to her about it, but I'm not sure what she'll say, okay? It's her decision."

"Okay."

"All right. I'm handing you back to your mum now. I'll text you my number, and you can message me anytime, you hear?"

"Thanks, Matt."

He looked at Noah's number and repeated it several times in his head, handed the phone back to Georgia, then left the room so she could talk to her son.

While he went to the kitchen and made himself a peanut butter sandwich, he could hear her talking, her voice gentle, so she obviously wasn't shouting at the boy. He was glad. What Noah had done was wrong, but he'd been driven to it because he was angry and confused, not because he was a bad lad.

While he thought about it, he picked up his phone, programmed Noah's number into it, and texted him. Then he poured himself a glass of milk, sat at the breakfast bar, and finished his sandwich. Her iPod was still playing Christmas songs, and he hummed along to *Let it Snow* while he ate.

She came out a few minutes later, wearing one of his shirts, looking gorgeous with her ruffled hair and smudged eyes.

"Hey." She sat beside him.

"Hey." He pushed the sandwich over to her.

She investigated what was in it, pulled a face, and pushed it back. "No thanks."

He finished it off. "Everything okay?"

"Well, as much as it can be. He's pretty sheepish." She picked up some crumbs with a finger. "He told me he'd asked you to go with me tomorrow."

"Yeah."

"I don't expect you to do that."

"I know." He drained his glass, put it to one side, and pulled her stool toward him with his foot. "Come here."

She sighed and leaned into his embrace, and he wrapped his arms around her. Over her shoulder, he saw that the night sky was reflected on his glass table, making it look as if the room was filled with stars.

"I'm so sorry," she whispered.

"Don't be."

"You really don't want this complication in your life."

He moved back a little and lifted her chin so he could look into her eyes. "You don't get to say what I do and don't want, okay?"

She nibbled her bottom lip, looking pained. "I didn't mean it like that..."

"I know, but I'm saying that you don't get to make my decisions for me. Georgia, I've just told you I love you. Doesn't that mean anything?"

Her anguish melted into a warm smile. "Of course it does."

"I was going to talk to you about this tomorrow but, well, here goes. I'm crazy about you. I know we don't want to rush anything, but it's already clear to me that I don't want this to end. I want to keep seeing you. I want you in my life—you and Noah. I like him, he's a good lad who's just a bit mixed up, and I think maybe I can help him a little. He reminds me a lot of me, and maybe that means I'm someone he can talk to. Or maybe not, I don't know, I'm hardly an expert on teenagers apart from the fact that I was one. What I'm saying is that I'm well aware he's part of the package, and I'm very happy with that."

Georgia didn't say anything for a moment. The room fell quiet apart from the music, Frank Sinatra's version of *Have Yourself a Merry Little Christmas*. Her eyes glistened.

"Hey," he said, "don't cry. Don't you want to be with me?"

She nodded. "Yes. I just... I can't quite believe my luck."

He chuckled. "You might change your mind when we've been together a bit longer."

She raised a hand to cup his face, brushing her thumb across his five o'clock shadow. "Are you sure you're ready for a relationship? Is that really what you want?"

"I can't say it doesn't scare the shit out of me. Not being with you," he added hastily. "The thought of loving and losing someone again. It's scary. But I want you. I don't want to be apart from you. And that feeling is strong enough to make me want to give it a go."

She nibbled her bottom lip. "In the taxi, you said something..."

His lips curved up. "About having kids?"

"Yeah." She almost giggled again, but managed to keep it under control. "Why did you ask?"

"I've been thinking about what it would be like to have children of my own. I know you have Noah, and he's eleven now, so it would mean a bit of an age difference, and I wouldn't want him to feel pushed out at all. But I wondered whether you'd ever thought about having more children."

"With you?"

He tipped his head to the side and studied her. "With me."

She laughed, but when he didn't laugh back, her eyes widened. "Oh. You mean it."

"Mean what?"

"You're serious."

"Of course I'm serious."

She blinked a few times. "Have a baby with you?"

"Yeah." He pulled her closer to him. "I like the idea. There's no hurry. We'd get married first. But maybe later next year, we could think about it. Would you like that?"

"Married?"

"Sorry, haven't I asked you to marry me yet?"

"Matt!"

He laughed. "Look, I don't want to rush you. You've got a lot on your plate with Noah, and I think we should wait until you—or we—get back from Christchurch before we make decisions. But I want you, Georgia. In my life. In my heart. Forever. You don't have to answer now. Think about it for a while. But I will be asking you in the not too distant future. So be prepared."

Chapter Twenty-Six

Georgia thought about it all the way down to Christchurch the following day.

If Matt was disappointed that she hadn't reacted with immediate excitement to his semi-proposal, he didn't show it. He'd talked her into taking the Kings' private plane, saying it would be easier than trying to get tickets through the main airline during the festive season, and he'd told her firmly that he was coming with her, unless she outright objected. She didn't, because the thought of having him by her side when she dealt with Noah and the inevitable fallout from her mother gave her the strength she felt she might have lacked on her own.

"Has she always been like that?" Matt asked.

They'd stopped to refuel in Wellington and were now well on the way to Christchurch. Georgia sipped the latte that the flight attendant, Pat, had just made her. She hadn't wanted an alcoholic drink, needing to keep her mind clear for the coming confrontation.

"Yes," she admitted. "She believes in being hard with your children. I remember calling her from the pay phone in the foyer in the reception at my boarding school, sobbing, begging her to let me come home. She just kept saying 'This will be the making of you,' and refused to listen.

"And was it? The making of you?"

She looked out of the window at the fluffy white clouds. "Not in the way she meant it, I'm sure. That phone call was the last straw for me. After that, I knew she was never going to be the sort of mother I wanted. I promised myself I would never do that to my children, just turn my back on them. She thought it would force me to stand on my own two feet, and it did, I suppose, but that came after months of misery and crying myself to sleep every night. I didn't want my son ever to feel like that." She swallowed hard. The terrible shame was that she knew Noah did feel like that, in spite of her best attempts to be a loving mother.

Matt took her hand. "It's not your fault, honey. Losing his father obviously had a huge impact on him, and he's still struggling to come to terms with that. It would make him question life, relationships, and being a father himself. That's a lot to heap on a boy not yet a teenager."

She rubbed her nose. "I never thought of it like that. Did losing Pippa do that to you, then?"

"Yeah. I watched what my parents went through, and from that point on, I started thinking I would never get married or have kids because I wouldn't be able to bear losing them like that. And of course when you start thinking things like that, it makes you question why you're here at all."

She warmed her hands around the coffee cup, cold in spite of the sultry day. "He's mentioned to me that he fears being like his father. He sees what Fintan did as weak, and he's frightened he's going to feel like that, and be so out of control that he doesn't want to carry on anymore."

"Has he talked about harming himself at all?"

"No. But I suppose it would be weird if it wasn't in the back of both of our minds. He'll be a teenager soon, and we both know all the joys that brings in terms of hormones and behavior. I'm terrified that if he's behaving like this now, what on earth is he going to be like when he's fourteen or fifteen?"

"Well, for a start, just because he's having a bit of trouble now doesn't mean he's going to be a nightmare teenager. He sounded pretty shook up about getting caught stealing. It might have been enough to wake him up, you know?"

"Maybe," she said doubtfully.

He lifted her hand to his lips and kissed her knuckles. "He did say something I think you should know. He seems to think you're moving back to Christchurch in the New Year." Matt's eyes were a cool green, calm but uncertain.

Georgia stared at him. "What?"

"That was what he said last night."

"Why didn't you say something?"

"I wasn't sure whether it was something you'd decided and you were waiting to tell me. But after what we discussed last night, I thought I might as well bring it out in the open."

"I never said that, Matt. That was my mother talking."

"Ah." He blew out a breath. "Okay."

"She never wanted me to move to the Northland. She thought I'd struggle without the support of my family. But to be honest, it's the best thing I've ever done. Obviously, I'm still having trouble with Noah, but we were working through things just the two of us. I'm sure his bad behavior toward the end of school was to do with knowing he was going back to Christchurch. To the house where it happened, for God's sake. Of course it's going to make him feel bad."

Matt's eyebrows rose. "They still live in the same house?"

"Yes. They've ripped out the old bathroom and completely renovated it, but I know I avoid it and use the downstairs one, and I'm sure Noah feels the same."

"Poor kid."

Georgia smiled. "Thank you for talking to him last night. I'm sure it helped."

He shrugged. "I didn't feel that I did much good, but it might help him to know there's a guy he can talk to if he needs to." Matt had showed her the text he'd received from Noah after Georgia had finished talking to him the night before. It had just said *58008. LOL.* Since then, she knew they'd texted each other a couple of times, and it warmed her through to think that Noah finally had a man he felt he could talk to, because he wasn't that close to her father.

She didn't want to make the mistake, though, of hooking up with Matt because of that. His little speech the night before had completely thrown her. She liked him—loved him, even, and she didn't want to stop seeing him. But marriage and kids? That was a whole new ball game.

She'd done the late nights, the toddler groups, the potty training, kindergarten, and primary school. She'd thought she was heading out of that time now Noah would be starting high school, and the idea of returning to being tied twenty-four/seven to a baby was a bit daunting. And yet she was only twenty-eight, younger than many women when they started a family nowadays.

If they did settle down together, she was certain that Matt would treat Noah like his own son, but it would be natural for him to want children of his own, and she didn't want to commit herself to him if she wasn't prepared to offer that.

Did she want more babies? She rested her hand on her stomach as she looked out of the window, the city of Christchurch appearing through the clouds. She hadn't let herself think about it since having Noah. In the early days, life with Fintan had been such a rollercoaster that it had never even been on the table, and then she'd gone to uni, and then he'd died. Maybe at one point she'd felt broody, but she'd averted her gaze from the shops that sold baby clothes and had boxed up all her maternity outfits and Noah's toys. They were still sitting in her mother's garage in case she needed them again, but she'd been considering getting rid of them.

She couldn't deny it, though—the idea of getting pregnant again, of having a baby with Matt and watching him be a father to their child, gave her a flutter in her belly she couldn't ignore.

But there wasn't time to think about it now. The plane had begun its descent, and in a short while they'd be back at her parents' house, and she'd have to deal with Noah and sort out what she was going to do over Christmas. Was Matt going to stay or would he return once things had settled down? They hadn't really discussed it, because she wasn't clear herself yet what she was going to do. Matt was supposed to be going to Brock's party on Christmas Eve, but she was pretty certain that if she asked him he would stay in Christchurch with her. Did she want that though? Maybe her parents would hate him. They hadn't liked Fintan much.

The plane landed, and they collected their luggage and made their way out of the airport. Gary Banks was standing by his car in the car park. Noah was with him, and she waited for her son to run over and hug her like he normally did. But he stayed still, his hands in his pockets, looking sullenly at the floor.

"Hi, sweetie." Georgia hugged him anyway, introducing Matt to her father over his shoulder while Noah stood stiffly in her arms. "Dad, this is Matt King. Matt, this is my dad, Gary."

The two men shook hands. She'd rung that morning and told Anna that Matt was coming with her, explaining briefly who he was and that they'd been dating for a few weeks, but that she wasn't to tell Noah until she'd had time to tell him herself. Anna had been quietly disapproving, but Georgia had ignored the long silences. She'd been single for four years. If her mother couldn't show some pleasure that her daughter was happy, Georgia wasn't going to spend time worrying about it.

Her cheeks warming at the sight of Matt and her father exchanging pleasantries and talking about the fact that he had a private plane, she kissed Noah's head. "Come on. Let's get in the car."

After giving Noah a manly handshake, Matt got in the front, continuing to chat to Gary while she sat with Noah in the back.

"Everything all right?" she whispered to her son.

He shrugged. The muscles of his jaw bunched at the corners as if he was clenching his teeth. She wasn't sure if it was her imagination, but he looked a little taller, and for the first time hair shadowed his upper lip.

"Has anything happened this morning?" she asked.

Gary glanced over his shoulder. "He had an argument with your mother. Something about not wanting to eat the boiled eggs she'd cooked for him."

"They were hard," Noah muttered. "I like them runny."

Georgia said nothing, knowing it would serve no purpose to give him a lecture about how he should have eaten them anyway because Anna had taken the time to prepare them for him. They'd passed that point, and he would only see any remonstration as further proof that everyone hated him and he couldn't do anything right.

Instead, she changed the subject, asking about the city, and let her father talk away about the changes that had taken place over the past year as Christchurch continued to restructure itself after the devastating earthquake. Matt asked questions, keeping Gary's attention, leaving Georgia's gaze to drift out of the window as the car wound through the busy streets.

What was she going to do about Noah? How could she break through the anger and resentment he'd built around himself and reach the boy she knew was still inside?

Chapter Twenty-Seven

Over the next few hours, Matt learned more about Georgia than he had in the whole year he'd known her.

Watching her with Noah and her family, in the house where her husband had died, made him realize how right she'd been to move away from Christchurch.

He couldn't believe that Anna and Gary Banks still lived in the house where Fintan had taken his own life, nor that they assumed that Georgia and Noah would stay there when they visited. The house was pleasant enough, large and luxurious, lying just outside Christchurch on a few acres of land, and he couldn't truthfully say he felt any kind of dark cloud hanging over it.

But Georgia and Noah were completely different while they were there. Noah—sullen and uncommunicative at the best of times—hardly said a word, went straight to his room when they arrived, and only came down when it was time for dinner and Georgia bullied him out.

Georgia herself was subdued, although he couldn't tell if it was because of memories of Fintan or being in the presence of her mother. Maybe both.

Anna Banks was a piece of work. She looked quite like her daughter, small and dark, but everything about her screamed control freak. She definitely wore the pants in the house, with Gary backing up everything she said, clearly unable to stand up to her.

Matt had wondered why Georgia hadn't been more rebellious as a youth, but after meeting Anna, he understood. Anna had a way of looking at a person if they disagreed with her with a stony glare that made them feel two inches tall. Clearly, she thought she was right about everything and would brook no argument. Kind, gentle Georgia had obviously tried to stand up to her over the years, but had been put down repeatedly until she'd learned instead to walk away. Once, Matt had wondered if that was a weakness—now he knew it was common sense. A person would never win in an argument with Anna Banks. The only answer was to remove yourself from the situation.

When he first walked in, he saw immediately that Anna disapproved of his relationship with her daughter. He had no intention of getting into any arguments with her, but equally neither was he going to let her think she could push him around. When she poured him a brandy after dinner and gave it to him without asking what he wanted to drink, he passed it back and politely asked if she had any whisky.

"We drink brandy after dinner," she said, meeting his gaze, her eyes—so much colder than Georgia's—a steely gray.

He smiled. "Not for me, thanks. Maybe I'll have a coffee later instead."

She continued to try to hold his gaze as if expecting him to apologize and back down, but he turned to Noah—who obviously hated every minute of the meal around the table—and said, "Fancy going out for a walk? I thought you could show me the river."

"He hasn't finished his dessert," Anna said crisply.

Noah had pushed the piece of rather bland pear tart around his plate for the last ten minutes, so Matt was pretty sure he didn't want it.

"Perhaps a walk will improve his appetite." Without waiting for her to answer, he got to his feet. He did glance at Georgia though. "If that's okay." She'd attempted to have a talk to Noah that afternoon, but had told Matt she'd drawn a blank and that all Noah had done was tell her he wanted to go home.

She gave a little nod and looked at Noah. "You want to go out?"

Noah got hastily to his feet. "Yeah."

"Okay. Be good for Matt."

Noah rolled his eyes and ran to put his shoes on. Matt tucked his chair under the table and said, "Thank you for dinner, Mrs. Banks. It was lovely."

Anna gave a wry smile, unable to find fault with his politeness. "You're welcome."

Matt slipped on his shoes and followed Noah outside. It was just gone seven, cooler than it would have been in the Northland, although still a balmy night, as the sun set later here than in the Northland.

"Which way?" Matt asked.

Noah pointed toward the fence, and they set off, heading across the paddock to the bush on the other side.

As he walked, Noah jammed his hands in his pockets and tucked his chin to his chest, his whole posture defensive.

"You come down here often?" Matt asked.

"Anything to get out of the house," Noah muttered. He didn't say anything else as they passed through the gate into the bush.

The trees closed around them, filling the air with the smell of wet leaves and wild garlic. Noah led the way down the bank to the river. Matt was surprised to find a proper bench there, with solar lights strung around the nearest tree. No doubt Anna had requested that, far too superior to sit on a tree stump.

He sat on one end of the bench. Noah stood on the edge of the bank and picked up a handful of stones to throw into the river.

Matt leaned back and stayed quiet for a while, thinking that eventually Noah would start talking, but eventually he realized that wasn't going to happen.

"You want to talk?" he said.

Noah shook his head and threw another stone.

"What *do* you want?" Matt asked.

"To go home." Noah threw a stone harder, and it pinged off a rock and landed with a loud splash.

"Don't you think it would be nice for your mum to spend Christmas with her family?"

"She doesn't want to. She's only doing it to keep Grandma quiet."

He was probably right, but Matt wasn't about to say that. "Maybe she misses her family. I know it sounds strange when it doesn't look as though folks get on, but at Christmastime it can be nice to meet up for a few days."

Noah said nothing, just threw more stones.

A small seed of despair took root in Matt's stomach. He'd thought he'd be able to get the lad to talk, but maybe this wasn't going to work. Just because he'd had a rough time in his teens didn't mean that Noah would realize or care that they'd had similar issues. What would happen if they couldn't get through to him? Would his behavior continue to deteriorate? It would make Georgia so unhappy, and Matt couldn't bear the thought of that.

"Come on mate," he said, trying again. "I know you can't talk to your grandparents, and you're angry with your mum for whatever reason. Can't you talk to me?"

Noah turned on him, clenching his fists, and it was only then that Matt saw the tears glimmering in the boy's eyes.

"What makes you think I'd talk to you?" Noah yelled. "You're nobody!"

Well, at least he was talking. Matt decided the best course of action was to be non-confrontational. "True. But I care about your mum, and she's upset."

"Are you fucking her?"

Matt held the lad's gaze, anger rising inside him for the first time. For a long moment, the two of them studied each other, Matt angry but calm, Noah rebellious and confrontational, his chest heaving. An image flashed through Matt's mind of two male animals, stags maybe, or wolves, fighting for the lead role in the pack.

He wasn't about to lose his alpha status to an eleven-year-old. He kept his stare steady, and Noah eventually dropped his gaze, his shoulders slumping.

"Sorry," he mumbled.

Matt blew out a silent breath of relief. "It's reasonable to wonder why I'm here, but you can't talk about your mum using that kind of language."

"I know."

He'd thought Georgia would have told her son why he was there by now, but she'd obviously not been able to broach the subject. He couldn't leave the boy wondering. If she wanted to tell him, she should have done so before now.

"We're dating," he said. "We have been since you left. I wanted to take her out a year ago, when she first started at the office, but she kept saying no to me until a few weeks ago." He tipped his head. "How do you feel about that?"

Noah shrugged and kicked at a rock with his toe. "I don't mind."

Well, that was a start. "You want to come and sit down?"

Noah hesitated, then came to sit beside him.

"I want to share something with you, but I'm only doing it because I feel that you're old enough and mature enough to understand the situation, okay?"

Noah's gaze, his amber eyes so like his mother's, flicked over to him. "Okay."

"I'm going to ask your mum to marry me. And I'd like her—and you—to come and live with me in Russell. I'm crazy about her, and I'd like us to all be a family together. The thing is, and I know it's not a very manly thing to admit, but I care about you. I can see myself in you. Did your mum tell you that my sister died when I was your age?"

The lad's eyebrows rose. "No."

"Her name was Pippa. I still get choked up a bit now when I think about her. She was eight, and she had an asthma attack. You've met my brothers, Brock and Charlie, haven't you?"

"Yeah."

"Brock was with her when she died. Charlie and I were out playing football. When we found out… it was awful. My parents were devastated. We all were."

Noah drew up his legs and wrapped his arms around them. The sun was low in the sky now, and it was darker in the forest than in the field where the last rays were still lighting the grass. The solar lamps flicked on, reflecting on the river like stars. Luckily, Matt thought, they'd both put insect repellent on earlier because the mosquitoes would be biting soon.

Noah chewed his lip. "Brock's a doctor, isn't he?"

"Yeah. And Charlie's a scientist."

"Were you all angry when she died?"

"Brock was upset—he blamed himself for a long time. It's the main reason he's a doctor, so he can try to stop it happening again to other children. Charlie doesn't get angry—he's like a teddy bear. He was more bewildered."

"Were you angry?"

"My anger was like a supernova. I went off the rails. Got into fights, smoke, drank. It took me a long while to get over it."

"How *did* you get over it?"

"By realizing that the only person you're hurting is yourself. It's natural to be angry, to blame everyone. Like with you, I understand why you might blame your mum for not being able to stop your dad, or your grandparents for not moving out of the house where it happened."

"I hate it." Noah looked suddenly upset. "I keep thinking maybe his ghost haunts it. And I don't want to see it. I hate him for doing it. It's so weak! It's the easy way out."

"It might seem that way. I do some work with teenagers who have mental illnesses, though, and I think it's difficult for people like us who don't suffer from depression to understand what it must feel like to get to a point where you can't face going on."

"But he had mum, and he had me." Tears tipped over Noah's lashes and fell down his cheeks, but he didn't seem aware of them. "He left us alone. Didn't he think about that?"

Matt said nothing for a second, conscious that this moment could be a pivotal one in Noah's life. There was no point in insisting that Fintan loved him, because he would just say that couldn't possibly be true considering what he'd done.

What would be the best way to approach this? He wasn't a counsellor. Maybe he shouldn't be talking to the boy about something so serious—he could be doing more harm than good.

And yet Noah's face was almost eager, desperate. He'd been to a therapist, and it hadn't helped. He was close to going off the rails, just how Matt had done all those years ago. Who could be better to talk to him than someone who'd been through a similar event, and who'd worked with teens who'd suffered with these kinds of problems?

Chapter Twenty-Eight

Matt wished he had the time to ring his brothers and ask their advice. But it was just him and Noah, and even though he'd probably do it all wrong, he couldn't turn his back on the boy now.

He leaned forward, his elbows on his knees, hands linked, his head close to the boy's. "It might sound harsh, but by the time your dad reached that point, he probably wasn't thinking about anyone but himself. He didn't take his life to punish you, Noah. Or because he didn't love you or your mum enough."

Noah put his face in his hands. His body was rigid, as if he was fighting hard not to give in to his sobs.

Matt carried on, speaking softly. "From what I understand, depression is like having a black dog living with you. Most of the time, it sits in the shadows and you don't really notice it. But from time to time, it prowls around you. It's big and dark, and it's scary, and it gets to the point where you can't take your eyes off it. Where nothing else matters except this huge beast."

"The doctor gave him pills," Noah said resentfully, his voice little more than a squeak, "but he refused to take them."

"That's quite common, and it can be for several reasons. Men especially see depression as a weakness, and feel as if they should be able to cope with it on their own. An ex-All Black, Sir John Kirwan, actually wrote a book about it, called *All Blacks Don't Cry*—did you know that? He says that it's not a weakness of character to suffer from it, and that you have to seek help."

Noah wiped his nose on his sleeve. "I didn't know that."

"The other reason some people don't take their pills is because they make them feel different. Pills take away the depression, but they can also take away your drive. Most people's lives have ups and downs." He drew a horizontal wavy line in the air. "Antidepressants smooth those lines out, so it's more like this." He flattened the line so the peaks and troughs were less marked. "And not everyone likes that."

"But if depression really makes you feel terrible, wouldn't it be worth losing the ups to feel better?"

"Yes and no. Our drive is what keeps us going. It gives us ambition and pushes us to try new things and to succeed." Matt knew that a person's sex drive and performance in bed were often affected by antidepressants too. He didn't want to raise that with the lad, but when Georgia had said that Fintan seemed to have lost his drive in his work, he'd wondered whether there had been problems for them in the bedroom that had forced Fintan to think a solution might be to abandon his medication.

Noah stared at the ground for a long time. Matt let him, falling quiet for a moment, content to listen to the sound of the cicadas in the trees. A fish jumped out of the river further downstream, landing with a plop, and a kiwi cried suddenly, quite near them, making them both jump.

"Will I have depression?" Noah asked eventually.

"It can be hereditary, but not always. And even if you do have it, if you handle it right and get help—speak to someone, take medication if necessary—it can be controlled. It's like keeping the black dog on a leash." He smiled.

"I don't want it," Noah burst out.

"Do you feel the way I was describing?"

"No. I don't think so. I just feel angry all the time, and lonely, like I'm standing in the middle of a busy street shouting at the top of my lungs but nobody can hear me."

"What would you say if you thought people were listening?"

Noah sank back onto the seat. "I don't know."

"Come on, Noah. It's just you and me. I'm not going to go running back to tell your mum or grandma what you've said. Why don't I start? When Pippa died, I remember hating Brock for a while because he hadn't saved her. I was horrible to him for a long time. Sometimes we even fought. But he's four years older than me, and he realized before I did that I wasn't really angry with him—I knew it wasn't his fault. Of course he would have saved her if he could."

He gestured toward Noah. *Your turn.*

The boy studied his hands. "I'm angry with Mum because she was married to him and she didn't know how bad he was."

"That's understandable. The first thing I'd say about that, though, is that you know it happened right after the earthquake?"

"Yeah."

"You know what PTSD is?"

"Yeah. Sort of."

"It's Post Traumatic Stress Disorder. It's what people can get after a traumatic event. It can affect them in all sorts of ways—sometimes they can't stop crying, or they can't sleep, or they sleep all day. It's like the body shuts off the bits that can't cope. Your mum had lost her home. You'd nearly died. She wasn't thinking straight. The more traumatized a person is, the more they have to concentrate on themselves as they try to get their balance back. Maybe if there hadn't been an earthquake, she would have spotted how bad your dad was. Hell, he might not have felt that bad if he hadn't been through that. But it happened. And now, just like the way the city has had to take time to put itself to rights, everyone who went through it has to deal with the aftershocks too."

Noah stared mutely at the ground. Matt could see his anger fighting with his guilt.

"The thing is," Matt carried on, "when someone close to you dies, especially when you're young, it's common to blame either yourself or those close to you. I'm not a counsellor, Noah, and I'm not going to sit here and tell you how you should be feeling. All I can do is tell you about my experience. And as I grew older, I began to learn how selfish everyone is, including me. We only think about ourselves. We assume we're being punished, and that others are being cruel to us on purpose. But that's very rarely the case."

"Unless it's Grandma."

Matt tried to hide a smile, and failed. Noah gave a wry grin. "I'll tell you a secret," Matt said. "Nobody knows what's going on inside you, what you're thinking and feeling. The secret is not to show it on your face or in your manners. Make sure someone can't fault you on your politeness. Then you can think and feel whatever you want."

"I like that. That sounds sensible."

"Okay," Matt continued, "so here's my second piece of advice. The one main thing my therapist taught me that has helped. Step out of reaction, and into observation. Do you know what that means?"

"Um… Think before you speak?"

"Almost. It means that before you react to a situation or a person, you take a mental step back and think about what's happening. So, let's say that your mate has asked you to buy those cigarettes for you.

Your first reaction was a normal, selfish one—'I'm lonely, I want to be in his gang, so I'll do as he says even though I don't really want to.' But if you'd taken the time to step back, you might have thought that what he was asking was unfair. That a true mate wouldn't expect you to get yourself into trouble for him. You might have thought he wasn't the kind of mate worth taking that risk for."

Noah met Matt's eyes. "I like the way you tell me off without it looking as if you're telling me off."

Matt gave a short laugh. "I'm not telling you off. I'm saying I've been there, in that pit you feel you're in at the moment. And I know how horrible it is, and how you feel as if you're never going to get out. But I did. It wasn't easy, and it took a long time. And I had to get help."

"You said you saw a therapist."

"Yeah, her name's Barbara. I still see her occasionally, if I'm feeling a bit blue. I could take you to meet her if you wanted."

"Is she nice?"

"She's funny, and she's clever. She knows how you're feeling without you saying it, and sometimes that can make you feel a bit uncomfortable, but then all of a sudden you realize she's on your side, and she knows the way out of that pit. She can give you little tips on how to cope in situations, and different ways to look at things. Often it's not about completely changing your life or situation. It's about altering the focus, and changing the way you think."

Noah slid his hands into his pockets and kicked his foot against the leg of the bench. "When are you going to ask Mum to marry you?"

Matt copied his pose, shoving his hands in his pockets and stretching out his legs. "I wanted to wait until after Christmas because you'd said about her moving back to Christchurch. But I don't think that's going to happen."

Noah's face lit up. "Really?"

"We'll talk to your mum about it later, but she told me she didn't say that."

"That was Grandma." Noah glowered at the river.

"Maybe. Remember what I said about stepping back, though? Put your emotion to one side for a moment. Why would your Grandma have said something like that?"

Noah thought about it. "Because she misses Mum?"

"And you."

"She thinks she can tell us all what to do."

"She's strong-willed, sure. We all do what we think is best for our families. She's not trying to be spiteful. She truly believes it will be best for you and your mum to live here so she can help out."

"She thinks Mum can't cope."

"Well, she knows you've had a tricky time and she probably thinks it would be easier for your mum if she was around. Everyone has different ways of bringing up children. Some people believe it's best to be really strict and come down hard on any misbehavior. Other people, like your mum, think it's better to talk about it, because sometimes shouting and punishment can make things worse. Has she told you about where she went to school?"

"She went to boarding school."

"That's right, and she had a tough time. Her parents were very strict with her, and she found it hard. That's probably why she's tried a different approach. Neither way is right or wrong. But your grandma sees anything but the hard line as weak, and she probably thinks your mum needs extra help."

Noah dug his heel into the soft earth. "I don't mean to be bad. Not all the time."

"I know. Sometimes you can't help it. And sometimes you do things because it's the only way you feel you can get people to take notice of you."

"Will you and Mum have kids?"

"I don't know. I don't have any children, so I'd quite like to have one or two. But your Mum has you, and you're very special to her, and I'm not sure whether she wants to have more."

Noah rubbed his nose. "If you did, I wouldn't mind."

Matt smiled, warmth spreading through him. "That's good to know."

"I could be, like, a big brother."

"And boss them about."

Noah laughed. "Yeah."

"It's very important to me that you know how much I want us to be a family. It's not about me taking your mum away, or taking your dad's place."

"Yeah, okay."

"It would be cool if we could both work together to make your mum's life better."

"I don't mean to make her unhappy."

"I know. But look, you have a new start next year. You'll be going to high school, where the teachers don't know you, and where you can begin all over again. Maybe it would be a good time to start practicing stepping back, and thinking before you react. It won't be long before you'll be thinking about getting a job or going to university, and it's really important that you start getting those grades under your belt now. What's your favorite subject?"

"Art."

"Of course. And that's something I can help with. When we get back, you can come and look around my studio. I can give you after-school lessons and tips so you'll be way ahead of the game."

Noah nodded. "Okay."

"You think we can be a team? Work together to make things better?" He held out a hand.

Noah looked at it. Then he moved forward and threw his arms around Matt's neck.

Surprised, Matt sat stiffly for a moment, then as his throat tightened with emotion, he put an arm around the boy and gave him a hug. Noah missed his dad, and it had obviously been a long while since he'd had this kind of connection with a man. Gary Banks didn't look the type to give hugs, and Fintan's dad had died. People would constantly be telling Noah to grow up and act mature, but he was still ninety percent child, and even adults needed a hug from time to time.

"All right." He rubbed the boy's back. "Your mum will be getting worried and think I've thrown you in the river. We'd better get back."

"Okay." Noah released him and they stood and started walking back up to the house.

"I wish we didn't have to spend Christmas here," Noah said.

"Yeah, me too. But we want your mum to be happy, right?"

"She doesn't want to spend it here either."

That was probably true, Matt thought. But he was certain Georgia wouldn't change her mind now. Anna would have gotten extra food in and made other preparations, and she'd make a big fuss if Georgia were to leave now. And gentle-hearted Georgia wouldn't want to upset everyone so close to Christmas.

Still, at least he seemed to have made some sort of progress with Noah. That would be a good present for Georgia, if nothing else.

As they walked back through the paddock, listening to the kiwis crying in the bush, Matt hoped she wouldn't mind that he'd told her son about their relationship. She wouldn't be angry, surely?

Chapter Twenty-Nine

Georgia was pacing the living room, fighting against the urge to flee the house and join Matt and Noah, wherever they were. If she was alone, she would have tried meditating, but just having her parents in the house was enough to disturb her concentration.

Anna looked up and gestured impatiently at her. "Sit down, for God's sake. You're wearing a hole in the carpet."

Georgia stopped, but remained standing, folding her arms. Why was it that her mother always made her feel as if she was fourteen again?

Anna continued to look at her, and raised her eyebrows as if to say *I've told you to sit down.*

At any other time, that look would have made Georgia collapse onto the sofa like a dog told to sit, but she set her jaw and looked away, pretending to stare at the rugby match that her father was watching on the TV.

Observing how Matt had politely refused Anna's glass of brandy had been like a revelation. He'd done so politely, but while making it quite clear that he wasn't going to let her bully him.

All her life, Georgia had longed to be able to react to her mother like that. She might have rebelled and made the move to the Northland, but deep in her heart she knew she'd only managed that because she'd told Anna it would be short term, almost like a long holiday, until Noah had sorted himself out. And in her head, Anna thought she'd 'let' her go.

Georgia looked out at the darkening sky, wondering where Matt and Noah had gotten to. Were they talking? What was Matt saying to him? She hoped Noah wasn't being rude or aggressive. If he was, maybe it would make Matt think twice about them staying together. She couldn't imagine why he'd want to take on a boy who wasn't his own son who was clearly only going to become more trouble as he entered his teens.

Her stomach was a jumble of nerves, and she began to pace again as her mother got up to draw the curtains.

"We've been thinking," Anna said, straightening the curtains before returning to her seat. "Your father and I."

"Oh…" Georgia knew from experience that didn't bode well.

"Yes. We've looked at our finances, and we'd like to offer to pay to send Noah to St. Sebastian's."

Georgia stopped walking and stared at her. St. Sebastian's was the boys' equivalent of the all-girls' boarding school they'd sent her to, where Fintan himself had gone.

"Absolutely not," she said flatly.

"Please wait and think before you react impetuously," her mother snapped. "I know you thought you could handle Noah, and you've certainly given it your best shot, but it's clearly gone too far now. He needs more than you can give him, and it makes perfect sense to place him in an environment where the elements that he reacts to are removed."

"Me," Georgia said. "You mean remove him from me."

Anna gave her a *Now, dear, don't be like that*, look. "Come on, darling. I thought you would want what's best for your son. Don't be selfish."

"I'm not being selfish," Georgia said, but she couldn't stop a flutter of doubt appearing inside her. Was she putting herself first? Anna wasn't lying when she said that Noah's behavior hadn't improved in the past year. If anything, it had gotten worse. Maybe he did need a firmer hand than she was able to provide.

"He needs some stability. The worst thing you could possibly do for him is to keep moving around and parading a trail of men in front of him in an effort to provide him with some kind of authority."

Georgia went still. "I beg your pardon?"

"Well, really, Georgia. Bringing that man all the way down here when we haven't even met him. What kind of stability is that providing Noah?"

"I haven't dated anyone since Fintan died," she said incredulously. "I'm hardly sleeping around."

Anna closed her eyes momentarily, clearly offended by the thought of her daughter having—or at least talking about having—sex. "Even so. Noah's too young to understand about 'flings' and 'temporary arrangements'." She put air quotes around the words.

186

"Mum, I've known Matt for a year. This isn't a fly-by-night thing. He loves me, and we've talked about getting married."

"Has he asked you?"

"Well, no, not yet, but he's going to."

Anna gave her a wry look, and inside Georgia something snapped. She opened her mouth to speak, but at that moment Matt and Noah appeared on the deck and entered via the sliding door.

"Hey," Matt said, slipping off his shoes and leaving them on the deck. "Sorry we're a little late. We got talking."

Noah also took off his shoes and came in. "Excuse me, Grandma," he said, "I'm sorry I didn't finish my dessert. I wondered if I could finish it now, please?"

Georgia recognized his politeness and realized Matt must have prompted him, but she was too angry to let him have his moment. "No time for that. We're going."

They all stared at her. Even her father turned in his chair to raise his eyebrows at her.

"What nonsense." Anna picked up her knitting. "Stop being so dramatic."

"No, Mum. I'm done with you making me feel as if I'm the one in the wrong." Now she'd made her decision, an icy calm settled upon her. "You have a way of making me feel as if I'm two inches tall, as if I'm hopeless and unable to make my own decisions. Well, I'm twenty-eight, and I know what's best for me and my son, and it's not staying here."

"Georgia…"

"No." The firmness of her voice made Anna's eyes widen. Georgia swallowed and forced her clench hands to unfurl. "I can't stay here," she said more quietly. "This is where Fintan died, and it just holds too many terrible memories for me, and for Noah I'm sure. It doesn't matter that you painted the bathroom. When I'm here I feel like the person I was four years ago, frightened and miserable, and I'm not like that anymore."

Anna stood, her face flushing. "If you feel like that it's your own fault. I'm not making you feel anything."

Georgia glanced at Noah, whose eyes had lit up at the news that they might not be staying. Then she looked at Matt. She'd wondered whether he'd be frowning, maybe cross that he'd made headway with

Noah and she'd taken the wind out of his sails. Instead, though, he winked at her, and that gave her the courage to continue.

"I've changed," she said. "I'm happy up in the Northland. I have a new job and a new life, and I know Noah's not perfect, but he's had a tough time. His father died, and he's still coming to terms with that. But he's getting there. My life is there now. And I like the person I am when I'm there."

"You're still the same person," Anna said, "don't fool yourself."

"No, I'm not. People can change, Mum. Or at least, up there I'm a truer version of myself. We've had a few tricky times, but we've got through them on our own. And I don't want to stay here. I'm sorry, I know you've got Christmas planned, but Leah's still coming tomorrow so you won't be alone."

"You can't go now," Gary said, also standing. "Stay tonight and go in the morning."

"No, I don't want to stay." She needed to leave, but she wasn't sure how much longer she could fight them. She looked at Matt, sending him a pleading glance.

He turned to Noah. "Go and pack your stuff." Then he smiled at Georgia. "We'll find a motel in the city somewhere."

"This is ridiculous." Anna looked upset now. "I haven't seen you for a year. You can't just walk out."

"I can't stay, Mum. Being here makes me sad. Don't you want me to be happy?"

Anna said nothing, watching Matt move quietly about, picking up their things. Noah came back into the room with his bag, and then Matt went to the bedroom to collect their cases.

Georgia saw her mother's lip wobble, walked over to her, and put her arms around her. "Come on. It's okay. Maybe in a few months you'd like to come and visit us in Kerikeri, how about that?" Her parents hadn't yet been up to the Northland to see her.

Anna nodded, but didn't say anything. Georgia let her go and hugged her father, who also looked upset, and then she sat to buckle on her sandals.

Matt came out with the cases and put them by the door. "I've rung for a taxi."

"I would have taken you," Gary said.

"Thanks, Dad," Georgia said, "but it's best we just go."

They spent another five minutes making sure everything was packed, trying to fit the presents that Anna had bought for them in their cases, checking to make sure they hadn't forgotten anything, and then the taxi drew up.

"I'll ring tomorrow when we get home," Georgia said, giving them a final hug.

Neither of her parents said much. Gary helped Matt take the cases to the car, and it was time to leave.

Anna hugged her grandson fiercely, and kissed him on the cheek. "I'll talk to you on Christmas morning on Skype."

"Okay, Grandma." Noah hugged her back, then got into the taxi. Georgia slid in beside him, Matt got into the front, and the car pulled away.

Georgia discovered her cheeks were wet, but she couldn't fight the rising sense of relief at leaving the house.

"Thank you." Noah wrapped his arms around her and squeezed her tightly. "I'm so glad."

Georgia hugged him back and pressed her lips to his hair. In the front, Matt glanced over his shoulder at her. She smiled at him, and he smiled back as the taxi headed toward the city.

*

They found a smallish bed and breakfast for the night, and headed out to the airport early the next morning. Luckily, the pilot and Pat the flight attendant had stayed in the city, so they were able to fly them back, and they landed in Kerikeri just after midday.

Matt loaded their bags into his car in the fenced-off carpark, and they got in. As he headed off, he said, "What do you want to do? Would you like to come back to Russell with me?"

Georgia hesitated. Matt had suggested they fly down to Auckland the next day for Brock's party, then spend Christmas with him, but she still wasn't sure what would be the best thing to do. "I think I might go home for a while, if that's okay. I need a bit of time to talk to Noah, and have a think."

To her relief, he didn't argue. "No worries. I'll drop you there."

It only took them ten minutes to get home. Georgia was almost dozing off in the car. She hadn't slept much the night before, and she felt exhausted from all the angst.

Matt helped them in with their cases, then to her surprise gave Noah a hug, who returned it wholeheartedly.

"See you soon, mate," Matt said. He turned to her and wrapped his arms around her. "Take care of yourself. You know where I am. You can call me or come over anytime."

"Okay."

He kissed her, just a light brush of his lips against hers. She accepted it, conscious of Noah glancing at them before he walked into his bedroom.

"Thank you," she whispered. "For everything."

"You're welcome. I just hope I haven't made things worse." A frown flickered across his brow.

Georgia gave him a surprised look. "Of course you haven't made it worse." He'd told her last night some of what he'd discussed with Noah. "You've helped me to see clearly, and you've given me the courage to be myself."

"I'm glad you see it that way." He gave her a final kiss. "All right. I'll see you soon, I hope."

He walked down the path to the car, then stopped and turned to face her, scratching his chin. "By the way, you can expect a parcel later today."

"A parcel?"

"A secret one. An early present for you both." He smiled, walked to his car, got in, and drove away.

Chapter Thirty

Puzzled, Georgia watched him go, then went in and shut the door.

She walked through her house, opening windows and the door to the garden to let in the fresh air. Then she went to Noah's room and knocked on the door. "Can I come in?"

"Yeah," came the reply.

She opened the door and went in. He was lying on the bed with his earphones in, listening to his iPod, but he sat up against the pillows as she perched on the end of the bed, and he took the earphones out.

The previous night, they hadn't had much chance to talk. They'd checked in at a motel, and had gone to bed straight away, her and Matt in one room, Noah on a sofa bed in the living room.

He hadn't commented on the fact that she and Matt had shared a room, so she'd guessed that Matt had told him about them being an item.

"How are you doing?" she asked, placing a hand on his bare foot.

He wriggled his toes. "I'm okay. Glad to be back."

"I'm sorry, Noah."

"About what?"

"Everything." Her throat tightened with emotion, but she held it in, not wanting to cry in front of him. "I understand you had a long talk with Matt."

"Yeah. We went down to the river."

She chewed her bottom lip. "He told you that we've been seeing each other?"

"Yeah."

"How do you feel about that?"

"I don't mind. He's cool." Noah met her gaze. "He said he's going to ask you to marry him."

"Oh. Um..."

"Will you say yes?"

"I don't know yet." Her face grew warm. "I'm sorry I didn't get a chance to talk to you about him first. I feel bad about that."

"I don't mind. Matt said we're a team and that we need to work together to make you happy."

Warmth spread through her. "That was a nice thing for him to say."

"He said he wants us to be a family. I told him that I didn't mind if you have kids because I can be a big brother then."

Georgia pressed her fingers to her mouth, unable to stop the tears trickling over her lashes.

"Aw, Mum. Don't cry."

"I'm sorry," she squeaked.

"It's okay. Things are going to get better. I know I've been difficult, but I promise I'll try to be good." He shuffled down the bed and put his arms around her, patting her on the back as if she were a child.

She stifled a laugh and wiped her face. "It's nice to know I have the two of you to look after me."

He sat back, crossing his legs. "Matt said Brock's having a party tomorrow. Can we go?"

"I'm not sure what to do yet. Would you like to go?"

"Yeah. Brock's apartment's really big, isn't it?"

"Yes, and very posh."

"I'd like to see it."

"What about Christmas Day? What would you like to do? Do you want to spend it here?"

"I don't mind, I'm just glad that we're not down there. If we go to Matt's place can I take my presents?"

"Of course. Well, let's give it a few hours, have a rest, and see how we feel."

*

Georgia lay down for a while, thinking she'd doze off straight away, but sleep wouldn't come, so in the end she just looked out at the garden, watching the bees buzzing around the flowers she'd grown in pots on the deck, the summer breeze puffing out the curtains every now and again. She was too tired to think straight, but her mind wandered through the events of the past few weeks like a hand brushing over the tops of a field of corn, not thinking, just remembering, contemplating, accepting.

She thought back over the previous year, about her job and meeting Matt, and how much she liked being in the Northland.

Then her mind wandered even further back, to the earthquake, and the events leading up to Fintan's death. And for the first time, she felt as if she was moving forward. The memory of those difficult years had clung to her for so long like a dark mist, full of negative emotions, of guilt, blame, and misery, but at last the sun was coming out and dispelling the mist, and it was time to move on.

The sun streamed into her room, falling across the bed in sheaves of yellow, and Georgia felt a calm contentment settle over her.

Later in the afternoon, someone knocked at the door. She answered it to find a courier standing there with two parcels—one large, rectangular, flat one, and one smaller parcel, also rectangular.

She signed for them and brought them inside. Noah had come out of his room, and they sat together on the sofa and studied the parcels.

"They're from Matt," Georgia said, seeing his handwriting on the label, distinctive with its elaborate artistic flourishes.

"Are they for Christmas Day?" Noah took the smaller one that was addressed to him and turned it over in his hands.

"No." Georgia smiled. "You can open it now."

He tore the brown paper off carefully to reveal a delicate wooden box. Opening it, he stared at the contents.

It was a handmade booklet, the first edition of *Rory and the Taniwha*, hand-painted and cut to size.

Georgia put her arm around him and they leaned back together as he flicked through the pages. Although obviously not the finished product—Rory's face and many of the pictures contained only a few broad strokes—it was beautifully made, and a great story too, about how Rory discovered that the *Taniwha* in Lake Taupo had travelled through a wormhole from Loch Ness in England, and how he managed to help it back to the Loch where it had left its family so it could become the Loch Ness monster again.

Noah looked up at her. "Is it really for me?"

"I'm sure he wouldn't have sent it to you if it wasn't."

"It's so cool."

"When it wins all the awards next year, you'll be able to tell your mates that you have the first edition."

He laughed. "Yeah!" He looked at the other parcel. "What's in there?"

"I don't know." She pulled it toward her. It was addressed to her, and she skimmed her fingers across her name before turning it over and removing the brown paper.

It was a large flat box. She loosened the lid and lifted it, and her jaw dropped.

"It's you." Noah lifted out the canvas inside. Matt had taken the sketch of her face he'd done the night she lay on the sofa and copied it onto canvas, completing it this time in oils, or maybe acrylics, considering that it felt dry. It wasn't like a photograph—he'd used bright, vibrant colors as if he was looking at everything through a colored lens. Her hair was brown but also contained strokes of red, dark blue, and forest green. Her lips were pink, with splashes of scarlet and purple that made her look as if she was pouting. But it was her eyes that were the most amazing thing about it—they flared with orange and touches of gold leaf that brought the whole painting alight.

"Wow," Noah said.

"Oh my God." She covered her mouth with her hand.

Noah tilted the canvas to catch the light. "You look beautiful."

"It's... not me. Is it?"

"It's how he sees you." He grinned. "Mum and Matt, sitting in a tree, K-I-S-S-I-"

She pushed him, and he fell sideways onto the sofa, laughing.

"I'm going to get a drink," he told her. He stood, then paused and looked down at her where she sat still staring at the painting. "Are we going to stay with Matt for Christmas?"

Slowly, her lips began to curve up.

*

Christmas Eve

"We're late," Georgia said.

"It's cool to be fashionably late." Matt punched the code into the elevator, and it began to ascend.

"Yeah, but that means everyone's going to stare at us when we walk in." She smoothed her skirt down nervously.

"You look great, Mum," Noah said. "Stop worrying."

"He ain't wrong," Matt advised.

"I suppose I'm going to have to put up with this now, aren't I?" Georgia scolded. "The two of you ganging up on me?"

"Yep." Matt grinned, pleased when she laughed. She looked gorgeous, he thought, glowing almost as much as she had in his painting. She wore her black mini skirt and a sparkly silver top, and she'd pinned her hair up with a pretty Christmassy red-and-silver clip.

He'd waited nervously the day before as one hour, then two, then several hours passed following the moment when the courier rang to tell him that his parcels had been delivered. He'd spoken to his brothers on Skype, revealing rather gloomily that he was almost certain he wouldn't be going to the party. But eventually, as the sun had set, his phone had rung, and it had been Georgia.

"You're a sweetheart," she'd said, her voice filled with emotion.

"Did he like the book?"

"He loved it, Matt. And the painting… I don't know what to say."

"You fill my life with color. I just wanted you to know that's how I see the world when you're around."

"Oh, Matt." And she'd burst into tears.

Noah had taken the phone then. "She's all right," he'd announced.

"Are you sure?"

"Yeah. They're happy tears. She's been doing it all afternoon. I think we're coming over now, by the way."

"Oh?" Matt's heart had soared.

"Have you got any mince pies?"

"Two boxes from the Bakehouse. Best ones in the Northland."

"Cool. I'm giving you back now. I look forward to seeing your studio, though."

Georgia had come back to the phone. "Sorry," she'd said with a sniff.

"No worries. I understand I might be seeing you soon?"

"Yeah. Is that okay?"

"It's wonderful. You want me to come and get you?"

"No, we'll drive over once we've packed."

"All right, honey. I'll see you then."

"Matt?"

"Yeah?"

"I love you."

He'd smiled. "I love you too."

They'd arrived within an hour, and the three of them had spent the rest of the evening watching Christmas movies and eating too many mince pies. Eventually, Noah had gone to bed in the spare room Matt had made up for him, and then he and Georgia had cuddled up on the sofa with a glass of wine before going to bed as well.

They'd made love, and it had been precious and sweet, because it had felt like the first day of the rest of their lives together.

He looked at her now, standing in the elevator, and an image flashed through his mind of her the night before, lying naked beneath him, eyes fluttering closed with pleasure.

Her cheeks flushed as if she knew what he was thinking about. "Stop it," she said.

"What?" he replied innocently.

Noah rolled his eyes. "Are you two going to be like this all the time?"

"Yep." Matt put his right arm around her. In his left hand, he held one of his awards. Georgia had insisted he bring it to show off to his brothers.

He kissed her cheek. "Merry Christmas."

The lift doors opened, and they walked down the corridor into the living room to see his brothers and their partners and friends waiting for them.

"Jesus," Matt said. "Charlie, what the hell are you wearing?"

Chapter Thirty-One

"I don't see what all the fuss is about. It's only a tux."

It was nearly five hours later, with only thirty minutes to go until midnight.

Brock and Erin, Charlie and Ophelia, and Matt and Georgia were all sitting around the table on the deck. Before they'd left, the staff who'd organized the party had cleared away the empty wine bottles that had littered the table, and now all it bore were their glasses, several candles, and some mint chocolates they were all nibbling at.

The last guests had gone, Ryan and Summer had crashed out in the bedrooms, and even though Noah had insisted he wasn't tired, he'd dozed off on the sofa while watching Jim Carrey in *A Christmas Carol*.

The six of them weren't quite ready to end the day. Charlie, Ophelia, and Summer were going back to Charlie's place eventually, but Brock had asked whether Matt, Georgia, and Noah wanted to stay over and spend Christmas Day at the apartment, and they'd decided to do that and then fly back on Boxing Day.

Consequently, they'd opened another bottle of champagne and topped up the girls' glasses. Brock had then cracked open the bottle of forty-year-old Laphroaig he'd been saving for a special occasion, and the guys had all poured it over ice and then *aaahhhed* as they took their first sip.

Charlie was referring to the fact that everybody kept remarking on how different he looked. He'd removed his jacket and his bow tie now hung loose, but he still looked unusually suave in his black trousers and crisp white shirt. "You all act as if I dress like a tramp the rest of the time," he complained.

"It's not that." Ophelia leaned forward to plant a kiss on his cheek. "It's just that you look like a cross between James Bond and—"

"Einstein," Matt said, referring to Charlie's hair.

"Ha ha." Charlie took a sip of his whisky, only looking mollified when Ophelia whispered something in his ear.

Matt chuckled, leaning back in his chair so Georgia could snuggle against him. He couldn't believe he, Brock, and Charlie had finally made it to Christmas Eve with the women of their dreams. Only the previous night, they'd all been certain things were going to end disastrously.

I guess there was enough magic left to go around after all, he thought, kissing the top of Georgia's head.

"What a beautiful night," Erin said with a sigh. They all looked out across the harbor of the City of Sails. The lights from the restaurants and clubs lay on the water like sparkling sequins. Carols sung by a church choir played in the living room, and Matt felt a little shiver as the haunting sound of *Silent Night* filtered out to them on the warm deck.

"Go on."

"What, now?"

Matt saw Charlie nudge Brock, who was looking alarmed. "What's going on?" Matt asked. The girls glanced around, similarly puzzled.

Brock scratched his chin, glared at Charlie, then gave a dramatic sigh. "Oh well. I guess it's as good a time as any." He stared at the table for a long moment. They all exchanged bewildered, amused glances. Charlie was the only one who grinned.

Brock cleared his throat, then looked at Erin. His lips curving, he got to his feet, and began to pace the deck. "I meant to do this earlier," he said, "but people started arriving."

"Do what?" Her eyes had widened.

Matt met Charlie's gaze and raised his eyebrows. Charlie gave a short nod and smiled.

"Holy fuck." Matt laughed.

Brock ignored him, slid his hand into his pocket, and pulled out a small velvet box.

Erin clapped a hand over her mouth. Ophelia gasped. Georgia went, "Aw!"

Brock glanced at the chair he'd been sitting in, picked up the cushion from it, and dropped it onto the wooden deck. "Getting old," he mumbled as Charlie snorted. Then, moving closer to Erin, he dropped to one knee and popped the lid of the box.

"Erin?" he said. "I fell in love with you online. I know it sounds mad, but it's true. And I've only fallen further in love with you since we started dating. I'm crazy about you, and I know I want to spend the rest of my life with you. Will you marry me?"

Erin stared at the ring, which glittered in the semi-darkness like a Christmas bauble. Matt fought not to swear out loud. He'd heard that a man was supposed to spend three weeks' wages on an engagement ring. This one looked as if Brock had flown to South Africa and hewn it out of the rock himself.

The six of them fell quiet, the only sound coming from the music inside, the delicate notes of *Silent Night* drifting out to them like snowflakes. Matt found himself holding his breath as he stared at Erin, waiting for her reply.

She continued to stare at the ring, her hand over her mouth. Brock blinked, and his gaze slid to meet Matt's opposite him. Matt winked at him, having spotted the way Erin's mouth was curving up behind her hand.

Brock look back at Erin, and she raised her gaze to his. Her eyes glistened, and she nodded. "Yes." It came out as a squeak, so she cleared her throat and said again, more clearly, "Yes, I'll marry you."

Brock inhaled deeply and then blew out a long, relieved breath, and Erin laughed and threw her arms around him. The others all cheered, and then everyone was standing up and shaking hands and hugging, congratulating the two of them, laughing at Brock's relief and Erin's happy tears as she slid the ring on and showed the others.

Matt looked down at Georgia and smiled, holding his arm out to her, and she moved beneath it for a hug.

"How lovely," she whispered. "She looks so happy."

"I'm pleased for him." Matt thought of the picture on his wall that Brock had never seen, his face filled with grief. He'd have to paint a new one to replace it now.

It took several minutes before they were all back in their seats. Matt topped up everyone's glasses and raised his. "To the happy couple."

"To the happy couple." They all cheered, laughed, and drank.

Brock took a big mouthful of whisky, swallowed, and sighed. Then he grinned at Charlie. "Your turn, dude. Try and follow that."

The others laughed. Charlie pursed his lips and studied his whisky glass. Matt knew him well enough to know his brother felt awkward and was trying to work out what to say.

"We're very happy," Ophelia said, "but it's too soon for a proposal. We might have been meeting at the breakfast cart for a while, but we've only been dating for a few weeks. And unfortunately, on paper I'm still married to someone else."

"Yeah," Brock said, but he had a glint in his eye, clearly buoyed up by his success and wanting everyone else to be as happy as he was. "Go on, ask him."

Ophelia's eyes widened and she gave him a *Don't you dare* sort of look.

Charlie's gaze slid to her, then to Brock. "Ask me what?"

Brock grinned. "She told me that she thought you liked her. *Liked.*" He snorted. "I suggested she ask you to translate what you told her in Italian."

Charlie's eyebrows rose. Ophelia winced.

"What's going on?" Matt demanded. "What did you say in Italian? And when did this happen?"

Charlie took a swallow from his glass. "I may have been a little overenthusiastic while we were… ah… for the first time."

Ophelia groaned and covered her face.

"Tell her," Brock prompted.

Matt frowned at him. Brock and Charlie had been like this since they were kids. It made Matt uncomfortable because he knew his middle brother suffered from terrible social awkwardness, but he did acknowledge that it often encouraged Charlie out of his comfort zone, which wasn't always a bad thing.

Charlie looked into his glass as if working out the cubic area of ice residing in it and how much whisky it was displacing, but Matt knew he was trying to calculate the outcome of what he was about to say.

Ophelia was watching him now, though, and her features were filled with such affection that Matt knew Charlie couldn't go wrong. "Tell her," he said, echoing Brock's words.

Charlie met his gaze, blinked a few times, then looked at Ophelia. "I said *Voglio stare con te per sempre. Sei l'amore della mia vita. Mi vuoi sposare?*"

"And in English?" Brock prompted.

Charlie sighed. "I want to be with you forever. You are the love of my life. Will you marry me? When you're not married to someone else, I mean."

Ophelia's eyes widened so hurriedly it was almost comical. "Oh God," she said, and burst into tears.

Charlie glared at his brothers. "This is what happens when I do what you tell me."

"It's okay," Ophelia squeaked, dabbing at her eyes as Erin hastily gave her a tissue. "I'll be all right in a minute."

Charlie pushed back his chair and held out his hand. "Come inside with me for a minute."

Ophelia took his hand, and the two of them went into the living room and through to where Matt knew Brock's study was. The door closed.

Brock looked at Matt and pulled an *eek* face.

"She's okay," Georgia predicted. "Those were happy tears. I know the difference."

Brock finished off his whisky, took some ice out of the bowl, and held it out to Erin as she pulled the cork from the bottle. "So come on then," he said to Matt as she sloshed the amber liquid over the ice. "Your turn."

Matt took a mouthful of whisky, thinking how much it looked like Georgia's eyes. He winked at her. "Want a shag?"

Erin and Georgia burst out laughing, and Brock rolled his eyes. "Mr. Romantic."

"I'm not going to propose now," Matt told him firmly. "It'll look like I'm only doing it because you guys have done it."

"All right, but you're the odd one out," Brock said. "As usual."

Matt gave him the finger. Brock laughed and drank his whisky.

"It's Christmas Day," Georgia said suddenly, looking at her phone. "It's gone midnight."

"Oh, merry Christmas." Erin gave her a hug. "We'll have to do this again. It's been such fun."

"You'll all have to come and stay at my place," Matt said.

"Wow," Brock commented. "Wonders will never cease. I didn't think we'd ever get to see your house. I was beginning to think it only appeared once every hundred years like Brigadoon."

"I like my privacy. So sue me."

Georgia smiled. "I feel honored."

He put an arm around her and pulled her close so he could kiss her nose. "I suppose I had locked myself away a bit."

"A bit?" Brock prompted.

"Okay, a lot. And padlocked the gates and put barbed wire on the walls." He smiled at Georgia. "You're the one who unlocked me though. You know that, right?"

She gave a little happy nod, and he bent his head and gave her a long kiss.

"Yeah," Brock said. "That'll do at a pinch."

Matt lifted his head to say something sarcastic, but saw that Charlie and Ophelia had left the study and were walking toward them. Charlie had his arm around her and was whispering to her. Her eyes were red, but she was smiling.

They stopped in the doorway to the deck. "We're off," Charlie said. "I'm taking her and Summer home."

"Sorry." Ophelia wiped under her eyes. "I'm tired and it's been an emotional week."

"Of course," Brock said as they all rose. "You've really been through it."

Matt knew that Summer had been in hospital with a chest infection. He'd seen the dress Charlie'd had made for her, a princess-style gown with sixty-five roses—the name that children called Cystic Fibrosis.

Matt held his hand out to his brother. "All the best, bro. When you get it right, you get it really right."

Charlie shook his hand, and then they bear-hugged. "Thanks," Charlie whispered. "That means a lot."

They all said goodnight, hugged and kissed, and Charlie retrieved Summer from the bedroom and carried her to the elevator, the girl still in her princess dress. They'd booked a taxi to take them home, paying through the nose for the privilege, but that was the least of their problems, Matt thought, hoping that Charlie's research would be able to help Summer in the long run.

As it was late, the rest of them decided it was time to go to bed too.

"Thanks for inviting us." Georgia lifted up on her toes to kiss Brock goodnight. "I'm glad it worked out for you." She smiled at Erin.

"Likewise." Erin hugged her, then went to check on Ryan.

"I'd better get Noah to bed," Georgia said.

"Okay." Matt kissed her on the cheek, then whispered in her ear, "I have a secret parcel for you to open, by the way."

"Oh?" Her lips curved up, and she grinned happily as she went into the living room to rouse a sleepy Noah from the sofa and take him off to bed.

Matt and Brock stood out on the deck and finished off their drinks.

"Feel good?" Matt asked.

"Not bad." Brock smiled. "You?"

"Yeah. I will ask her, you know. To marry me. When the time's right."

"Good."

Matt lifted the hand holding his glass and pointed to the east, where Sirius and his partner sparkled in the night sky like the diamond in Erin's ring. "They make me think of Fleur and Pippa."

Brock followed his gaze and studied the stars. "Yeah."

They both stood there quietly for a while, looking at the sky, listening to the carol playing in the living room. *Star of wonder, star of light, star with royal beauty bright...*

"We three Kings," Matt said. "We've done all right for ourselves, haven't we?"

"Yeah. Could be a lot worse." Brock gave the stars a last look, then finished off his drink. "I'm going to bed. Merry Christmas." He went in, left his glass on the table, switched off the music, and disappeared into the room he shared with his fiancé.

Matt turned back to the stars and raised his glass to them. "Merry Christmas." He finished off the whisky, welcoming the burn down to his stomach, then went inside.

Chapter Thirty-Two

Georgia had taken Noah to his room, brushed her teeth, and changed. Now she lay on her side on the bed facing the door, waiting for Matt.

She didn't have to wait long. She heard Brock go into his bedroom and the door close, and then it was only a minute later that Matt's footsteps padded along the corridor to the bathroom. Shortly afterward, the door opened.

He walked in, saw her on the bed, and stopped, his eyes widening.

She raised an eyebrow. "What?"

He gave her a wry look and started unbuttoning his shirt. "Like you don't know."

"I have no idea what you're talking about." The giggle wouldn't be suppressed though. She wore a scarlet lace teddy and matching panties, and white thigh-highs with red glittery fur around the top. "Merry Christmas," she said.

Matt's fingers were fumbling, so he tore open the rest of the shirt, sending buttons popping across the room.

"You're in a hurry." She rose to her knees, her heart racing.

"Ready for your secret parcel?" He slipped off his trousers and boxers to reveal an impressive erection—complete with a big red bow.

She burst out laughing. "Have you had that on all night?"

"No... Thank God. The ribbon itches like a bastard. Quick, untie it."

Chuckling away, she pulled the bow undone, taking her time and enjoying every moment. He held out a hand, and she placed hers into it and let him pull her to her feet. Placing his hands on her hips, he steered her to the window so her back was against it.

She glanced over her shoulder at the harbor. Down below, the pier was still busy, and lights showed from the boats where parties were still going on. "Matt! People can see us!"

"Don't care." He covered her mouth with his and pushed his naked body up against her, pressing her to the glass.

Georgia didn't complain, because that was pretty much what she'd hoped would happen, and she just rose up onto her toes and wrapped her arms around his neck, opening her mouth to his hungry kiss.

"I want you," he said hoarsely, kissing around to her ear, and down her neck.

"I'd never have guessed," she said, panting, the feel of his rock-hard erection against her more than enough clue as to how turned on he was.

She hooked a leg around his waist and rocked her hips against him, and he cupped her breasts through the skimpy fabric and covered her nipple with his mouth. Georgia closed her eyes, no longer caring that people might be watching, thinking only of the gorgeous man in her arms, desperate to feel him inside her.

"Now," she whispered, and he slipped his fingers into the elastic of her panties and pulled them down her thighs. As he dropped to his haunches, she steadied herself on his shoulders to step out of them, then gasped as leaned forward and slid his tongue into her folds.

"Matt!" She leaned back on the glass and closed her eyes, groaning at the feel of his slick tongue slipping in and out of her, his fingers following it and delving into her moist depths. "*Ohhh...*" Slowly, expertly, he teased her until she could stand no more.

Pushing himself up, he placed his hands beneath her bottom and lifted her easily into his arms. She wrapped her legs around his waist, and he pushed her back against the glass as he lowered her down until the tip of his erection parted her folds. Keeping his mouth over hers, their breaths mingling, he lowered her a little further, sliding deep inside her until she was impaled on him.

Georgia's fingers dug into his back as he began to thrust, hard enough to make her gasp with each push of his hips. Already, she could feel her muscles tightening as he ground against her sensitive clit. The sensation of the cold glass on her back, his warm skin pressed to hers, and the hard heat of him inside her, all conspired to tease her to the edge. Within minutes she came, fast and hard, only realizing she was crying out when he covered her mouth with his. Pinned to the glass, she gave in to the waves of pleasure, and let him thrust away until his climax claimed him too, his hips jerking as he spilled inside her until he was spent.

"Jeez," he said when he finally lifted her off the glass and carried her to the bed. "How long did that take us? Five minutes?"

"A Christmas quickie." She smiled sleepily as he lowered her to the mattress and carefully withdrew, then climbed on beside her and took her into his arms.

"Sorry, but that's what you get when you wear such a saucy outfit," he grumbled, turning her so her back was to his chest.

She chuckled. "You're welcome."

He kissed her hair. "I'm glad you came with me tonight."

"Me too. And Noah had a great time." He'd spent the evening with Summer, Ryan, and the kids of the other guests, and had seemed to enjoy himself. "I think he might have turned a corner."

"If he has, that would be the best present I could think of." He nuzzled her neck. "By the way, about earlier, when I said I'd ask you to marry me…"

"It's okay, Matt. There's no rush. We both need to be sure."

"Oh… I'm sure. That's why I've decided. I'm going to ask you every night when we go to bed until you say yes."

Her eyelids were drooping, but that made them fly open temporarily. "Seriously?"

"Seriously." He kissed down her neck to her shoulder. "So… Georgia Banks, will you make me the happiest man in the world and be my wife?"

"I'm asleep."

"Fair enough. Guess I'll have to wait until tomorrow." He sighed and wrapped an arm around her. "Sleep well, sweetheart."

"You too." She yawned, linking her fingers with his.

They'd left the curtains open. Outside, she could see Sirius, shining brightly against the velvet darkness. For some reason, it made her think of Fintan.

Since she'd moved to the Northland, she hadn't thought of him as much, maybe because there weren't memories waiting for her around every corner. That made her partly sad and partly relieved. It had been hard, having one foot in the past all the time. Everyone was talking about the new Christchurch and how it had improved since the rebuild, but it was only now that she realized how much seeing the broken city had made her unhappy. The crumbled cathedral, the torn roads, the houses with huge chasms in the floors, and sky where glorious buildings had once stood. She'd done the right thing moving up here, and life would only get better after she moved in with the man lying beside her, whose breathing had turned deep and regular.

"Matt?" she whispered

"Mmm?" His hand splayed on her belly. She thought of what Noah had said about not minding if they had more kids, and she warmed right through.

"The answer's yes," she said, and closed her eyes.

THE END

Other Books By Serenity Woods

If you liked Three Wise Men, then you might like my Treats to Tempt You series. These stories feature a group of friends who run a chocolate, ice cream, and coffee shop, set in Doubtless Bay, New Zealand. Check them out at your favorite retailer.

Book 1: Treat with Caution
Book 2: Treat her Right
Book 3: A Rare Treat
Book 4: Trick or Treat
Book 5: A Festive Treat

Newsletter

If you'd like to be informed when my next book is available, you can sign up for my mailing list on my website, http://www.serenitywoodsromance.com

About the Author

Serenity Woods lives in the sub-tropical Northland of New Zealand with her wonderful husband and gorgeous teenage son. She writes hot and sultry contemporary romances and would much rather immerse herself in reading or writing romance than do the dusting and ironing, which is why it's not a great idea to pop round if you have any allergies.

Website: http://www.serenitywoodsromance.com
Facebook: http://www.facebook.com/serenitywoodsromance
Twitter: https://twitter.com/Serenity_Woods

Printed in Great Britain
by Amazon

60544703R00122